THE
LAST
CITY
ROOM

Also by
Al Martinez

THE
LAST
CITY
ROOM

Al Martinez

Thomas Dunne Books
St. Martin's Press ⚏ New York

THOMAS DUNNE BOOKS.
An imprint of St. Martin's Press.

www.stmartins.com

Design by Heidi R. R. Eriksen

Library of Congress Cataloging-in-Publication Data

Martinez, Al.
    The last city room / Al Martinez—1st ed.
        p.   cm.
    ISBN 0-312-20901-0
    1. San Francisco (Calif.)—Fiction.   2. Newspaper publishing—Fiction.
    3. Journalists—Fiction.   4. Newspapers—Fiction.   I. Title.
PS3563.A7333 L37 2000
813'.54—dc21   00-031738

First Edition: November 2000

10   9   8   7   6   5   4   3   2   1

For my joyous, loving, unstoppable Cinelli
and for those who left their
marks on the calamitous city
rooms of the past

THE
LAST
CITY
ROOM

PROLOGUE

T he 1960s were more than a decade. They were a dance, a rush, a war, a song, a dream. They were a kind of madness that swept the land, a sudden, terrifying realization that parties end, drugs wear off, and heroes die. If you think of the sixties in terms of a parade, it would be led by lacquered nymphets followed by roaring lions and naked marchers. There would be soldiers with blood on their bayonets and flowers in their helmets. There would be bands that played words and screams, and a route that led to a crimson sea, where strings of poetry and human entrails washed ashore.

The 1960s neither began in 1960 nor ended in 1970. States of mind overlap, and that's what the decade was, a condition of *being,* jump-started by a 1957 student riot on the steps of the San Francisco City Hall aimed at a congressional committee hunting Communists, and ending in an indifferent 1970s protest at U.C.'s Sather Gate. I don't remember what that final protest was. It doesn't matter. Everyone was fully clothed by then, the joints all smoked, and the mind-bending acid used up. What mattered was the stuff in between, the drums and hymns, and the vast movements of moral imperatives. What mattered were the old institutions, social and governmental, that were swept away like sand castles in a hurricane. A way of thinking died then. Watts burned and so did Detroit and Newark, and the Black Panthers warned that this was just the beginning.

To fit the story of the *San Francisco Herald* and its players into that strange psychedelic pulse of time, one must understand that it probably didn't belong there in the first place. Its demise began at the hour the decade rolled around, falling at an inverse ratio to the rising calamity that surrounded its old brick tower. The *Herald* held solidly to a fading ethos even as its publisher composed screaming editorials at those who tore at the fabric of the past, and who in turn shouted obscenities at what the newspaper had come to represent. The middle finger was invented in the 1960s, thrust grandly upward in an icon of defiance more familiar than the peace symbol.

The *San Francisco Herald* wasn't the only large newspaper to go down. More than 150 dailies across the nation fell in the 1960s, from the *Boston Traveler* to the *Houston Press* and from the *Portland Reporter* to the *Indianapolis Times.* They blamed the unions, the rise of television, and the increased cost of equipment and newsprint. They blamed a generation whose loss of faith in government had splashed over to the most traditional of media. "The times," Bobby Dylan sang, "they are a-changin' . . ." Indeed they were.

We were young in that decade and strong and righteous. We knew what mattered and what didn't. We could smell the bullshit as neatly as we smelled the roses. We shouted peace in the world and made war in the streets. Compromise was an old shoe, sex was important. The *Herald* was both confused by the new morality that shot up like weeds through cracks in our culture and intrigued by the heat the morality generated. Its publisher was a patriot past his time with enemies he didn't understand.

Into the calamitous mix came the observers and the leaders, the users and the visionaries, each with his own agenda, each with her own singularity. They comprised the humanity of the sixties and were both witness to its dissonance and participants in its movements. They wrote, marched, made love, OD'd, shouted defiance, gave morality the finger, and created the whole new world in which we live today. This book is about them, about the decade, and about what happened to a fictional daily newspaper that suddenly found itself in the path of a tsunami in an era beyond its capacity to understand.

CHAPTER ONE

William Colfax, limping slightly, entered the city room of the *Herald* with the wariness of a cat, hesitating long enough to assure himself that something on the other side of the doorway wasn't going to get him. For a cat caution is instinctive, for Colfax it was a response conditioned by combat that would leave him eternally suspicious of whatever lay ahead. But there was something of a cat in him too. Despite the limp, he moved with a feline's canny grace and with an intensity that made him all the more noticeable as he passed by the rows of ancient wooden desks that lined a pathway from a back elevator to the interior of the newsroom, prowling slowly through the intermingling sounds of typewriters and telephones as though he were stalking a ghost.

It was that quality you noticed first about the man. One looked up as he passed, aware of his presence alone among all the others who came and went, an intriguing stranger among the familiar. Trager noticed him too. The old copy chief, a perpetual scowl etched into his face, had a limp of his own, and as he passed Colfax limping in the opposite direction he studied him carefully, wondering if the stranger had somehow heard of his deformity and was mimicking him or if instead they shared a common malady. That wasn't the case. Colfax's was more a hesitation, while Trager's polio-induced stomp was an obvious limp-drag, a clump that gave his withered frame an angry forward thrust.

Moving past the edge of rewrite, Colfax spotted the city desk just about the moment Gerald Burns, telephone in hand, noticed him and gestured for Colfax to come forward. Colfax tried a smile in response, but it didn't work and he scolded himself silently for even attempting it. He was not a smiling man, but rather somber for someone so young, and it gave him the kind of serious, important appearance women were especially attracted to, as though he bore an infinite responsibility no one else could possibly understand.

On his mind at the moment, however, was not responsibility but a sense of shabbiness. He felt awkward in the outfit he'd bought specifically for this interview. The dark jacket and light slacks were wrong. Hadn't he worn something like this at his junior high graduation? His tassled loafers reminded him of a tap dancer's.

For a moment Colfax thought of turning away quickly and returning to the safety of Edenville, where he had hidden himself for the past months among the trees and the mountains and a small daily newspaper only very few gave a rat's ass about. Two years in the Marines had deadened any sense of style he might have had and dulled his ability to survive in an urban society. Laura would have helped him once, laughing at his color-clashing outfits and loving him for it, but now she was gone and he was left with a junior high graduation suit, a tap dancer's shoes, and an emptiness he couldn't fill.

Turning away, however, was out of the question. This was what his whole life was destined for, where he had always wanted to be. A fifth-grade teacher, a woman with short dark hair, a poet hiding in the mountains of Edenville, had ordained it. Colfax remembered her even to the faint, rosy glow of her face, leaning over him in a classroom that smelled faintly of pine and saying, "You will write someday." She had read his essays written in pencil on lined paper and she knew. She saw. And from that moment, he knew too.

The city room wasn't what he'd expected of a newspaper that towered in his imagination. It smelled old and its dark wood paneling had been painted over a hundred times, adding a dull luster to its veneer. Bare fluorescent tubes hung from a high ceiling, adding a dimension of flatness to the sunlight that filtered into the room from a row of dusty windows looking onto Mission Street. Outside, the city's skies were heavy with dark clouds. Rain tapped at the windows. It was September in San Francisco.

"Mr. Burns?"

Colfax tried to make his voice sound even and his manner confident, but night patrols in the Mekong Delta had involved less strain. Burns was studying him curiously over the top of rimless glasses, smiling like a man about to play a huge trick on an unsuspecting victim. He was in his mid-fifties and slightly built. His white nylon shirt was buttoned at the top and his muted blue tie straight and even. Not a strand of his thinning sandy hair was out of place, in contrast to the disarray that seemed to surround him.

"Hi," Burns said in a voice that was disarmingly soft.

"I'm William Colfax."

Burns took his hand and shook it. There was an air of concentration about the city editor. It made Colfax uncharacteristically nervous, as though he were something very small and wiggly under a microscope. Adding to his discomfort was a knowledge of Burns's reputation. Henry Dustin had stood in absolute awe of the man, and when Colfax decided it was time to abandon the *Edenville Messenger* for something better, the *Messenger*'s editor had urged him to go to the *Herald,* if only because that's where the legendary Gerald Burns presided.

"I have some clips and a résumé," Colfax was saying, opening a manila folder he carried and looking around for a place to sit or be interviewed. None existed. Burns took the material and set it aside after glancing through it in a perfunctory manner.

"Dustin says you're a good man," Burns said. "He vouches for you a thousand percent. That's a good vouch. Henry and I worked together on the old *Bulletin.* He doesn't belong in Podunkville. How old are you, William Colfax?"

"Twenty-four," Colfax said.

He was about to elaborate on his limited experience in newspapering—high school, some college, part-time at a throwaway, six months at the *Messenger*—when a commotion from the far side of the room caught his attention. Both men turned in time to see the approach of two medics pushing a gurney with someone on it. They wheeled toward double doors that led to the front lobby, and as they passed, Colfax could see it was a man on the gurney and instantly knew, by his gray skin and blue lips, that he was dead.

Across the city room, reporters were standing, more out of respect than curiosity, and the noise that had filled the room was suddenly muted. Then one of them, a woman with a cigarette in her hand, began clapping, scattering ashes on the wooden floors and sending up a puff of smoke with each clap. Soon she was joined by others until the whole room was applauding in a slow, rhythmic cadence until the doors to the lobby swung shut and the gurney was out of sight. Only then did they resume their work and the pace of the room continue. Colfax, unnerved by the sudden appearance of death, turned questioningly to Burns.

"That was Jonathan Blair," the city editor said. "This was his fifth heart attack and, as we have observed, his last."

"Does the clapping mean something?"

"It began a long time before I came. You clap for someone you like who dies at his desk. Later, they'll drink to him across the street and buy him a snort whenever they order a round."

"What happens to the drink?"

"Someone throws it down in his honor, then the glass is placed upside down on the bar. It's a tradition, you know? A drinker's last rites."

"Jesus," Colfax said, still thinking about the face of the dead man. He couldn't remember ever having suffered a flashback to the war, but the thick, sweet smell of death was never far away. He could summon it with only the slightest concentration and it was filling his head now, taking him back to fields of bodies that lay in the humid sunshine.

"He had a good life," Burns said, sensing Colfax's unease. "He knew he was going to die. And he'd have admired your timing, William Colfax. Thanks to Jonathan Blair's sudden departure, we have an opening on cityside. He covered chaos for us. Any kind of chaos. Are you good at chaos, William Colfax?"

There was neither mockery nor false sympathy in Burns's voice. Only a trace of weariness hinted at the feelings he might have been experiencing.

"We didn't have a lot of chaos in Edenville," Colfax said, drifting back from the aroma of the killing fields and trying to focus again on the business at hand. As he did, he suddenly realized that Burns was telling him he had the job.

"You'll need a car," the city editor said. "You have a place to stay?"

Without waiting for an answer or even expecting one, Burns rose, came around his desk, and said, "You've got to meet Stafford first."

"Am I hired?" Colfax asked, trying to conceal his surprise at the speed with which it had occurred. It was a question he hadn't intended to ask, ringing with childlike anticipation. The moment demanded cooler tones.

"If the man says you are, you are. He likes to think he's the one who builds the staff. He isn't."

Burns led the way toward a half-glassed door next to the line of windows that eased in a mottled gray light. The woman who had led the applause for Jonathan Blair, a new cigarette in her mouth, looked up from her desk in annoyance as they passed, as though their mere proximity had dislodged a blossoming idea now lost forever. Burns returned a mock scowl.

"That's Sally Bell," he said loud enough for her to hear. "Avoid her. She's carnivorous."

Burns pushed the door open into a small inner office where a middle-aged secretary worked at a typewriter that was only slightly newer than the ones Colfax had observed on rewrite.

"You getting any?" Burns said as he passed.

"Never enough," she replied without looking up.

Burns led Colfax across the room and into a larger office of rich oak paneling and thick dark carpeting. There were vertical blinds on the windows, books in cabinets that lined the walls, and a large, polished-wood desk in a half circle that filled a whole corner of the room. The American and a California flags flanked the desk, adding an air of officialdom to the office. There was also an aura of quiet intimacy in marked contrast to the city room's noisy disorganization. It took Colfax back to a glade in the woods he had often visited outside of Edenville to remind himself of who he had been before the war.

On the desk an ornate gold and crystal nameplate announced that this was the domain of Jeremy Lincoln Stafford III. Above him, the mounted head of a lion, its teeth bared, looked down. Its expression was almost a smile.

"This is William Colfax," Burns said. "He has no body odors and speaks adequately good English. Unless you find him otherwise offensive, I would like to hire him." Burns laid Colfax's clips-laden manila envelope on the desk. "He writes good too. I know his work."

Stafford laughed loudly at Burns's introduction and strode around the desk like Teddy Roosevelt on a campaign trail. Colfax wondered briefly if Stafford had killed the lion himself. He was a large, red-faced man with the imposing bulk of a grizzly bear and the handshake of a wood clamp. As Burns left the room, Stafford motioned for Colfax to sit and returned to the high-backed leather swivel chair behind the desk.

Colfax had done his homework and knew that Stafford was the third family publisher of the *Herald* from a genealogy that dated back to the city's gold-rush days. The newspaper was stolen by his antecedents from an elderly widow who made the mistake of trusting them to sell it for her. There was no sale. They took it the way a bully grabs crutches from a cripple, but they transformed it from a small waterfront journal into what it was today, an imposing champion of family values and a trustworthy disseminator of the day's news.

"I like to meet those who wish to work for my family's newspaper," Stafford was saying in the formal stentorian voice of a man addressing a high school graduation. He was leaning forward across the large and meticulously organized desk and looking directly into Colfax's eyes. Having said that, he withdrew the résumé from the manila folder and studied it in silence. Much of the giddiness Colfax had felt entering the city room had vanished. Like a man committed to battle, he felt oddly at ease, his fate in the hands of a power beyond his control. There was no turning back. The lion's head over the desk seemed to nod.

"I like the United States Marine Corps," Stafford finally said, isolating each word of the title. "I would sentence every rabble-rouser off the street to a term in the United States Marine Corps if I could. It would teach them discipline and loyalty to our country."

"It would teach discipline, all right," Colfax said for lack of anything more profound, thinking of a drill instructor in boot camp who had beaten bloody a recruit, a Jew, he accused of being a Communist. The man had lain in a fetal position on the floor of the barracks during the beating, but no one would lift a hand to help him because they had been ordered to attention and the Corps had drilled them well in the conduct of obedience. The D.I. was court-martialed and transferred. The recruit was given a medical discharge.

Aware that Stafford was waiting for him to continue, Colfax felt he ought to say something positive about his brief experience at war or, at the very least, sing a verse of "God Bless America." Instead, he nodded somberly and sat a little straighter in the hard-backed leather chair he occupied. There was something about straightness that implied sound values. His father never slumped and Colfax could see the angry old man standing as unbending as an I-beam on their porch in Edenville, hardened by prison, silenced by the emptiness of his life, looking toward the woods that sheltered the last memory of his wife.

"We expect loyalty from our staff," the publisher was saying. "We're a family here. What affects one, affects all. We work together and sometimes play together. Our Christmas parties and Independence Day picnics are solid traditions. World Communism would take all that away from us, son." His voice dropped. "We've got to cling to it with all of our might!"

A vision of Red Army troops parachuting into a company picnic flashed briefly through Colfax's mind, but he squelched it. This was no time for whimsy. His future was at stake.

"You've done your part and I'm proud of that," Stafford said, his voice choking with genuine emotion, reaching across to shake Colfax's hand again, half pulling him out of the chair. Colfax felt the man would drag him across the desk, so deep and sudden was the outpouring of his gratitude.

"Thank you, sir," Colfax said, finally sliding free of his grip. He felt the "sir" suddenly necessary.

"There's a war going on out there, Mr. . . ."—glancing again at the résumé—"Colfax." He paused suddenly. "Colfax. What is that?"

Stafford's tone was intended to be matter-of-fact curiosity, but Colfax sensed something he couldn't quite put his finger on.

"It's a mix. English, French, and Irish, I think. I'm Episcopalian."

"Good, good," Stafford replied, glowing with relief. "Fine people, the Episcopalians."

Colfax resisted the urge to say he considered himself an agnostic and hadn't been in a church in twenty years. Instead, he only nodded, suddenly experiencing the same kind of intense dislike for Stafford that he'd felt for the local preacher when he was a kid, keeping his distance from the man for reasons emerging from instinct rather than reason.

"You know," the publisher said, dropping his voice to a conspiratorial tone, "there's a war going on out there, Mr. Colfax. Not across the ocean. Here, in our own backyard. The Communists can't beat us on the battlefield so they're finding different methods." He let that sink in. "Methods we've all got to be aware of or we'll perish, Mr. Colfax. We'll die like dogs in the street, and newspaper people will be the first to go."

Colfax caught himself staring at the publisher in open disbelief, but changed his expression quickly to one of intense interest.

"I understand."

"Good! Well, we're proud of what you've done to help your country and we expect good things from you here, Mr. Colfax!"

As suddenly as Stafford's emotional gratitude appeared, it vanished. "Mr. Burns will handle the rest," he said, abruptly turning to paperwork.

"Thank you," Colfax said. "I appreciate that." He felt he ought to end the conversation with a salute or a bow, but instead watched for a microsecond as Stafford lowered his head to concentrate on a story he appeared to be editing. The lion's head on the wall seemed similarly preoccupied.

Colfax had turned to leave when Stafford's voice, still stentorian, rose from the man at the desk, who continued hunched over his work. The voice seemed to come from everywhere at once. "Do you have a suit?"

"Well . . . yes."

"We require our reporters to wear suits."

"All right."

"Good."

Nothing else was said. Colfax returned to the city room, where Burns waited, still wearing the amused smile.

"Do you love America?" Burns asked.

Colfax nodded. "I love it even more now," he said, grateful for the man's sense of humor.

"You find him a little strange?"

Colfax shrugged noncommittally.

"He's always been . . . different," Burns said, "but he's gotten even more . . . different . . . since his wife died. She was his balance."

"How'd she die?"

"Her heart stopped."

Burns smiled as he said it, the same kind of secret, muted smile he wore when he first met Colfax. It said he knew something. It said he'd keep it to himself. Colfax received it with a nod that accepted its ambiguity without further question.

"We have a deal with the hotel across the street," the city editor said. "You can stay there for two weeks free until you get a check and can rent your own place."

"That's fine with me."

"Did he tell you to wear a suit?"

"He did."

"You don't have to. But shower regularly. Stafford likes his people clean. Start tomorrow. Six A.M." Burns extended a hand. "Welcome to the ruins. By the way," he added, "you're going to be handling some student demonstrations in Berkeley. They've got antiwar rallies going on, and they're raising noisier hell every day." Pause. "You were wounded?"

"Some shrapnel. I can handle it."

"Yes . . . I'm sure you can."

Burns turned away to say something to a scowling Trager, who had walked up behind him. Colfax, thus dismissed, headed for the door. As he did, he noticed a woman near Stafford's office watching him limp across the room. She was young, strikingly beautiful, and had the straight, flaxen-blond hair that illuminated the era. The interest in her expression was obvious. Colfax smiled slightly, but in the moment it took her to appear, she was gone into Stafford's office.

He felt light-headed as he left the Herald Building, absorbing the elation as though it were some kind of odd and compelling energy filling him to the point of flight. It had been a strange and unsettling morning, from the body on the gurney to the meeting with the George Patton of newspapering, a test of both his wit and his tenacity. He felt a surge of pride for having endured, the way he'd felt when he stepped on American soil again for the first time in eight months. He had come through it, by God. He had weathered the war . . . or in this case the interviews. Now it was on with his life. This was where he wanted to be.

As he crossed the street toward the Mission Hotel, ducking against a light rain, he turned to look back at the high brick tower of the *Herald,* thrust arrogantly upward from the main portion of the building. For a moment, Colfax had the strange impression that the tower was giving him the finger. It was a sign he wasn't taking lightly.

· · ·

Across the bay in Berkeley, Vito Minelli was mounting a platform at U.C.'s Sather Gate before a small crowd of students bearing antiwar signs. It was late afternoon on a day softened by gentle rain. Minelli's voice, amplified to the limit of its decibels by a public address system, stabbed into the softness with the intensity of a bayonet. "No more war!" he cried. "No more fucking war!"

The year was 1965.

CHAPTER TWO

The road to the *Herald* hadn't been easy for him. Colfax lay fully clothed on a couch in the semidarkness of his hotel room listening to the rain, his unfinished dinner growing cold on a table in a far corner. Nondescript music played on a radio. The hotel was old but in better shape than he'd anticipated despite a dank odor to his room. He wondered vaguely why he was more aware of smells than he had been before Vietnam. War, he decided, must sharpen the senses. If he concentrated, he could even evoke the wet-pine fragrance of Edenville, which he recalled now with mixed pleasure and sadness for all it reminded him of.

There was something else that he thought of, an essence that lay in his memory like a dream, the perfume in Laura's hair. It was a whiff of roses that left traces in a room she had occupied or a mist on a pillow where her head had lain. He had never asked what it was in all the months they had been together and he regretted it now. Not that it would have made any difference. She had slipped from his life like a passing breeze, leaving him filled with the possibilities of what might have been. He could still hear her voice on the phone saying good-bye, arranging each word like sounds from an old movie, amplified and hollow, crying as she told him it was over. A year together, a war, and then she was gone.

. . .

In a bar called the Three-Oh on the main floor of the hotel, the remnants of the Jonathan Blair party continued to drink in the dead man's honor, waited on by a large-breasted barmaid named Patty who, it was clear by the nature of her tilt, had joined in much of the gathering's noisy grief-drinking.

"Well," she announced in loud acknowledgment of Blair's passing, "someone has to drink what the poor bastard left!" and downed the bourbon that had been poured for him. The glass was placed upside down next to four others in a ritualistic fashion. Coming up would have been Blair's fifth drink had he survived the heart attack that clobbered him in midstory, a piece about domestic violence that now would never see the light. Its pages, a half dozen sheets of copy paper that remained at his desk, would be buried with him.

In his day, a fifth shot of Old Yellowstone would have been only the beginning of Blair's evening. Single and with no one to be responsible to (although it was said that in his forties he was sleeping with a nun), Blair would often stay late into the night at Three-Oh with only a bartender for company and stagger out to a waiting taxi when the place was closing down. He never drove. He didn't know how. When he tried to learn, he took out three parked cars, a fire hydrant, and a hearse. He never touched a wheel after that.

Trager was at the head of the long table arranged in a corner of the place for Blair's wake. His demeanor had softened not at all away from the city room, the scowl fixed like a permanent imprint on his craggy face. Sally Bell, the woman who had led the clapping in the city room, sat across from him. It was said that once she and Trager were lovers but it had ended in a bitter public brawl, a fistfight at the Three-Oh which, according to eyewitnesses, Sally had won. Now they were friends. Sally smoked Camels, lighting one from the other, and stared with the intensity of a laser beam at wherever her attention was directed. Her knowledge of cops and crime was phenomenal, and there were some who called her Suicide Sally simply because it seemed to fit, but never to her face.

There were two others at the table and a half dozen empty chairs which, up until an hour earlier, had been occupied by friends or co-workers of Blair, including two from the *Daily News* two blocks away. The noise had abated from its earlier din. The toasts to Blair had all been made, the stories all told, and now a silence of memory overlay the small group that remained. Talk, when there was any, was muted. Death at last was being looked in the face and acknowledged.

Colfax entered the bar from a side door that led in from the hotel lobby and hesitated before making his final move into the room. Part of the reason was to allow his eyes to make the adjustment from the brightness of the lobby to the dimness of the Three-Oh, framing him in the doorway long enough for the outlines of the room to take shape. The motif of the Three-Oh was what its habitués liked to call neo-defecation, a combination of heavy browns and tarnished golds that absorbed whatever light was allowed in. Part of it came from a stained-glass window adorned with a series of flute-playing angels and the numeral 30 in Old English script. Contrary to first opinions, the number and the name of the bar had nothing to do with the classic "thirty" that once ended newspaper pieces, but was the address of the bar on Mission Street. It disappointed those who surmised otherwise but did nothing to detract from the mystique that already surrounded the *Herald* and all of its associations. It was a newspaper with a character all its own, a mixture of waterfront muscle and gold-rush sophistication, luring the hardest drinkers and fastest writers to its brick tower. Jack London and Ambrose Bierce had polished both their boozing and their writing skills at different times in a city room that had not changed much since the turn of the century. They were the fast guns on rewrite, transforming the scattered facts of breaking stories into the kind of prose that set a standard for good writing no other newspaper in the state could match.

The Three-Oh was the *Herald*'s chapel, where staffers went to drink and argue and evaluate each other's work. The room was dominated by the bar and included three booths composed of cracking artificial leather, small round tables in the center, and the long table at the end that was traditionally occupied by staffers from the *Herald* at lunch and after work. The owner-bartender, who seemed to be on the job at any hour, was a tidy fat man named Danny Doe, whom everyone called John Doe after the unidentified bodies toe-tagged at the morgue. Doe accepted the name with jolly good humor and had his own pet names for those whose favorite drinks he poured automatically as they walked in the door. It was a relationship that was both warm and distant, forever separated by the bar between them but linked by the needs of their separate yearnings: booze and company for the *Herald* staffers and an essence of power and importance by association for Danny Doe.

Colfax remained in the doorway long enough for Trager to spot him and motion for him to come over. As the others observed Colfax, Trager said, "New man," without further explanation, because he had none. Trager introduced himself in a slurred voice and then Sally Bell, who responded with a wave of her cigarette, leaving a thin trail of smoke in the darkness. Others at the table were an assistant city editor, Sam Perkins, a trim, hard-muscled vegetarian who hated germs and drank nothing but branch water because he had heard it increased a man's testosterone, and Gwen Ballard, the only other woman on rewrite. She was in her late thirties and wore a miniskirt that sometimes seemed to edge up to her waist. Gwen fought to remain painfully thin as though to be otherwise were an abomination in the eyes of God. Colfax guessed she was one of those women who could never accept growing older and clung to her sexuality the way a shark clamps on its prey. Her hair, dyed to a subtle shade of blond, lay in a frizzy clump atop her head as though it had been placed there as an afterthought.

Of those at the table, Gwen was the one who shook his hand and who held it a fraction of a moment too long, sending a message not lost on Colfax. As Colfax seated himself, Trager explained the death ritual Colfax had already heard, but he nodded in response as though he hadn't. He found himself fascinated by Trager's ability to speak without appearing to move his lips, his voice emerging in the combination of a growl and a mumble, but clear enough for him to hear.

The waitress Patty, by now walking with difficulty, brought Colfax a scotch and water, sloshing a little on the table as she placed it in front of him, apologizing and wiping up the spill, then spilling more as she set it down a second time.

"She isn't usually that way," Trager said. "This is a special night. She had some kind of arrangement with Blair."

"He was porking her," Sally Bell said.

"Porking her?" Gwen said it in a tone that was both smirky and incredulous. "Since when did porking replace fucking?"

"He's a new man, for Christ's sake," Sally said, gesturing toward Colfax. "Spare him your piggery."

It was obvious that this kind of bickering went on all the time, but it lacked the teeth of a bitter assault. Ignoring it, Sam Perkins welcomed Colfax warmly and asked a line of questions intended to lay Colfax's history before them. He told them about his birth in Edenville, his two years at North Pacific State College, and then jumped to his tour in the Marines, omitting any of the details that would have fleshed out his story. He was single (Gwen smiled), knew almost no one in the city (she smiled harder), and had come to the *Herald* on the recommendation of the man he'd worked for in Edenville.

Perkins was ready to continue his questioning, sipping at his water like a food critic tasting a new sauce, but Trager waved him off and turned to Colfax.

"You ask the questions," he said. "You've got to have a zillion of them."

They waited as Colfax considered the offer. Patty brought another round of drinks, compliments of Danny Doe. He did that when it was getting near the time he wanted to close. That could be any hour he deemed appropriate. It was ten o'clock now and still raining outside. Gwen's leg was touching Colfax and rubbing slightly. He felt both aroused and uneasy. It had been a long time.

"The *Herald* is non-Guild?" It was both a question and a statement.

"For now," Sally said enigmatically. She lit another cigarette from the glowing end of the one she held, coughing slightly.

"We have an association," Gwen said, turning toward him at a harder angle. There was no place for Colfax to move. His chair was against a wall. He bore her advance without response.

"A *family* association without the power of a baby's dick," Sally added.

"There was an NLRB vote five years ago," Trager said. "The Guild had people lobbying the hell out of us and we were ready to go, but Stafford lowered the boom."

"Go Guild and you end up in the toilet," Gwen said, paraphrasing.

"Burns carried out the old man's word," Trager said. "He hated being the bearer of bad news, but he knew what the score was. He stayed because he wanted to protect us if he could."

"I wonder," Sally said.

The intimidation had been successful. The American Newspaper Guild lost by a landslide vote. The *Herald* Employee Association continued to represent the editorial department, but talk of union had never subsided. It had begun when Stafford's father, a tough and cranky old man, died at age ninety-one and the son moved up from assistant publisher to publisher. Stafford Two was a no-bullshit *news*man, Stafford Three was never considered more than his dumb, slightly awkward son. They thought him too conservative, too profit-conscious, too close to the city's business community. Stafford Three made them nervous three years ago when he took over. He still made them nervous.

Despite the bartender's gesture, the group stayed. Colfax drank scotch and water to a degree he had never done before. Generally he disliked the taste of liquor, but you just didn't drink beer in a crowd like this. Hard liquor was a reporter's sacred wine, the blood of drinkers who had gone before. Downturned glasses continued to line the table, but Patty had long since gone home and the job of downing the contents was passed around.

As the scotch worked on him, Colfax felt increasingly easy with his new colleagues. Only once before, drinking gallons of beer in a squad tent outside of Saigon, had he bonded this much, except maybe for the times he'd shared joints with two *Messenger* reporters in Edenville. It was just after he'd come home. Laura was still strong in his memory and war still had him by the throat. Their willingness to listen to him in the drowsy mist of their smoky conversations was helpful in reestablishing himself stateside.

The time at the Three-Oh slipped easily past midnight. Danny Doe had turned off the exterior neons and closed the bar, sitting on a stool and waiting patiently for the wake to end. He never hurried the *Herald* people, feeling he owed them for having turned Three-Oh into their special place and allowing him into the area of their comradeship, however peripheral that was.

Perkins left when it became obvious that Danny would prefer not pouring any more of anything, even water. Sally Bell departed shortly thereafter. Trager walked her to her car and while they were gone, Gwen, her voice dropping to a husky whisper, gave it everything she had: She had liked Colfax the moment she'd seen him, there had been a flash of something, she felt a warmth she had never known, did he feel something too? As she spoke, she plopped a leg across his lap and smiled suggestively, if drunkenly. Whatever subtlety might have existed had been washed away with alcohol. Colfax could sense the heat of her body enveloping him. He wondered if her next move would be to drag him to the floor and rip off his clothes. Danny Doe watched with interest. Colfax tried to figure out what to do. It was not the best way to launch a career.

"I have to use the bathroom," he finally said, pushing himself free.

"I'll go with you," Gwen said, still leering.

There was no doubt in his mind that she intended to follow. He wasn't ready for that. "That's okay," he said, resigning himself. "It can wait."

She shrugged and threw her leg back over his lap. "Suit yourself."

When Trager returned, Gwen pulled her leg back and Colfax tried to sit upright, but he could tell by Trager's expression that the copy chief knew what was going on and didn't care. It was almost a tradition at the *Herald* that Gwen Ballard tried to hump every new man who walked through the door and only occasionally succeeded. Trager accepted her current attempt nonchalantly while sympathizing with Colfax's discomfort, and opened a large leather case he was carrying to reveal a gilt-edged harp. Both Gwen and Danny Doe responded with enthusiasm, and Colfax with curiosity. To see a man like Trager with his permanent angry scowl holding an instrument as gentle as a harp was a clash of realities that Colfax couldn't compromise.

"You play that?" he said to Trager.

"He plays it beautifully," Gwen said, slurring. She meant it.

"I'll say," Danny Doe added, moving his bar stool closer.

"I found a harp in a dump when I was a kid," Trager said in a voice that was uncharacteristically soft. "Can you imagine someone throwing away a harp? You wonder just what the hell was going through their head." He plucked a few strings. "Maybe someone died. Maybe there was a divorce. It was in good shape, so I kept screwing around with it. A guy in a music store heard about it and gave me lessons. Pretty soon . . ."

He began playing. The sweetness of the music drifted through the darkness like ribbons of light, enveloping them gently in a sadness that music by its very nature creates, holding each in an isolation of individual memory, yet somehow binding them. Colfax only recognized one of the tunes, "Danny Boy," but it didn't matter. They blended together as Trager played. No one spoke a word, no one moved, and Colfax, glad he had come here, closed his eyes and let himself sink into the comfort and camaraderie of the harp.

In an alley off Van Ness Avenue, two men huddled together in the rain, looking down the eastern end of the corridor toward a large building across the street. One of them was Vito Minelli. A beard and mustache covered most of his face and his long dark hair stuck out from under the cloth seaman's hat he wore pulled down to cover his forehead. He was a slightly built man with eyes that glowed in the faint illumination of streetlights that cast shadows from Van Ness into the passageway they occupied. Neither man spoke, their attention focused tightly toward the alley's end.

"They're coming," Minelli finally said, cocking his head toward a sound the other man was only now beginning to hear, the faint padding of someone running, shoes slapping on wet pavement, the tempo growing quicker as the sound grew louder. Then faint silhouettes appeared at the eastern end of the alley, two men running fast toward Minelli and his accomplice, a thin, edgy man named Ted Strickland.

"It's done," the larger of the runners said, puffing from the exertion and excitement.

The other, dressed in a janitor's uniform, held his watch up to the existing light, squinting to see the minute hand sweeping around the dial.

"Two minutes," he said.

"You placed it in the receptionist's office," Minelli said, verifying.

"Under the desk," the large man said. They stood silently, listening.

"One minute," the other said.

They waited, their stares fixed on the building across the street.

"Thirty seconds."

The rain had abated and only a soft mist fell now. It was the kind that touches with the softness of a baby's kiss and dampens a woman's hair into gentle curls. The four men who waited were unaware of the rain or of a cold wind that swept down the alley.

"Ten seconds."

And then it blew.

The explosion, coming from within the building, was the quick, muted *harrummph!* of a fat man's indignation, following by the tinkling of breaking glass and the scattering of debris over Van Ness. Smoke rose in large, dark billows from several windows of the third floor and then flames licked at the sky's soft mist. The two who had set the bomb yowled in delight. Minelli nodded with satisfaction. Strickland remained silent, staring at the smoke that thickened over the Federal Building. Then, at Minelli's gesture, they headed almost casually down the alley in the opposite direction, where an old Volkswagen van waited. They piled in like kids going to a party and then van sped off into the night.

Had they been inside the building, they would have heard a man's anguished scream piercing the silence, segueing into the sounds of sirens. . . .

The red phone rang at Three-Oh, jangling into Trager's music, an intrusion that startled them. Trager stopped playing instantly. Danny Doe grabbed the phone by reaching over the bar, and handed it to Gwen Ballard in one quick movement. It was Mel Collins on the night city desk, looking for any reporter available. Gwen listened, acknowledged, threw the phone back to Danny Doe, and was halfway to the door, suddenly sober, before she said a word.

Then she called back, "Someone's blown up the FBI, you wanna come?"

It was directed at Colfax, who shouted, "Hell, yes," and followed her out the door, leaving the old copy chief and his harp and Danny Doe sitting alone in the bar.

A photographer's car, emerging from the *Herald*'s underground garage, made a wild U-turn in the middle of Mission and skidded to a wet stop in front of the Three-Oh. Gwen and Colfax piled in and the photographer, a bulky man in his thirties, his face bright with anticipation, gunned the car away from the curb as though he were racing at Indianapolis, three radio scanners going at the same time, one hand holding a microphone that linked him to the city desk, the other hand gripping and spinning the steering wheel as though it were a toy.

"The madman at the wheel is Milton Travis," Gwen shouted over the sound of the scanners. "This is Bill Colfax," she said to the photographer.

"I'm part monkey," the big man shouted back, "which makes me a little crazy!" He laughed loudly.

"Pleased to meet you," Colfax shouted back. "I'm part Irish."

Now both men were laughing while Gwen shook her head,

thoughts of a sexual encounter with Colfax out the window. "Jesus," she said in mock disgust, inwardly glad that the new man could see her at work, all of her senses tingling.

"Anybody killed?" she asked Travis.

"Maybe," he said. "An agent was probably the only one on duty monitoring the phones. They're still digging through the mess. A hell of a story!"

The car raced up Mission, swung right on Van Ness, and headed toward the dark smoke still rising in dying puffs from the Federal Building, illuminated in spotlights that gave it form and substance. Sirens continued to sound with the rising intensity of a scream.

Back in Berkeley, Minelli and the others had gathered in Minelli's basement apartment, watching the one television station that had managed to get a camera to the explosion. An open bottle of Jack Daniel's was on the floor before them. A joint was passed around.

The reporter on the scene, an almost pretty man in Levi's and a leather jacket, was describing what he saw with broad gestures and an edgy excitement at odds with his carefully created appearance. A camera panned across the area of activity: firemen running in and out of the building carrying hoses, others on ladders spraying water from the outside through windows from which smoke poured, policemen holding back a surprisingly large crowd of those still up at two A.M. who had stopped to watch.

The reporter, handed a piece of paper, read it quickly to himself and then, his voice lowered to an appropriate tone of remorse, said, "We have just learned that the victim, identified as FBI Agent Leonard Rose, badly injured in the explosion, has died on the operating table at St. Mary's Hospital. I repeat, agent Leonard Rose has died of his injuries. . . ."

"I thought there was nobody in there!" one of the men in the room suddenly cried out, abruptly turning down the sound. Silent images moved across the television screen.

"I didn't think there was," the man in the janitor's uniform said. "What the hell do we do now?"

Vito Minelli, watching the images with almost scientific curiosity, frozen into a posture of concentration, said nothing at first.

"We killed someone." The words, dropped into the room like the lower tones of a dirge, came from the lips of Ted Strickland, who stared at the screen with the intensity of an animal suddenly, chillingly, aware of a predator.

It was only then that Minelli pulled himself away from the forms and faces that rushed like mimes across the picture tube.

"People die in wars," he said. "This is a lesson no one will soon forget."

Then, to the surprise of the others, Vito Minelli managed a smile.

CHAPTER THREE

G wen Ballard wrote the main story of the FBI explosion and Colfax composed a sidebar. It was not something he had intended to do, but Burns, as calm and clear-eyed as a surgeon, was waiting in the city room when they returned from the Federal Building and ordered it done for the first edition. It was almost three A.M. and the night and the liquor were taking effect on Colfax. His eyes were heavy and his head ached, but he'd felt worse at war and managed to survive; he'd manage here too. He drank yesterday's coffee from an urn that was never switched off, a thick, strong brew which, if allowed to gel, would have become a solid block. Then he went to work trying to re-create on paper the vision of chaos he had witnessed a short time earlier. He pored through clips from the *Herald*'s library to flesh out details of the old building on Van Ness and the woes which of late had befallen the FBI in the midst of antiwar protests sweeping the country. Though the experience was new to him, being at the scene of the explosion had somehow seemed perfectly natural to Colfax, a soldier in the army of reporters and photographers moving in on the fire with the intensity of a combat team. He could easily superimpose the faces of the men he knew at war over the faces of the journalists who plucked words and pictures from the inferno.

But mostly Colfax remembered the people who had gathered

around the building, the agents who had suddenly lost their stiff and faceless placidity and become, in the hard emotions of reality, true humans, angry and vulnerable, and the bystanders who licked up the elements of calamity as though it were a spiritual aphrodisiac. He remembered the voices, the shouts and murmurs, and the sizzle of rain on hot timbers. He remembered the isolated vision of heat and fire and smoke rolling into the dark sky the way he remembered it from Vietnam, and wrote as though he were possessed. Image blended into memory with the heat and intensity of a napalm explosion, blowing away the barriers that limited journalism to its cautious form. Colfax didn't think. He just wrote.

Across the room, Gwen alternated between telephoning and writing, the mouthpiece of her telephone headset jammed so close to her face she appeared somehow robotic. The clatter of their Remingtons dueling in the otherwise predawn quiet of the city room created flyspecks of sound that seemed at odds with the pervasive silence. Without making a conscious decision to do so, Colfax held nothing back and in the end wondered if he had created something, as Dustin had once said, that made dogs howl. It was not intended as a compliment but as criticism of prose that was garishly florid. Colfax, however, made no effort to significantly alter what he'd written, other than changing a word or two, committing himself to the emotions that had swept over him at the scene of the explosion, never compromising, never limiting. A sidebar was intended to flesh out the main story with the kind of color that hard news ignored, adorning fact with parallel observations.

Burns said nothing as he read the piece, marking with a pencil here and there and finally handing the story back to a night copy editor, who bent over it as though he would devour the words and the paper like a plate of chow mein, never once looking up until he rolled the copy paper up, placed it in a vacuum tube, and sent it hissing down to the composing room. Colfax would learn later that the man was almost blind and, refusing glasses, needed the proximity to what he read in order to make out the words he was editing. His ability to catch the smallest of errors, however, exceeded his physical disability and few complained. His name was Moses Moore. Reporters, not unkindly, called him the Bat.

Gwen finished her story, argued with Burns about her lead, and finally stomped off without a word to Colfax, the early evening ardor gone in the new heat of a major story. The argument was a short one, which the city editor would tolerate without once raising his voice, his quality of amusement maintained even during debate. Few had ever heard him shout, defying the image of the city editor as bellowing monster of the newsroom. Burns allowed protest, knowing it was good for his people to blow off their energies, remaining implacable in the face of the worst assaults. But in the end his editing almost always remained intact. Not even Stafford was inclined to alter it.

As the door closed behind Gwen, Burns shrugged and said he was going to lie on a couch for a while. Colfax should go get some sleep. Having said that, he disappeared down a far bend in the hall that led to the Sunday Department, where a couch waited in a corner office. It was also where a bottle of Smirnoff waited. The city editor would drink exactly two shots and then lie still, resting with his eyes open, as though he had ascended into a state of limbo where no one and nothing dwelled. He had learned the technique early in his career, working days on the waterfront and nights on the police beat of the old *Seattle Crusader.* You grabbed sleep where you could and buried your exhaustion in the secret places where the Smirnoff took you.

Colfax and the Bat were left alone in the city room, now cloaked in a hushed silence following the burst of activity. Even the wire service Teletypes, normally chattering in the background, were momentarily still. Colfax slipped into his junior high jacket and headed for the back elevator. As he passed the city desk, its telephone suddenly rang into the stillness. The Bat looked up, first at the phone, a fuzzy image on the main desk, and then at Colfax. The phone continued to ring.

"Answer the damned thing," he finally said.

Colfax hesitated and then reached out. Without preamble a voice said, "The People's Voice has spoken to the federal pigs who perpetuate war. Now the war comes to them. Is the *Herald* next?" Then the phone went dead.

Colfax had never said a word. He didn't have time to. He wrote what he had heard on a half piece of copy paper on Burns's desk and then wondered what to do. Was it the real bomber or only some nut cashing in on the calamity? Colfax returned to his typewriter, wrote a paragraph about the phone message, and left it for Burns to use or discard. Weariness had suddenly enveloped him like a thickening fog and he didn't really care what happened from that point on. His work was done. Then, still trying to place the voice, he limped across the room to the elevator and then to the Mission Hotel. It was four in the morning. Rain continued to fall into the sad and weary night.

The first newspaper off the large, noisy Hoe presses was traditionally delivered to Stafford at his sprawling Colonial-style home in the Marina, a monstrous, gleaming white neighborhood anomaly the staff referred to derisively as Tara. He read it in robe and slippers in a growing rage. This was the street edition and its headline in large black type was splashed across the top of the page with biblical condemnation: FBI OFFICE BOMBED! The subhead said, AGENT KILLED IN TERROR ATTACK. As he read the stories, his face reddening, a television set in the background reported the same bombing in its morning news report, repeating what little was known about the explosion.

It was six A.M. and the sun was beginning to rise through the mist that lay over the hills of Marin County in the distance. From his window, had he chosen to pull away from the front page of his newspaper, Stafford could look down to the bay and then to the ocean that spread out in gray masses below his compound, and to the Golden Gate Bridge that connected the city to its suburban neighbor. But Stafford was in no mood to enjoy the view as he hurled the newspaper aside with manic force and telephoned his city editor.

"It's the goddamn Communists!" his daughter heard him say as she came down the stairs from her bedroom, still soft with sleep, her blond hair touched by the muted light from a high window, wearing the dreamy sunrise as though morning were created for her. She crossed the large room silently, her bare feet sinking into the thick carpeting, and picked up the newspaper her father had flung across the room. She knew he'd be talking to his city editor and wondered what had ignited his rage. She sat on a sofa and tucked her feet up under her as she read, clutching a robe around her against the grayness outside that somehow seemed to seep up from the bay and into their home.

"They attack the government and the newspapers," Stafford was saying into the telephone mouthpiece, his voice rolling with the tonal qualities of a distant thunder, "and we will be prepared for it. Security will be doubled, and I want to know exactly what was said and precisely how it was said! Send him over immediately. Have someone drive him. Gerald"—his voice dropped—"this is what I have often predicted and anticipated. We must take measures."

As he hung up, Stafford turned to his daughter, his features drawn into an expression that foresaw doom. "These are dangerous times," he said. She watched him curiously and, knowing his deep concern was real, she put down the newspaper, crossed the room, and embraced him.

She had seen his anger growing over the years since his father had died and wondered, as she had learned in class, whether he was suffering feelings of abandonment and in response was looking around for the comfort of a cause. He had come to see the existence of Communism as a personal affront and resistance to the war in Vietnam as a kind of blasphemy. His anger, as she embraced him, was palpable.

A pounding on the door awakened Colfax like the distant drumming of artillery. He bolted upright from a paralyzing sleep and, still in his underwear, opened the door a crack to peer out, trying to focus, his vision blurry, for a moment confused by his surroundings and by his own sudden response to the pounding. The door pushed open and a woman entered. She wore a yellow slicker but no hat, and her short dark hair was plastered by rain against her head. She was petite and perky, as though she had bounced out of a fairy tale holding a magic wand, and for a moment Colfax stood by the door staring at her, and she stared back, admiring what she saw, not displeased with his near nakedness.

"I'm Jill Carter," she said, thrusting out her hand. "I'm a copyboy. Well, actually a copygirl, but we're all called boys. You're Colfax."

"Yes," he said, hurriedly slipping on his pants.

"You're all over page one," Jill said, handing him a newspaper tucked under her arm.

He scanned the front page. His story was given equal play to Gwen's and it bore his name, a rare occurrence at the *Herald*. Bylines were given sparingly and only for extraordinary reporting or writing. Gwen's story was unsigned, a fact that caused a feeling of apprehension in Colfax as he wondered how he would deal with it later. Additionally, a box reporting the threatening phone call had been rewritten to include the fact that it had been Colfax who had received it. His first day in the big city had been a heady one. The realization of what had occurred washed over him, and while the weariness of the night remained, the sleepiness was disappearing. He felt as though he were once more at war and expected to endure the long days without sleep, replacing exhaustion with the notion that to stop was to die. "Stay awake," a gunnery sergeant had said to him once. "Life is short and death is long."

"Not bad for the first day," Jill was saying, pulling Colfax's attention away from his own prose.

"Why are you here?" he said.

"To deliver you to Stafford."

"The publisher?"

"He wants you now, like chop-chop, and I'm supposed to take you there. It's a copyboy's job."

"What's he want?"

"I don't know, but I wouldn't screw around, if I were you."

Colfax dressed quickly while Jill watched. He thought for a moment she would follow him into the bathroom and he locked the door very deliberately while he was in there.

The *Herald* was like nothing he had expected. It was happening too fast for Colfax, the drunkenness, the story, the people. It was a world in microcosm, a kingdom unto itself that operated with a disturbing sense of isolation even as it reached out to cover the news, bold in its mission yet somehow uncomfortable with its station. Those he had met so far were almost excessively individualistic and yet, in their way, seemed to fit perfectly into the whole unit.

He was wearing his only suit when he moved quickly up the stairs to the door of Stafford's home, leaving Jill waiting in the car. The suit was a brown corduroy and decidedly rumpled. Colfax tried his best to straighten his tie and smooth back his hair, but everything about him seemed rumpled, and as he waited for someone to answer the door, he gave up smoothing anything and left himself to fate, like a man facing a firing squad, watching his executioners lock and load.

Stafford himself opened the door, still in his robe and slippers, wearing an expression of deep concern. He was on the phone and motioned Colfax to enter while still talking to someone, expecting the reporter to follow him inside. Once Colfax was there, the publisher motioned for him to sit, then vanished into another room, following the long telephone cord into privacy. As Colfax waited, the woman he had seen the day before in the city room entered.

"I'm Ellen Stafford," she said, then added somewhat whimsically, "the boss's daughter."

Colfax rose quickly, as much in respect of her beauty as her position.

"I'm William Stafford . . . I mean Colfax," he said, wincing at his error. "It's early," he added lamely.

Ellen's laugh bore the quality of wind chimes. "Maybe some coffee would help," she said. She walked toward a kitchen, leaving Colfax silently cursing himself, and returned with two cups.

"Nice job today," she said. "You blew my father away."

"Is that why he wants me?"

"Ask him."

As she said that, Stafford reentered the room, done with the other distracting business, concentrating completely now on Colfax. It wasn't the reporter's prose he was concerned with. It was the telephone threat he wanted to know about, the message that resounded like a bugle call from a distant enemy to attack all that Stafford held dear.

War had left Colfax often detached from his surroundings, as though from a position in a corner of his own mind he could observe the goings-on without involvement. He experienced uneasiness, to be sure, but he faced what was necessary with quiet aplomb. Fear was not a quality that affected him easily. It had burned itself out in Vietnam, so intense were the fires of terror that possessed him at different times during combat.

Stafford sensed in the man who sat across from him in the vast open living room of the publisher's home that Colfax was someone to be dealt with, not treated like most of the reporters who populated the beats and the city room of his newspaper. Here was a United States Marine who had carried America's might to a far corner of the world, unlike the dirty, bearded slobs, the queers and the Communists, their minds fried by drugs, who waged war against their own country on the streets.

"Mr. Colfax," Stafford said, "we have arrived at a most serious moment in our history and you and I are playing a significant role." Both Colfaxes watched and waited. Ellen sipped coffee and listened.

Vito Minelli scanned the newspaper with satisfaction, ignoring Ted Strickland's nervous pacing. Strickland had brought him the paper and now, his T-shirt and jeans drenched from the rain, he abruptly stopped pacing and faced Minelli. "I can't believe you *telephoned* the newspaper!" he said incredulously. Minelli continued to ignore him, even though he had absorbed the words written about the explosion and the telephone call. He was thinking, dwelling in the kind of enclave of silence he often created when there was something to explore that was beyond anyone with him.

"You'll catch pneumonia," he finally said, observing Strickland for the first time. "Don't you have a poncho or an umbrella or something?"

"I can't believe you telephoned the newspaper," Strickland said again.

"How do you know it was me?"

There was little furniture in the room of the small apartment in the basement of a converted Victorian building on Channing Way, a mile from Berkeley's U.C. campus. Minelli sat on a cushion propped against a wall. His sleeping bag lay in disarray on one side of the room under the only window in the place that looked upward toward the street level. Cardboard covered the window's lower pane. Paper bags that had once borne fast food into the room lay crumpled in a corner.

"It was you, wasn't it?" Strickland demanded.

"For Christ's sake, man, go into the bathroom, get a towel, and dry yourself off. There's some extra Levi's in the closet, and a T-shirt. They're dirty, but they're dry."

"Goddamn it, Minelli, tell me!"

"I don't know who called them, okay? Maybe some nut, like when there's a murder that gets a lot of attention, everyone confesses. It's a human instinct to be heard, to be noticed. Don't worry. Now get dry."

"But they knew our name!"

Minelli shrugged. "Someone came up with it by accident. We'll change it. From now on we're the People's Army."

"I don't like messing with the FBI. We never should have bombed that place." Strickland began to pace again, his voice breaking. "God, man, we *killed* somebody! *We fucking killed somebody!*"

It was not Minelli's habit to placate or comfort. He sat watching Strickland for a long moment, wondering about him, observing the trail of water the man was leaving around the room. His sneakers sloshed and squeaked as he walked.

"Dry yourself."

There was something in Minelli's voice that caused Strickland to hesitate and then finally to head for the bathroom to dry off. He had known Minelli only a short time, but sensed in him an ominous quality behind what he considered a brilliant mind. He was convinced it had been Minelli who had called the *Herald,* but there was no proof. Had Minelli known an agent remained in the building they had bombed? Strickland found himself suffocating, frightened in his tenuousness and doubting the man he had committed himself to follow in the name of peace and a new government.

When Strickland emerged from the bathroom still trying to dry himself with a large red bath towel, Minelli was ready.

"Remember this," he said without preamble, "we are a people's army, at war with forces that are killing us overseas and subjugating us at home. We are the strike force of those without recourse, the dispossessed, the victims of America, the politicians who feed our brothers into a war machine that eats them alive."

Minelli stood, triumphant in his logic, ludicrous in his underwear, jabbing his rhetoric home with a finger pointed like a gun at Strickland.

"We are the one hope that America has, an army of intellectuals who can outthink and who will ultimately surround and destroy them. If we don't, Ted, they'll destroy us. It is our wits that will win the war we wage on America's soil, but the battles will be fought on their own savage levels until our point is made."

Minelli ended his speech by putting his arm around Strickland's soaked shoulders.

"Believe me," he said, "I know this."

After Strickland had left the apartment, Minelli rolled a joint and sat contemplating the events that had thrust him abruptly into the mainstream of the news. Then he picked up the newspaper and looked at its front page again. Satisfaction, he thought, was a very good feeling.

"I want you to find these people for me, Mr. Colfax," Stafford was saying. "That is your prime mission at my newspaper. Find and expose them. Think of yourself in the jungles of Vietnam. You know that somewhere in the underbrush an enemy is waiting." Stafford crossed the room and sat next to Colfax. He leaned close to him, so that their noses were almost touching. "They have killed our President and now they have killed an agent of the Federal Bureau of Investigation. God only knows who might be next. Flush them out, Mr. Colfax. Do that."

Images of John Kennedy, head thrown back, clutching his throat, flashed through Colfax's mind. Had it only been two years ago? Time was stretching out behind him, moving slowly into the mists that clouded his life before the war. . . .

As he had done the first time they met, Stafford ended the conversation abruptly, this time leaving the room. Colfax could hear his voice on the telephone again. He turned to Ellen. "I guess that's all," he said, couching it so it was half question and half statement.

"This is very personal to my father," Ellen said. Colfax sensed a tone of apology. "He feels very strongly that our country is in danger from the radical left."

"How do you feel?"

Ellen smiled. It was golden. "Probably not quite as strongly."

Colfax nodded. He knew he should get up and leave but didn't want to. There was something in Ellen's manner that reminded him of Laura: a way of speaking, a vulnerable self-assurance, a presence, a radiance.

"Do you work at the newspaper?" he finally asked.

"I'm full-time at Berkeley," she said. "My dad keeps wanting me to come aboard and I suppose someday I will. But right now it's study, study, study. Even rich girls have to pass tests."

She said it with a kind of piquancy that teased a chuckle from Colfax. He didn't laugh any more easily than he smiled, but he felt relaxed with Ellen.

"You know," he said, opening up, "this may have been the strangest two days in my life. Stranger even than boot camp."

"Stick around," Ellen said, her eyebrows arching, "they're bound to get stranger."

Jill bitched on the way back to the hotel that she had to wait a hell of a lot longer than she'd expected, but Colfax wasn't listening. He kept thinking of Stafford and Ellen and his mission to flush out a bomber hiding in the jungle. . . .

CHAPTER
FOUR

C olfax slowly ceased to be the new man and began to blend into the pattern of activity that was the *Herald*'s city room. His surroundings lost their odd foreign glow and began to settle into tones of familiarity that told Colfax he was assimilating. It had been that way when he'd first arrived in the battle zones around Saigon. The landscape, with its rice paddies in the foreground and hazy mountains in the distance, had worn the same glow of unfamiliarity accentuated by new smells and the unsettling, pastel-washed color of the sky. Only when he had settled in did the glow vanish and the hard colors of reality stand out in harsh relief, transforming anticipation to acceptance with a rush that told Colfax he was, without doubt, at war.

To say he was no longer new to the *Herald*, however, was not to say he had been embraced by the regulars who inhabited the newspaper's third floor. There were undercurrents he was not privy to, whispered asides he was unable to decipher. His explosive entry at the paper had placed Colfax in a strange position. He was simultaneously viewed with awe and envy, a combination that shattered old attitudes of what new people were supposed to be. They were to be taken around, shown the ropes, and patronized to the degree that they didn't know what the old-timers knew, what the past hid, what the present foretold. Instead, his prose had rung with emotion and authority, the anguished outcry of someone who had been hurt and survived and, by the brutal cleansing of pain, had emerged with better vision.

Oddly, this denied Colfax the patronization necessary to acquaint him with the strange surroundings he found himself in. He was new, but he wasn't. His position was unclear due to that first story and to Stafford's anointment of him as a kind of chief investigator who would save the *Herald* from the mad bombers that ran amok around them. Colfax hungered for the insights that an informal orientation would afford, but, to an extent, they were withheld from him by his sudden stature, except for those who had been a part of his birth at the *Herald*: Gerald Burns, Sally Bell, Trager, Gwen Ballard, and, to a lesser degree, the assistant city editor, Sam Perkins. Colfax realized what little knowledge he had of the place when it occurred to him one day that he didn't know Trager's first name. When he asked Sally Bell, she replied around the cigarette in her mouth that copy editors didn't require first names, and then as she walked away she said, "Shit." That was part of the *Herald*'s lore, created some years before by a reporter named O'Neil, who, the victim of severe Trager editing, had stood on his desk and announced grandly that henceforth Trager would be known as Shit. In some ways an elegant man though a notorious drunk, O'Neil had died of cirrhosis, but had at least added to the mythology of newspapering in one fine moment of defiance that lived on among those who had witnessed it. Trager's first name, Colfax learned later, was Shuit.

Only Corona McGee seemed willing to treat Colfax as a pathetic beginner. A staff artist who occupied a closet-sized office in a back corner of the *Herald* called the Tomb, her job was mainly to size and airbrush the photographs rushed in by copyboys, although it was rumored she was an accomplished painter on her own. Colfax had met her at the Three-Oh. She was at a booth with Trager, who motioned him over and introduced him to the dark-haired woman, who observed him with almost open disdain. "You could use some editing," she said to him after the introduction. He could see it was a comment not intended as humor and yet there was a look to her that said neither was it intended as malice. "An adjective that runs like lava buries the essence of the content." She paused. "Whatever that means."

Colfax wasn't sure how to handle her. There was a flash of intelligence in Corona McGee which, while she wasn't a knockout, added an element of knowing that was beauty in itself. She was alert, quick, almost cobralike in her assessments, striking suddenly and then backing off to wait while her victim writhed. But in her case there was no venom to her bite. It was a mind game played by a wicked cobra and its prey.

Trager managed a smile through his scowl. "Corona is kept in seclusion most of the time, which limits her degree of humanity. You might say she hasn't evolved as far as the rest of us."

"Bullshit," Corona said. "They're protecting me from the contagion of mediocrity."

"Well, anyhow," Colfax said, a little nonplussed by the encounter, "I'm glad to meet you." He would have extended his hand but knew she would have left it untouched, hanging in midair like a fish whose flopping about is over.

"Whatever," she said, downing her drink. "I'm just telling you to cool your passions. Take that for what it's worth. New people have to learn discipline." Having said that, she slid down the seat of the booth, got to her feet, and headed for the door. It was the first time Colfax realized that she was barely four feet tall.

"Christ, she's a midget!" he said aloud.

"There's some debate about that," Trager said, watching as she pushed aggressively through the doorway onto the street. A flash of sunlight caused them both to squint.

"What debate? She's short! *Real* short!"

"True," Trager said, nodding wisely, "but whether she's a midget or a dwarf has never been established. Her upper body is normal, but her legs short, making her small. As such, she could either be a midget or a dwarf. Or maybe a fucking elf."

"It seems odd."

"Burns hires people like that once in a while. We had a deaf guy covering sports for us for six years. He read lips. That's all he needed. Covering baseball demands little else. Burns believes that journalism does not require full faculties. That's why I got hired. He found me limping around a butcher shop once and asked if I could read."

"You were a butcher?"

"For a while."

"And the limp?"

"Polio as a kid. By the way, I've been meaning to mention this. Don't ever walk side by side with me. Both of us limping, we look like a comedy team."

Colfax saw Corona McGee in the elevator. He said hello, then, after an appropriate pause, added wryly, "It's a simple word but slightly overblown and possibly in need of editing." She looked at him without answering, as though it were beneath her, but glanced back as she left. He thought he detected a smile.

Colfax had begun researching the FBI bombing by heading for the U.C. campus, where it seemed a hundred revolutions were stirring simultaneously. Their presence became evident as he aimed his company-owned Chevrolet off the Eastshore Freeway onto University Avenue. It had been declared Peace Day in Berkeley, during which the city and the students at the university were gathering signatures to send to Washington demanding that Lyndon Johnson meet personally with Ho Chi Minh to stop the war.

Blue and white flags emblazoned with peace symbols hung from cables strung across the main thoroughfares, and students in cars and on foot chanting, "No more war," trailed down San Pablo Avenue, blocking the traffic that headed east toward the sprawling university campus. Colfax's car was first in line at the intersection waiting for the parade to pass, affording him an unblocked view of the marchers, some of them young women without the benefit of tops, their naked breasts thrust proudly forward in symbols of youth and arrogance on a day washed into high gloss by the cleansing action of a passing storm.

Colfax watched with fascination, intrigued by the world that was presenting itself, a world twisted into a new form in the two years he had been gone, a world with new goals, new sounds, new clothes, new symbols, and a new morality. It was a world in which blacks marched, revolutionaries shouted, buildings blew up, and women thrust their legs apart more as an element of defiance than a sexual invitation. He felt no part of this generation that was essentially his own, as though in his absence it had been shifted onto another plane, leaving him to study it from afar, as he studied the passing parade.

The marchers cleared the intersection in less than fifteen minutes and Colfax drove on beneath the city-sanctioned peace banners that fluttered in a cool and gentle breeze. The antiwar movement was reaching a wild pitch and Berkeley, alone among cities, had spear-headed it by declaring its intention to send a peace delegation to Hanoi in defiance of State Department restrictions if the war was not ended by Christmas. As he parked and walked, limping slightly, toward the campus, a young woman, one of it seemed hundreds, pressed a small peace flag in his hand, kissed him, and said, "Fuck the war," as she moved on to down the block. It was offered in a tone that was more mechanical than passionate, reflecting a detachment that repetition creates, though the wetness of her kiss lingered on his mouth like a taste of rain, fresh and unflavored, stirring memories.

His own feelings about the war were rooted in a far different place, where only raw emotion existed, without banners and slogans or marchers, without tits and beards and acid trips, without youth or the party atmosphere that revolutions invariably engendered. Whenever Colfax thought about the war it was with a sense of repressed sadness for the shadows behind the word itself. War, the word, meant nothing to those who had never been in one. Lurking behind the simple word were moments so violent and grief so profound that even if there existed a movie lens so wide-angled it could capture the entire field of conflict, it would still not properly represent even an instant of what war involves. No lens looks to the soul, and that's where war exists on its most elemental level.

The peace movement neither appealed to him nor offended him but remained in a neutral area of his brain as he observed it from the distance of a journalist. He would remain thus detached, he promised himself. That was his job.

He found Schroeder Hall with difficulty. It was an older, two-story building on the far eastern end of the campus, built during the Second World War to house military personnel attending classes as part of an officer-training program. After the war it was given over to faculty offices, and still later, considered too remote for the faculty, sat abandoned until world media focused on the university as a headquarters for whatever revolution was blowing in the wind. Eucalyptus trees planted during the war now surrounded the colorless square building, their fallen leaves creating a soft walkway, the reddish bark pealing and their branches untended. This was a forgotten place only newly stirred to life, and the *Herald*'s Office of the Revolution, as it was called, was located here.

As Colfax walked down the hall looking for the office, he became aware of footsteps behind him and turned to see an older man enter the building. From a distance, Colfax could see he was in his fifties or even early sixties, balding, slightly overweight, and moving slowly in Colfax's direction. He could have been someone's grandfather except . . . Colfax was not sure what the except would have been. There was simply an aura about the man, a strength, a presence, that didn't include anything small and cuddly bouncing on his knee.

Colfax found the *Herald*'s office. It was the last one in the row of offices, from some of which he could hear voices or typewriters and once or twice the direct-wire sound of Teletype machines. Someone had cut out and pasted the masthead of the *Herald* on the door; otherwise there was nothing to identify it, or any of the offices, for that matter. Without guidance, a stranger would have to knock on every door to find what he was looking for.

Rather than knock, Colfax simply pushed the door open into an empty room. "Hello?" There was no reply to his call. "Anyone here?"

Still silence. He poked his head into another room, which held a desk with a typewriter and telephone. Next to the desk were stacks of newspapers and in a corner a television set that played with its sound muted, silent images of a game show moving in ghostly cadence across the screen. Diagonals of sunlight streamed through the dusty windows, casting the room in a surreal glow. "Hello!" he called again, louder.

Before the sound had faded, a door on one side of the room was thrust suddenly open and a woman emerged straightening her skirt, startling Colfax with her sudden appearance. "What the hell are you shouting for?" she demanded angrily. The sound of a flushing toilet trailed behind her. "I was in the goddamn toilet!"

"Sorry," Colfax said. He watched her cross the room and then said, "I'm William Colfax."

"I know who you are," she replied, sitting at the desk and spinning the chair to face him.

Her name was R. B. Kane and, only in her late twenties, she was already a legend. She had covered every major story since the day she'd entered a newspaper office, including a stint in Vietnam as a correspondent for the *Herald.* They had sent her to Washington when John Kennedy was assassinated, and the odd, clipped tone of her prose had brought the city to tears. She was a tall, rawboned woman with dark hair cut short around her face and a mannish way of moving, and it was suspected that R. B. was a lesbian, but no one would ever say it to her face. She was a powerful woman, both physically and psychologically, and one feared the latter more than the former. Her temper was quick and her rage terrible, but her value to the *Herald* was indisputable.

R.B. was a reporter, and she wore the title like a uniform. She knew every cop and federal agent from San Jose to Santa Rosa and eastward into Contra Costa County. She called politicians, including the governor of California, by their first names. It was said that twice she had been nominated by Burns for Pulitzers on her brief coverage of the war, but was bypassed by a committee that didn't want to recognize women in the role of combat correspondents despite their ever-increasing numbers in the fields of blood. Now the war she covered as a legman was in the Eastbay where the revolution festered.

"Let's get to it, I've got things to do," she said as Colfax waited until she had finished assessing him.

"I'm ready when you are, Rosebud."

The voice came from behind Colfax and he turned to face the man he had seen down the hall. He had entered the room soundlessly and stood leaning against a wall, waiting for his entry to be acknowledged.

"Up yours, Bruno," she replied, but not without amusement. Then, realizing the two men had never met, she added, "Bruno Hagen, meet William Colfax."

"You're FBI?" Colfax asked, unable to conceal his surprise.

"You had expected J. Edgar Hoover?" Hagen said.

"He had expected something better," R. B. interjected, enjoying Colfax's predicament.

Hagen was dressed in the disheveled manner of a shoe clerk, his suit wrinkled, his tie slightly askew, and held the butt of an unlit cigar in his mouth. The FBI agents Colfax had seen were young, sleak, cookie-cutter figures in immaculate dark blue suits and not a hair out of place. They didn't smoke, they didn't smile, and they didn't look as though they were dying for a drink. Hagen fit no mold. Colfax liked him immediately.

"You two talk or bark or whatever," R.B. said, rising. "I've got work to do. Don't piss on the floor. I'll be back in two hours and I expect you to be gone by then."

She was out the door without another word. Hagen watched her leave, then turned back to Colfax. "You think she's queer?" he said.

Colfax shrugged. "I have no idea."

"No, of course you wouldn't have." He lit the cigar. "You talked to the mad bomber?"

"I listened to him. It wasn't a conversation."

Hagen nodded. "Rosebud's her real name, you know. That's why she calls herself R.B. Can you imagine a woman like that calling herself Rosebud?"

Colfax smiled. "No, I guess I can't."

Hagen sat in R.B.'s chair. "Her father was city editor of the old *Mirror*. Harry Kane. He felt it was some kind of act of God when *Citizen Kane* hit the movie houses. Same last name. So when he had a daughter he named her Rosebud, you know? After the sled."

"Jesus," Colfax said.

"That's probably why she's queer," Hagen said, nodding assurance. "I'd be queer too if someone named me Rosebud."

He knocked ashes from his cigar on to the floor, then ground them in.

"That's not likely," Colfax replied, picking up the tempo of Hagen's conversation.

"No, I guess not."

A moment passed in which neither man spoke. They could hear shouting from somewhere outside. Music played. A dog barked. Then Hagen said, "Tell me about the phone call."

He wanted to know about the voice quality of the caller, the rhythms of speech, the pauses, the inflections, his respiration rate; he wanted to know them over and over again. The same questions were asked in different ways as they walked together across the campus toward a student hangout just outside of Sather Gate where Hagen suggested they have lunch.

"Take each multisyllable word," Hagen said as they entered the noisy restaurant. "And tell me how it was emphasized."

"That would depend on the word."

"That's right," Hagen said in a tone of annoyance. "So pick a word from his message. 'The People's Voice has spoken to the federal pigs who perpetuate war,' " he said loudly, repeating the message from memory. " 'Now the war comes to them. Is the *Herald* next?' "

They were in a restaurant called the Rathskeller that served large pitchers of beer and knockwurst sandwiches at wooden picnic tables. There was sawdust on the floor and there were antiwar posters on the wall. One was a dove with an arrow through its heart that said, WAR KILLS. Another looked straight into a woman's vagina, wherein dwelt a miniature army of armed men. The caption said, RESIST!

"So pick a word," Hagen said again.

The noise in the room was almost overwhelming, shrouding even Hagen's booming bass. No one had even looked their way as the FBI agent recited the phone message.

"Perpetuate," Colfax said. They ordered German beer and knock-wurst. "Per-PET-yew-ate." He overstated the syllable's emphasis to make clear to Hagen what he meant.

"That's the way it's supposed to be said," Hagen said argumentatively, "but is that the way he actually said it?" He paused then added: "PER-pet-yew-ate. Per-pet-yew-ATE. Per-pet-YEW-ate."

Colfax sat in silence surrounded by the din, staring straight through the older man, searching the darkness in his memory for a light that would illuminate sound. He finally was able to hear the voice again *(The People's Voice has spoken to the federal pigs . . .)* and isolate the words. As he did, the uncomfortable, compelling notion swept over him that the malice in its tone was real.

The police chief of Oakland, Wallace B. Korchek, was a tall, broad-shouldered man in his late forties who had come up through the ranks from patrol into the Subversive Intelligence Unit and finally to the position of assistant chief through the simple expediency of an almost pathological hatred of Communism. His brutality toward those in his custody was legendary. It showed on his face, a hard, deeply lined mask of iron that rarely changed expression, and in eyes as dark and ominous as a window into hell. Even his elevation to chief by the Oakland City Council six months before had not ameliorated his hatred. It continued to burn with the heat of magnesium deep within the man's finite core, fueling his attitudes toward the student revolution just north of the city limits. Only weeks before he had personally stopped a peace parade at the line that separated Berkeley from Oakland, bludgeoning the face and head of a parade leader who had approached him to discuss the possibility of continuing a nonviolent march down Telegraph Avenue to 13th Street. Every moment of the beating was filmed by television cameras and the cry for his dismissal was loud, but the City Council was of the notion that the nation was in peril and the chief stood between them and calamity.

He had become a familiar figure of late in the city room of the *Herald,* striding through the double doors like Douglas MacArthur on a mission, the epaulets of his deep blue uniform glistening under the pale neon tubes. Colfax looked up as he strode past headed for Stafford's office and for a moment their gazes locked. When the chief had disappeared into that inner sanctum, Colfax turned to Sally Bell, who sat next to him on the back row of rewrite. The fast writers, the big guns, occupied the privileged first row, and the feature writers and new people were relegated to the second, except for the specialists, who sat in corners by the window. Sally had chosen the second because that's where she wanted to sit and such was the force of her personality that no one questioned or really cared where she sat.

"Why is he always here?" Colfax asked, still staring at the publisher's door.

Sally stopped typing and removed a cigarette from her mouth, scattering ashes over the typewriter. She blew them away and watched thoughtfully as they floated into the city room, as though she were buying time to formulate a response. Then she said, "Who knows?" and returned to her typing.

"He's here every other day."

Colfax had learned not to bother her when she was working, but his curiosity was intense. It was what propelled him, a terrible need to know. Sally Bell tolerated him because she knew more than most how essential the hunger was to a good reporter, whose last question is never answered. It was the first lesson she had learned from Burns, who, when she had failed to come up with a needed piece of information, had said simply, "Ask, ask, ask."

"They think alike," she finally said with the patient tone of a third-grade teacher. "One is the alter ego of the other. Korchek has the muscle, Stafford has the voice. I don't know what else might unite them. Now leave me the fuck alone."

"The thing I like about you," Colfax said, "is your patience."

"Shit," she said.

Reporter Paul Lowin, a small, tense man who sat directly in front of them on Rewrite Row, turned to face Colfax. "They're both fucking Nazis," he said. "Right-wing bastards who think they have a special duty to save the world from people like me."

"Paul's a Maoist," Sally explained without looking up. "Someday they'll drag him off and stand him against a wall and shoot his ass. You want a blindfold, Paul?"

Lowin stared at Sally with a deep animosity and then turned abruptly away without responding. Older than most, Lowin kept pretty much to himself except for outbursts of left-wing rhetoric, explaining to Colfax during his first week that the world would someday belong to the people. He said "the people" in a way that gave them special status, the way Lutherans discussed Christ's Disciples. *The People.* Some said Lowin carried a gun, a sweet little snub-nosed .38, as Trager described it, and they avoided him for that reason too, in addition to the fact that he was considered odd. But no one could beat him for his typing speed or his ability to slap stories together with only seconds to spare before deadline. It was for those abilities he'd been hired and why Stafford tolerated him. A dedicated loner, he ate from a brown bag on the roof and read obscure books on the New Left, sometimes taking notes. "He wants to die for China someday," Sally said. "I'm sure Stafford and Korchek would be happy to arrange that."

Vito Minelli led a sit-in at U.C.'s Sproul Hall when the university refused to reinstate a political science professor fired because of selling grades for sex. He was a sexual predator and everyone knew that he deserved to be canned. It was a nonissue, but Minelli managed to turn it into a cause with the flip of his middle finger. He accused the administration of firing the man for political reasons and filled Sproul Hall with his followers for three days before campus police flushed them out. They called it the Sproul Hall Sprawl and it gave Minelli the kind of publicity he needed. When it was over, the professor stayed fired and no one really gave a rat's ass.

Colfax made an effort to meet Minelli but was turned away by his lieutenants, who considered the *Herald* a tool of the right wing and therefore Colfax a soldier in the pay of the devil. After six months of hearing that off and on from the student left, Colfax ignored the invective and went on about his work, the slurs whistling over his head like bullets wide of their mark.

Colfax set out on a mission to find out as much about Minelli as he could, so when the sit-in ended he presented himself at the university Registrar's Office, identifying himself to an assistant registrar. She was a frail, sour woman in her late thirties with dark hair pulled tightly into a bun and eyes that blinked and shifted in an endless pattern of random response to her own inner tensions. As he studied her, Colfax could detect an odor that reminded him of the burning insulation around an electrical circuit. He felt she might explode at any moment, showering the room with sparks, like fireworks blasted into a holiday sky.

"What do you want?" Her manner was abrupt but not hostile. The Bay Area's attitude toward the *Herald* was mixed. A conservative afternoon newspaper, its news coverage was thorough and immaculate, but its editorial policies were rooted in opposition to just about every movement that was sweeping the country. Stafford had taken to writing many of the major editorials himself, assuming the job normally left to others. He stood firmly in favor of the war in Vietnam and against rioting in the streets for whatever purpose, and there were hints of racism in his attitude toward blacks. His editorials made serious enemies. Radicals hated the *Herald* and even conservatives weren't sure. The paper had come to exist in a twilight zone of its own creation, covering the revolutions in the streets without bias even as its publisher despised them.

"I want to know about Vito Minelli," Colfax said, responding in a tone similar to the woman's. "His background, his address, anything in the records that would give me a fix on him." He remembered reading the text of a speech by Gerald Burns when he was still at the *Edenville Messenger* that admonished new reporters to enter a room as though they were delivering the First Amendment. Colfax took that to mean you operated from a position of power on behalf of the people's right to know and he tried never to wilt in the face of authority.

"I would like to know why you need that information," the woman said, fidgeting with papers on her desk. She wore an identification badge that said her name was Iris.

"Why I need it doesn't matter," Colfax said, "but I will tell you that it concerns some investigative work I'm doing."

"I'm not sure we're authorized to reveal that information," the woman said, her attitude now assuming a hostile tone.

"I'm sure you are," Colfax replied, matching her hostility. "This is a taxpayer-supported institution and the information contained therein is in the public domain. Look it up. I'll wait."

Unsure now, she rose and abruptly left the room without speaking. Colfax could hear her talking on a telephone but couldn't make out the words. There followed five minutes of silence, during which he sat thumbing through enrollment pamphlets that trumpeted the renown of California's oldest university, including its nine Nobel laureates, its academic standards, its worldwide satellite units, even its location near San Francisco. When the door opened, the woman stood triumphantly framed by its archway.

"There is no Vito Minelli enrolled at this university," she said, her gaze as steady as a light beam. "Nor has there ever been."

With that, she turned and left, striding off almost in the manner of a general who had just scored an impressive victory. Colfax shrugged, amused by her attitude. There probably weren't a hell of a lot of victories in the Registrar's Office.

Colfax knew that not everyone who marched in the student protests were students, but it seemed odd that Minelli, who had become so visible as a leader in the movement, had not bothered to register as a pro forma gesture. Playing a hunch, Colfax stopped by the office of the university's newspaper, the *Daily Californian,* figuring that student journalists, whatever their political cants, would be anxious to help a real reporter for the sake of a good word later on. He was right.

A *Daily Cal* columnist who used the byline Hector agreed to sit down with Colfax in a back room of the office. They passed through a newsroom that was a miniature version of a city room, with the sound of typewriters, an AP wire machine and ringing telephones. Hector had interviewed Minelli once but didn't know much about him except that he was brilliant and believed the world would be a better place if he were running it. Hector had eaten it all up as though it were cotton candy and fed it back in a series of three columns extolling the virtues of political activism generally and Vito Minelli personally. It wasn't until the end of their conversation that Colfax wondered why Minelli had never bothered to register at the college.

"He's registered," Hector said. He was a tall kid about nineteen with a shock of red hair and deep green eyes which he squinted in an effort to look more reporterish, more intense.

"They said there was no Vito Minelli registered here."

"He uses his real name in official things."

"Minelli isn't his real name?" It was the first time Colfax had heard this. "What is his real name?"

"Epstein," Hector said. "Jules Epstein." Then he added unnecessarily, "He's a Jew."

Crossing the campus again, Colfax could see a large gathering of students near the Campanile, the tower that had become the logo for revolution in America. He headed toward it. Armed with Minelli's real name, Colfax had confronted the assistant registrar again and this time got what he'd needed, some basic background on Minelli and a home address. A speaker's platform had been built to accommodate the university's activists, proving to those who despised the upheavals that the college administration was party to the chaos and, in fact, encouraged it. As he approached the gathering, Colfax could make out the speaker, a slight man in dark clothing with a seaman's cap covering his face down to his eyes and a thick dark beard covering most of the rest. It was Minelli. He wore sunglasses to complete what appeared to Colfax to be almost a disguise, or at least an effort to create a persona that would stamp its imprint on those who listened.

The words, shouted through a bullhorn, were unintelligible at first, but as Colfax approached the edge of the crowd he began hearing them amplified into segments that pieced themselves together as he listened.

"We have come to the crossroads," Minelli said, raising his voice to be heard, the primitive amplifier creating a ringing echo of his words. "It is time for pamphleteering to end and active resistance to begin! The government pigs have no intention of stopping the war! Death is a factor that they accept! The blood spilled in Vietnam is nothing more than the ink of reelection posters aimed at benefiting every fascist son of a bitch in Washington!" Shouts of agreement greeted the phrase. "They're killing our brothers to advance themselves!" The response grew louder and stronger. "Who will join me in stopping them now?" The response was a roar. "Now!" Louder. "Not next week, not tomorrow, *now!* Not later, *now!* Freedom *now,* peace *now,* equality *now,* justice *now . . .*"

The speaker's voice became a chant picked up by the growing crowd around him, its combustible energy exploding into noise and movement, fists thrust upward, signs held high, a roar that seemed never to abate. Colfax, zeroing in on the speaker, pushed toward the front of the gathering, shielded by his own determination to move forward. He wasn't sure whether Minelli had spotted him pushing his way toward him but sensed that he might have, glancing his way quickly and then leaving the podium. The crowd dispersed still shouting antiwar slogans, sizzling with the energy Minelli had ignited in each of them.

Colfax pushed through them. His leg ached from the effort it took to hurry, but he was determined to reach Minelli and to at least make contact. There was no response when he shouted Minelli's name across the expanse of lawn that separated them. He called it twice, three times, and then, as the distance between them grew, he raised his voice to its fullest extent and hollered, "Epstein!" Minelli stopped and turned to face Colfax. "Jules Epstein!" the reporter added in a quieter voice.

Minelli studied him carefully as Colfax limped toward him.

"I'm William Colfax," he said, "a reporter for the *Herald*."

"I know who you are," Minelli said, "and you know who I am. I work for the people. You work for the pig press. What is it you want?"

The men with Minelli had formed in a half-circle around him the way Secret Service agents surrounded a President. They were large and hostile and, Colfax assumed, would have gladly beatten him to the ground to win their leader's approval. But Colfax was unintimidated by their presence and took a half step toward Minelli, to face him directly.

"Talk," Colfax said.

"You want to talk." Minelli looked around. "Anyone here feel like talking?"

No one responded.

"Nobody wants to talk to you."

"It's you I want," Colfax said, playing along.

"I don't want to talk to you. That makes it unanimous." He turned to leave. "Just make something up." He allowed himself a grim smile. "That's your job."

And he was gone.

In his office, darkened by the movement of the afternoon sun away from his window, illuminated only by a small lamp near the door, Jeremy Lincoln Stafford III hunched over his massive desk, writing with a pencil on a lined yellow legal pad. The words "SUNDAY EDITORIAL" were written across the top of the page in bold, printed letters, and under that, "Use on Page One." He wrote with a determination rarely seen in the man, outraged by the growing revolution around him, fueled by the energy of his own commitment to the American Way. Chief Korchek was right. These were dangerous times and he, as owner of a major newspaper, had to take a stand again the anarchists and Communists who were hell-bent on destroying their system of government. History would remember him and his newspaper as leaders of a counterrevolutionary movement that would not surrender to Communism. This was war and he had to draw the battle lines. His father would have understood.

"We can no longer sit idly by and allow the revolution to destroy everything we love and have worked to build," he wrote. "The *Herald* will not be a party to passive resistance. We must erect barricades to stop the advance of those who would tear down our flag, and then round them up to pay the penalties of treason. The time to start is now. We have waited too long."

Stafford hesitated and looked up for a moment before continuing. There was a ferocity in his expression that matched the lion's head that looked down on him. They would remember him for this, he told himself. He would make history, standing as Winston Churchill had stood before the gathering storm, inspiring his people to resist the Nazis. Stafford envisioned himself as Churchill on the balcony at Number 10 Downing Street, looking over the masses that had gathered. And, alone in his office late on a quiet afternoon, Jeremy Lincoln Stafford III thundered aloud, "We will never surrender!" And when he said it, there were tears in his eyes.

CHAPTER FIVE

The home of Theodore and Emily Strickland was large even by the standards of Mill Valley, a massive wooden structure tucked into the west face of Mount Tamalpais with an unrestricted view of the ocean. Standing in any one of the windows that faced the Pacific, one could see from the Golden Gate Bridge to Drake's Bay, and on a clear day the view extended out across the water all the way to the Farallon Islands. Emily had seen the lights of her son's car through the trees and was waiting for him at the front of the door with hugs. There were always hugs. She made a noise half purr and half giggle as she embraced him, held him back to observe, then hugged him again with the eager enthusiasm of a reunion, calling him Teddy as she always had. Strickland returned the hug as best he could, taking in the clean, cool aroma of the perfume his mother had worn as far back as he could remember. He denied that he had lost weight, insisted that he was feeling fine, and repeated three times how glad he was to be home for the long Thanksgiving weekend.

In another room, his father Theodore sipped at a vodka martini and waited for his son to enter, not rising from the heavy leather chair when he did. Their greetings were perfunctory, almost ritualistic, as Strickland leaned down to give his father a quick hug and as his father returned the gesture with a pat on his son's back.

The elder Strickland had never been able to figure out their only child. There was something secretive about him, a knowledge tucked away somewhere in a corner of the boy's brain that perhaps the boy himself didn't understand. Teddy was bright enough, all right, the top of his class at the Wilden Academy, but never outgoing or *involved* with anything. He wondered if his son was smoking dope or had an emotional problem, but the subjects were never broached. That line of communication, the personal thread that connects fathers and sons, had never been established between them.

They sat immersed in cool banalities about classes, about football, about fraternities, about grades, about anything that wasn't important or political or in any way significant. Later, in his room, Ted Strickland turned on the television and stretched out on his bed. Around him were the familiar relics of his growing-up years, a poster depicting the cover of *The Catcher in the Rye,* another from Voodoo Comics showing the gory killing of a vampire, stacks of paperback books, and rows of LPs in alphabetical order.

He had sunk into a half sleep as he lay on the bed, the low-level noise of the television set droning like white sound in the background, until a name floated across his consciousness, rousting him abruptly into full awakefulness. The name was Leonard Rose. Strickland rose quickly from the bed and turned the set louder. A television anchorman was at his desk and the word BULLETIN flashed alternately off and on below him. ". . . found shot to death in her car in an isolated area near Land's End on the edge of Lincoln Park. A note in the car indicates that Mrs. Rose was in deep grief over the recent bombing death of her husband. To repeat our bulletin, the body of a woman identified as Nadine Rose, the wife of slain FBI agent Leonard Rose, was found less than an hour ago shot to death in her car, an apparent suicide. . . ."

In the few moments that Strickland had stood staring at the screen of the television set, the words had wound about him like the coils of a serpent, tightening to the point of suffocation. All the breath in him was sucked inward and only with great effort did a gasping sob emerge, finally freeing him from the coils. His hand moved slowly to his mouth and his voice said, "Dear God . . ." as though the movement and the sound were involuntary.

Shaking free of the coils, he reached for the phone by his bed and dialed. The voice of Vito Minelli said simply, "Yes?"

At first, Strickland was unable to speak, though he tried, until finally the words tumbled out. "Did you hear?"

Minelli sat on the floor of his apartment, leaning against a wall. The television set was across from him, figures flashing across the face of the tube without sound.

"I heard," he said, instantly recognizing Strickland's voice and the anguish in it.

The others had disassociated from Minelli after the bombing, stunned by the enormity of what they'd done, scattering in different directions, resuming normal lives, isolating themselves in their studies as though they had never been a part of the violence at the Federal Building. Strickland was different. He had clung to the moment and to Minelli with the clamp of a shark's bite, and Minelli knew that he represented deep trouble.

"What are we going to do?" Strickland asked, as though there existed somewhere an answer that would ease his panic and regret.

"There's nothing to do," Minelli with as much equanimity as he could. To the tense silence at the other end of the line, Minelli tempered his voice. "No one wanted that agent to die," he said. "We didn't plan it that way and of course we regret it. And most of all we didn't want what happened tonight. But there's nothing we can do about it now. We just have to grieve quietly." He almost choked on the words. "Do you understand?"

"I . . . I can't believe this is happening," Strickland said, unable to internalize Minelli's words. "We've killed two people!"

Softer: "We can't do anything at the moment. Someday we will, when all this is behind us. Pray for their souls. Light a candle. But do nothing else. And don't call me anymore."

Minelli hung up abruptly, unable to carry on the facade. He was angry with himself and with the weak, frightened man he had recruited to be one of them. At least the others had remained detached. Strickland, he knew now, was different. He was dangerous.

There were no streetlights along Channing Way and the addresses of the old homes that lined both sides of the thoroughfare were difficult to see, so Colfax drove slowly. When he finally spotted the number he was looking for, there were no immediate parking spaces available and he had to drive another block to find one. Walking back in the darkness, favoring his aching leg in the cold wind, evoked glancing memories of Vietnam and his own soundless movement through thick underbrush on night patrols. It was on just such moonless nights, as black as death, that terror lurked on the edge of his emotions, when the urge to turn and run was the strongest, an urge he never allowed to fully surface. Unconsciously, he listened for snapping twigs as he walked, for the rustle of vines or undergrowth, crouching slightly, slowing, the cat in him piercing the darkness. . . .

Twenty-one "B" was a basement address in a two-story Victorian that no one had bothered to restore. Colfax descended the stairs slowly, and as he was halfway down, the door of the apartment suddenly opened. Vito Minelli, seeing him, stood motionless in the doorway, silhouetted by the light from the apartment. For a moment the two men simply studied each other, and then Minelli, looking past Colfax, said, "You alone?"

"I'm alone."

Inside the apartment, Colfax looked around at the sparse furnishings, finally settling on a worn, overstuffed chair, sinking deeply into it. Minelli sat on the floor and leaned against a wall. Again they studied one another under the dim glow of a single light that hung from the ceiling of the room. The only other piece of furniture was a small television set atop a wooden crate. Minelli was shirtless and shoeless.

"I'm here to profile you for the *Herald,*" Colfax said without preamble.

"I don't do interviews," Minelli said, adjusting his position. His voice was uncharacteristically soft, almost whispery, not the resonating roar Colfax had heard on the campus.

Colfax toughened. "I've been asked to profile you," he said evenly, "and I'll do that one way or another. Our lives are trails of records: friends, enemies, and relatives. I could follow that trail and write your life without you saying a word, but it would be a hell of a lot better balanced if you did. This is your life, Minelli. How will you have it?"

Minelli glanced toward the window. The lights of a passing car flashed across his face and then vanished. He chewed at a cuticle, spitting out the bits of skin that came off, licking a spot of blood from his finger. Colfax decided it was a game Minelli played, a power trip, psychological warfare, leaving an enemy in the dark, unable to anticipate the next move. It made Colfax uneasy, staring at the jungle, watching the shadows.

"Why're you working for that pig outfit?" Minelli finally said.

"I ask the questions, you answer them. That's the way this works."

"You want to know my life, I want to know yours. You first."

There was a mocking tone to Minelli's voice, a ring of familiarity and danger that slipped by like a stray breeze.

"This is bullshit, Minelli. Do you ask every goddamn television cameraman you court where he's from and what his father did for a living?"

"It's my right!" Minelli said, his voice rising.

"Your right is to cooperate or not cooperate and at this point I don't give a possum's dick whether you do or don't, but I guarangoddamntee I'll be on your ass from now on."

"Welcome to my ass, then, reporter. You'll be good company."

As Colfax was about to leave in disgust, the door burst open. Strickland filled the doorway, his face ashen, his expression anguished. "It isn't right!" he shouted, staring directly at Minelli.

"Shut up," Minelli said quickly.

Colfax, standing to one side of the doorway, watched with interest the interplay between the two men, the bursting pain of one and the intensity of the other. Strickland saw him just as Minelli ordered him into silence.

"I didn't know . . ." Strickland began, and then stopped.

"Aren't you going to introduce us?" Colfax said.

He studied Strickland carefully. The man was in deep emotional pain. He had seen faces like that after an engagement, when the friends of the dead sat by their inert bodies like dogs at a master's grave, grieving beyond the ability to cry.

"I don't think that's necessary," Minelli said. "You were just leaving."

"Is he one of your 'soldiers'?" The word dripped with sarcasm. "I wouldn't send him to the front if I were you."

Colfax smiled, stared hard at the shaken Strickland to fix the man's face in his memory, and left. As the door closed and Colfax's footsteps faded, Minelli turned to Strickland and said, "You asshole."

The next day an editorial written by Stafford appeared on the front page.

"The idiot sees Communist conspiracy everywhere," Sally said around a cigarette in her mouth, laying the front page out on a table at the Three-Oh, coughing slightly.

"They're everywhere," Gwen said, sipping at a Bloody Mary. It was too early in the day, she explained, for real booze. "They're in his closet, his fridge, his fucking chicken soup . . ."

"In his bed," Corona McGee said, picking up the tempo, "his Bible, his strawberry jam, his toilet . . ."

"Especially in his toilet," Sally said, "looking up and waiting."

"It's his goddamn paper," Trager said sternly. "He can see Communists if he want to." He couldn't help adding, "Even in his toilet."

" 'America must stand firm against the Red Threat,' " Sally read. "The 'Red Threat?' It sounds like a fucking outbreak of the plague. 'The campi of the nation boils with conspiracy.' The '*campi*?"

"He looked it up," Colfax said, joining in. He hadn't touched his own Bloody Mary. Ordering it was a gesture.

"All right, good for him, but campi's plural and the campi of the nation should fucking boil not *boils,*" Sally declared with finality.

"Christ," Corona McGee said, standing, "why are we debating the literature of a third-grade mind?"

"Somebody should be editing the asshole," Gwen said, waving away the smoke from Sally's cigarette. "Christ, can't you blow in a different direction?"

"Nobody edits the publisher," Trager said, feeling offended by the remark. "Burns's orders. 'Run it as it is.' "

Sally nodded. "I see Burns smiling," she said.

Corona McGee opened the door. Her small frame was silhouetted against a glaring morning sunlight. "I hear the city laughing," she said, and left.

It took Colfax weeks to gather enough for a profile on Minelli. Bruno Hagen offered off-the-record help for two dinners at expensive restaurants and one free drink a week for life. They settled on one free dinner and two weeks of free drinks. The FBI agent was becoming a fixture on the Berkeley campus. Colfax ran into him at surprising moments: in a crowd or down a hall, and once even in the back of a lecture hall where Minelli was auditing a class, leaning against a wall, listening.

Minelli was born Jules Epstein in the South Bronx. No one knew why he had changed his name. No warrants were outstanding. Colfax guessed the intent was to remove the issue of ethnic hatred from the role he chose to play in life. Everybody hated Jews, nobody hated Italians. He had left New York as a teenager and began floating across the country from hot spot to hot spot, leading or playing an active role in student uprisings ranging from civil rights to antiwar. In Brooklyn it was a series of black marches. In Chicago, rallies at a political convention. In L.A., he was a Brown Beret agitating for Chicano rights. The profile hinted at the itinerant nature of his personality, a modern-day drifter living off the land when he had to, off the revolution when he could. He left a trail of violence behind him, either in bloody confrontations or bombings. Burns edited the bombing out of the profile.

It pointed the finger at Minelli and there was no proof to substantiate it. But as Colfax thought about it, he began to realize why Minelli's voice had sounded familiar. It was the voice on the phone the night the FBI building was bombed.

"We're working on that angle," was all Hagen would say.

"Work with him," Burns advised. "You may be on to something."

The profile was Colfax's first major story since the bombing, two front-page efforts separated by a lot of boilerplate, workday inside-page stuff. No one said much about it, but Colfax could sense it had elevated him in the eyes of the staff. Corona McGee walked by one day, pointed at him, and winked. It was considered a compliment. Only the presence of another-page one Stafford editorial lessened the glow of the profile's prominent play. Shrill and poorly written, it placed the blame directly onto Minelli's shoulder as a leading agitator for Communist causes and condemned the university as a breeding ground for the violent overthrow of America. What bothered Colfax most was that Stafford identified him specifically as a Jew, a fact Colfax had not written into his story. The anti-Semitic slant of the editorial did not go unnoticed. The switchboard reported at least fifty calls from those who dropped the paper.

Two days later an Oakland cop shot and badly wounded a student trying to stretch an antiwar banner across Telegraph Avenue just inside the city limits. Covering the incident, Colfax was awash with the uneasy feeling that the war at home, just as the war abroad, was escalating, and he wondered how much he had to do with it.

CHAPTER
SIX

C olfax was given his first permanent desk almost a year after he'd begun at the *Herald*. It was January 1966. Jonathan Blair had been a floater until the day he died, a man without a desk, and Colfax, his replacement, had similarly floated until now. Trager bought him a drink to celebrate. Anytime was party time. Up until then he'd used the desk of whoever wasn't there at the time, except for Paul Lowin's. Lowin informed Colfax that his desk was for him alone, and since the man carried a gun, Colfax took him at his word and avoided it. He hadn't lived through Vietnam to be murdered in San Francisco.

His new desk had been occupied by Homer Follett, who had drowned himself in his bathtub one Saturday night, a method which had opened up a whole new area of conversation in the city room. Gwen suggested it might not have been a suicide at all but a case of Follett having fallen asleep and slipped under the water. Follett was a Texan, and Texans, she lectured, slept soundly.

"You ought to know," Sally said. "I'm sure you've slept with a whole posse of them."

"Up yours," Gwen replied.

Trouble began just as the day's first street edition was slapping off the presses. The circulation trucks were already waiting at the shipping dock, their hard-ass drivers lounging at the foot of the dock, smoking and talking among themselves. Husky laborers manhandled the bundles of paper into the cavernous bellies of the vehicles as the roar of the presses vibrated in the background and out into the open street. The drivers were members of the Teamsters Union, the only collective bargaining unit at the *Herald*, and their contract limited them to driving, not loading; they weren't about to breach that contract. A new member defied that separation of labor once by insisting he help load and paid for it with a broken nose. One challenged Teamster traditions at one's peril.

The Berkeley PD reported crowds of students massing around Sather Gate. An hour later, more than fifty vehicles in tight formation were spotted by a Highway Patrol helicopter as they crossed the bridge to San Francisco. The parade pulled off at the Fifth Street ramp and parked in a vacant lot just south of Mission, leaving no doubt as to their ultimate destination. Then the mass of students, sometimes jammed twenty to a van or pickup, piled out and began a noisy march toward the *Herald.* There was a formless, roaring rage to the procession, undulating in intensity in a kind of oceanic rhythm, attacking then receding as it flowed down Mission. Only if one listened carefully could one define shouts of "Stop the presses"—which is what the banners they carried said—and "Down with the fascist pig press!" Police would later estimate the initial crowd at three hundred, but it grew as it approached, fed by others alerted to its presence, drawing from the side streets that intersected Mission, swelling to as much as a thousand in a well-organized demonstration of strength and solidarity. At its head, walking alone and slightly ahead of the mass, marched Vito Minelli.

Colfax had been assigned to write the main story. He observed the marchers first from the third floor and then from the street. Jeremy Lincoln Stafford III, looking grandly combative, was ready for them. He stood atop a makeshift stage at the main entrance of the tower, bullhorn in one hand, the other fist clenched, and stared down Mission at the advancing horde. He reminded Colfax of the Minuteman of a poem he'd learned in grammar school: *By the rude bridge that arched the flood, their flags to April's breeze unfurled./ Here the embattled farmers stood and fired the shots heard 'round the world....* Next to him in full uniform with gold-trimmed hat and epaulets stood a police captain, also equipped with a bullhorn, grimly sharing Stafford's view of the advancing parade, ready to call out his troops if necessary. They hid clustered together, helmeted and armed with riot batons, inside the *Herald* and down the alleys across Mission, waiting.

On the third floor of the *Herald*, reporters and editors watched the growing confrontation with mixed feelings of anticipation and un-easiness. Gerald Burns said nothing but observed it all with the barest hint of a smile, as though he knew, and the others didn't, that this was simply a small patch of history to be stitched into a larger tapestry by which they would all someday be known. It didn't worry him and it hardly concerned him beyond the question of how Stafford would want this handled. Looking down, he could see Colfax standing slightly apart from the stage and wondered if his newest reporter was wishing he'd stayed in Edenville and had left the clamor of the metropolis to those who lived like rats in its shadows. Burns daydreamed sometimes about a place far from the bedlam, an island warmed by the serenity of silence . . . but secretly he knew, the way he knew everything, that he would never have it. He longed for a drink now, to feel its burn and later its brief sedation, but remained instead by the window, as Stafford remained at his post, each in his own way duty-bound.

Minelli spotted Colfax as the students reached the front of the tower and spread out to form a roaring half circle around its main entrance. He nodded in slight acknowledgment and gestured with his head at the masses that surrounded him, as though to say, *Look at me and look at what I've gathered.* Colfax made no attempt to respond. Surrounded by journalists from television and radio stations and from other newspapers, he stood with notebook in hand waiting, jostled slightly by both still and TV photographers pushing ever forward, trying to position himself so that Milton Travis, one of three *Herald* photogs covering the march, would have a better view of the action.

Behind Colfax, crowding into him and sometimes looking over his shoulder at the notes Colfax took, stood the *Daily News* reporter Leo Kaminsky, the ultimate journalistic leech, who had tried to pick his brain for information after Colfax's story on Minelli-as-Jules-Epstein had appeared. Oddly, rather than diminishing Minelli by exposing him, Colfax's story in juxtaposition with Stafford's vitriolic editorial had increased Minelli's stature as both victim and leader. It was how he had been able to gather today's crowd, rising as a kind of bloodied savior from their ranks and promising the vengeance of a terrible swift sword.

"You are blocking our doorway and illegally impeding entrance to our building. I am asking you to disperse." Stafford's voice, filtered by the bullhorn, still rang with stentorian authority, but the crowd's response was a roar of mockery and, like laughter at a eulogy, lessened its impact. At Minelli's gesture, the crowd quieted in waves, the surf receding back to its massive sea.

"You are blocking our lives and our fucking progress and we are asking you to cease and desist!" Minelli's voice, seeking higher ranges, reached the perfect pitch of challenge and warning, mastering the demagogue's art of piercing to the heart of the crowd. Colfax could feel a surge that ran through the mass, igniting fires which, he knew, would be difficult to extinguish. In a way he couldn't explain, he envied Minelli's power, his ability to rise from a whispery, almost amiable persona to that of a strident demagogue who could rally thousands in a voice edged with thunder. He was a Shakespearean actor who stepped from anonymity to center stage playing Hamlet.

"I am saying again," Stafford boomed, "that this is an illegal assembly and you are to disperse immediately. If you fail to do so, I will order the police to disperse you by force if necessary!"

What the hell's he doing? Colfax wondered. He would *order* the police? Colfax glanced at the police captain next to Stafford. The man seemed untroubled by the publisher's assumption of power. For the first time, Colfax had a glimpse into just how much muscle his boss had and it gave him an uneasy feeling.

"And we will say to you, you fucking fascist, that you stop your dirty warmongering and race-baiting or we will tear down your fucking tower brick by brick!"

Minelli's voice, ranging even higher, struck like lightning at the combustible core of the crowd, igniting its fury. A large rock shot through the air, smashing into a front window of the Herald Building. To Colfax, the window seemed to shatter in slow motion. Shards of glass hung suspended in the morning air, glistened in the gray light that filtered between tall buildings, then settled with the tinkling sounds of wind chimes into the building itself, onto the street, and over the crowd. A second rock flew and another window exploded, but this time in quick motion, and the response was instant.

At a barely perceptible signal from the police captain near Stafford, the doors of the *Herald* burst open and what seemed a regiment of police rushed out. The crowd's roar grew louder and Colfax swore he could hear Stafford shout, "Attack!" over the din, reprising Teddy Roosevelt at San Juan Hill, shaking his fist at the angry demonstrators before being whisked away by the police captain and two other officers. As they left, Colfax thought he caught a glimpse of Wallace Korchek in the background and wondered fleetingly what the Oakland chief was doing there glaring into the mob with unmasked hatred as it undulated with a rage that fed on itself.

Simultaneously with the rush of the police out of the *Herald*'s door, others came from the alleys behind the crowd and from each side. A helicopter appeared almost magically overhead, the *thrump-thrump-thrump* of its rotary blades beating an ominous rhythm, its PA system warning the demonstrators to break up, to disperse, to move on. The level of noise approached the bedlam that Colfax remembered from war, evoking all the emotions he thought were buried beneath unyielding layers of resistance. Fear was there, and so was anger and acceptance and an almost overpowering urge to die and end the pain. He wanted to cover his ears and turn away but instead stood his ground as the army of police, wearing gas masks and swinging their batons, rushed into the crowd. Clouds of tear gas billowed up from canisters fired by officers at the edges of the demonstration, filling the air with screams and violent coughing and with canisters hurled back at their sources.

A slight breeze that blew down the valley between the buildings directed the clouds of gas away from where Colfax was standing, so he could see with only slight discomfort the violence being played out before him. Flashbulbs exploded into the calamity like canonfire with Travis leading the way in the number of pictures being taken, his large, tanklike bulk burrowing into the mass of humanity. What had seemed only a war of words was now a commitment to brutality. Blood spattered and students, both men and women, fell beneath the incessant battering and were dragged screaming to police vans that approached from two directions. Colfax watched stunned as time after time policemen used fists as well as batons to subdue individual demonstrators, continuing to beat them even as they lay unconscious on the ground. Those who had tried to go limp in passive resistance soon decided it would be an unworkable ploy in what had become a police riot. The demonstrators who tried to fight back were soon in flight, tripping over each other to escape both the tear gas and the beatings.

Colfax and the other reporters took notes even as they sought to avoid the violence themselves. Two women were seen being dragged almost naked to the police vans and soon reports of rape circulated. Teamsters who had witnessed the confrontation, mostly strong supporters of police authority, now rushed in to fight the cops and shield those who lay bleeding and helpless in the wake of their billy clubs. They themselves, the truck drivers, were hurled back and bludgeoned and others inside the loading dock rushed forward to face the same cruelties.

Minelli had remained clear of the core of danger but realized as the street was cleared that he had to be bloodied to be credible and walked into the midst of the swinging batons like the Messiah he thought he was. He fell to only a single swing of the club and Colfax, watching, knew that it was as Minelli planned, to continue the role of victim-as-leader, the One Who Fell With His Troops, fighting all the way. He was dragged to a van, one fist still clenched in the air, and the confrontation was over, leaving the street littered with broken protest signs, bits of clothing, empty tear gas canisters, splotches of blood, and violent emotions.

Colfax's story appeared on the front page of the afternoon street edition under the banner headline ATTACK ON THE *HERALD*! in bold black type. Travis's photograph of Minelli being dragged off by two patrolmen, his clenched fist raised high in defiance, was placed next to the piece. Colfax had written it the way he always wrote, with fire and meaning; it had become the imprint of his style. All the violence was there along with the number of arrests and the names of the injured. Stafford's words through the bullhorn were quoted and so were Minelli's. Despite his own feelings of repugnance at the police action, Colfax kept in check a tendency to tilt the story in the lead, instead placing the undisciplined attack of the cops in the body of the piece.

The only editing Colfax wondered about was the deletion of Korchek's name from the story. Burns explained that Stafford, who had approved the final editing, felt Colfax was incorrect in placing the Oakland chief at the scene of what the publisher called "the attack." Colfax had seen the chief only once and, without actually saying so, conceded he could have been wrong. He was grateful otherwise that no effort had been made to cant his report of the confrontation. Once more, however, the front-page proximity of an inflammable Stafford editorial associated his byline with the publisher's barely literate diatribe against the "Communist revolution infiltrating our shore." Colfax felt uncomfortable with the juxtaposition, but Burns only shrugged in response to his complaint. It was what Stafford had wanted, to associate his words with the news to which its message was directed, and there was nothing Burns could do about that.

"The general is telling us what the battle plan is," Burns said, "and that's the way it is, William Colfax. You ever hear the story of the tiger cub who didn't want to follow his mother's directions?" Colfax shook his head no. "The mother says, 'Okay, go see your father.' So he goes to see the father to complain and the father eats him."

Colfax looked at the city editor for a moment, confused. "What are you saying?"

"That the father tiger ate the cub."

"If I confront Stafford he's going to eat me?"

"The human equivalent thereof. As you saw, he doesn't like challenges."

"You know what it was like out there?"

"I have a vague idea," Burns said, never losing the edge of a smile.

"Stafford *encouraged* all that. I don't want anyone to think I'm in favor of what he's doing."

Burns studied the younger man for several minutes. He figured that Colfax was recoiling as much from his memories of war as he was from what had happened that morning in front of the *Herald*. He couldn't erase those memories with a few words and he wasn't even going to try. The inability left him sighing deeply. These were the times he felt most inadequate, unsuited to lead this varied force, but he knew there was no choice for him. Where would he go? What would he do?

"This won't last forever," was all he could finally offer Colfax, feeling uncomfortable with that. "Do the best you can." Then the city editor turned away and Colfax knew the conversation was over. As Colfax returned to his desk, Paul Lowin said, "Nice try." It was almost a compliment. Later on his desk he found a large manila envelope. Inside was a photograph of Korchek at the edge of the crowd and a note from Milton Travis: "He was there." Colfax put the picture in his desk and stood there wondering what in the hell was going on.

He worked late that night on a story for the next edition and when he was done accepted an invitation from Corona McGee for a drink. But as he started across the street with her trotting at his side, she jerked his arm in the opposite direction. "Not here," she said. "I'm tired of the same old clowns with their same old red noses and their same old bag of tired tricks. How many floppy shoes and baggy pants can you take, you know?"

They ended up at a place in North Beach called Louie's Post-

Expressionist Café, down an alley off Columbus. Artists painted in a back section. Two old men played chess by a window. The walls were covered with paintings. "That's mine," Corona McGee said, pointing. It was a city scene, color-dabbed to a high glow. The quality was apparent. The scene looked out past Russian Hill over the tops of buildings to the Bay Bridge.

"I like it," Colfax said, not quite knowing whether he did or didn't. "I didn't know you did anything beyond cropping and airbrushing."

"Why would you?" she said, ordering them a drink. "It's my secret. Now it's your secret too. I copy Monet's style. You know Monet?" He shrugged. "A French impressionist. He knew all of the colors inherent in a single-colored object." She paused. "You don't give a crap."

"I'm just not into that kind of thing, I guess."

"Oh, William Colfax, you have a lot to learn."

Trager had informed him one day that she was the only truly smart person at the paper. "But nobody wants smart people in any position of authority, especially short smart people, so they lock her in a dungeon and let her work in silence. She's happy I guess."

"What do you want out of this place?" she asked him, waving casually at a man in a paint-spattered smock who passed.

"To write," he said. "To grow old writing. To cover great stuff."

"But not here," she said.

"Why not?"

"Go south or go east but get out of this town. It's too inbred. It'll wear you down and then eat you up."

He nodded, not quite knowing what she meant. It was something he'd think about. That was his nature, to respond casually and form an opinion later. Corona McGee had warned him. He'd ponder that.

"It was a happy shop when I got there four years ago," she said. She wore jeans and a plaid shirt. She always did. The same thing every day. "It ain't happy no more."

"When did it stop?"

"Who knows?" They were on their third drink. It was beginning to rain again. Locals were saying this was the worst weather in forty years. The Yuba River was flooding its banks. The Sacramento was seeping into nearby towns. The storm of the century. It was Paul Lowin's story and he was in ecstasy. It was said that Lowin wasn't happy unless the world was ending.

"Last call for drinks," the bartender said.

"One more," Corona McGee said.

They finished the drink. Colfax found the world blurry. When he drank this much, colors changed. Everything turned amber. Tonight it was liquid amber, a glowing, iridescent hue that momentarily blinded him when they stepped into the rain. He stood there for a moment, getting wet and oriented.

"This way," Corona McGee said, jerking his arm. He followed her unsteadily for a half block into a doorway. She unlocked the door and half dragged him up a flight of stairs.

"Where are we?" Colfax said. The sound of his own voice startled him.

"My place. Take off your clothes."

He blinked. "Isn't thish . . ." Had he really said "thish"? "Isn't . . . *this* . . . a little abrups . . . abrupsh . . . a-brupt?"

"You're soaked," she said.

"Shit," he said. And that was all he remembered until the next morning when he found himself on her couch wrapped in a blanket, his dry clothes over a chair in front of a wall heater. There was a painting on the ceiling above his head. It was the Herald Tower. He wondered vaguely if he'd slept with Corona McGee but didn't care. There was more to life, he reasoned, rising slowly, than sex and midgets.

An earthquake of 4.5 magnitude shook the city on the first day of spring. It was remarkable for three events. It sent the *Herald* clock crashing down from the tower in a shower of bricks, crushing a dog that had been trotting by; it put one of the paper's two presses out of business; and it had been predicted by the Young Emperor Oscar de la Life. Well, almost predicted. Oscar de la Life had predicted a 6.7, due to the year being '67. Though his magnitude was off, the very fact that there was an earthquake at all created new interest in a character the *Herald* staff had adopted as its own.

Oscar de la Life, whose real name was Oscar Gibbs, lived on Skid Row not far from the *Herald* and drank sixty-nine-cent red wine in a bottle unecessarily hidden in a paper bag and ate from the Dumpsters behind the city's better restaurants. One day he appeared wearing a soiled blue cape with red lining and a crown cut out of cardboard and painted gold. He stood on the hood of a car parked in front of the tower and declared himself the Young Emperor Oscar de la Life, Protectorate of San Francisco and Keeper of the Bay. Some said he had once been a prominent public relations man in L.A., but drink had destroyed his career and driven him to San Francisco, where all drunks eventually wind up.

Colfax, both amused and sympathetic to the Emperor, did a short piece on him, television picked it up, and before long Oscar de la Life was famous. Passersby gave him money, improving the brand of wine he drank and affording him the luxury of a tin crown purchased in a Halloween costume store.

Colfax became a kind of official guardian to the old man, whom everyone now called the Emperor. More than once he suggested that the Emperor ought to use some of the money he was getting to buy real food and get himself a room now and again in one of the nearby flophouses. Colfax even paid for a room for three nights at the Mission Hotel, but the old man sold the room to a whore named Naomi who enjoyed the luxury of a bed for three nights on the job instead of the abrasive feel of a cold wet stairway on her ass.

Stafford was told that the press damaged by the earthquake was irreparable, but he refused to accept the verdict. Though he seldom shouted, his face reddened with the exertion of squelching a shout whenever rage filled his ample figure. Word reached the city room that he had thrown a team of experts out of his office. He then ordered his composing room machinists to fix the press so that it ran, which they did, although privately telling Burns, who told everyone else, that if the goddamn thing lasted another year it would amaze them all. What had irritated Stafford the most, it was said, was the suggestion that the *Herald* explore the possibility of a computerized composing room, which was the talk of the day in newspapering. The *Daily News* had already installed two computers in its newsroom for experimental purposes and young reporters on the staff were eating it up. But Stafford would hear none of it.

Two Linotype machines had also fallen victim to the Emperor's Earthquake, which is what the *Daily News* was calling it, but there was little other collateral damage. The clock was replaced but never worked thereafter and the holes left by the fallen bricks were never filled. The city cleaned itself up quickly, grateful that no one was killed, and Colfax wondered why, of all of San Francisco's great institutions, the *Herald* seemed to lie struggling in the midst of progress.

That was not the least of Stafford's troubles. Minelli, whose power was rising in direct proportion to the escalating antiwar movement, had called for a boycott against what he described as the right-wing, fascist, warmongering, race-baiting, pig-press *Herald* from a stand near Sather Gate. Flyers were distributed throughout the city and television jumped on the story like flies on dog shit, turning the notch up two turns on a battle that increasingly focused on Minelli and the *Herald*. In the spring of '67, the city and the *Herald* trembled ever so slightly.

The Founder's Day Dinner celebrating the ninety-eighth anniversary of the *Herald* was held in an upstairs room of the Fairmount Hotel, looking eastward across the bay to Oakland and the mountains surrounding Berkeley. It was held by tradition every other year, and this was Colfax's first. He bought a new suit for the occasion, a plain brown single-breaster that he adorned with a nondescript red tie. When he walked into the room, the publisher's daughter, Ellen Stafford, glanced at him the way Laura used to in a kind of quizzical, wondering manner that somehow embraced both disapproval and amusement, and he knew right away that what he was wearing was probably wrong. The shirt was a soft blue and now that Colfax thought about it, blue and red and brown probably weren't the world's best combination, so he veered off to the free bar for a drink, silently cursing his bad taste.

He'd been at the *Herald* for two years and in some ways it seemed like forever. Drinking was a big part of what they did and, though reluctant at first, Colfax fell into the routine but in a manner less dedicated than the others. There were morning drinkers, lunchtime drinkers, and after-work drinkers, and he'd joined the latter group, turning down offers to join Chip Dawson's Bloody Mary Breakfast Club after the first-edition deadline had come and gone.

Colfax had moved out of the Mission Hotel and was living upstairs in a two-story flat just outside the Haight-Ashbury District a few blocks from Golden Gate Park. It was a year past the Summer of Love and a meanness had set in where once the blossoms of the flower children had bloomed. A woman downstairs had been raped two weeks earlier walking home from classes at S.F. State by a guy flying on mescaline, and when he sobered up and realized what he'd done, he jackknifed off the fourth story of an old office building down the street, a place that housed Guido's Groceries. Guido found him the next morning, his head smashed open, and wanted to leave him there until the television cameras came and gave his store a little boost, but the cops wouldn't allow it. He had to settle for an interview later on KBAY, less than the best station in town, but it was better than nothing.

Stafford and Ellen greeted their guests at the door except those who came early, which was just about everyone in the city room. Trager had informed Colfax that it was best to arrive an hour before Stafford's annual speech in order to drink enough to numb the boredom. They gathered at the bar like it was the Three-Oh without Danny Doe and talked about nothing in particular. Gwen Ballard, who had tried to seduce Colfax on his first day, had given up on the effort that same day, in half a pique since he'd beaten her on the bombing story. He had received both a byline and top play while she had suffered the indignation of a severely edited lead. "Ballard's got principles," Sally Bell informed Colfax as they stood at the bar. "She'll never fuck anyone who makes her look bad, and since that's just about everyone, she hardly ever gets laid." Cigarette constantly in hand, Sally's laugh ended in a fit of coughing. When it was over, she muttered and doused the cigarette, but it wasn't much longer before she lit another.

Chip Dawson was first at the bar, appearing reasonably sober at the outset but assuming a heavy-lidded look as the cocktail hour progressed. He was their courthouse reporter, covering trials with an easy precision that belied his drinking habits, and to the best of everyone's knowledge he'd never made a mistake. He was a lumbering kind of guy who had been a Golden Gloves champ in his youth and could still handle himself in a fight. Smart people avoided Dawson when he was in the middle phase of drinking. At the beginning he was almost amiable and at the end he was usually too drunk to care, but in between those two phases he could be dangerous. His temper was like a missile blasting suddenly into space without a lot of warning. Twice he had punched out those who had somehow offended him, and in one case dumped a woman photographer named Sandra "Peter-Killer" Peterson into a trash can at the front of the darkroom. He sent her roses the next day, a dozen long-stemmers, and she was so moved she went to his place to thank him and was then rumored to have given him a head job.

The only man who'd managed to deck Dawson in his middle phase was, oddly enough, the religion editor, Carter Blake, a small, ferretlike man with beady eyes and the quickness of a cobra. It surprised the hell out of everyone because Blake, an ordained Lutheran minister, was a nondrinker and essentially a pacifist, but he put old Chip right on his ass with a combination that was so fast it blurred. Dawson just got up, dusted himself off, and walked away. He left the Good Reverend Blake alone after that.

Stafford's speech was all about the Communist attack on America generally and on the *Herald* specifically. He surprised everyone by revealing with dour sobriety that the newspaper's circulation had dipped below three hundred thousand for the first time since it had achieved that mark, forcing a downward adjustment in the ad rate. This was due, of course, to efforts by the leftist Communist underground to discredit both the *Herald* and Stafford personally. What he hadn't mentioned was the fact that the *Daily News,* once reasonably friendly with the *Herald,* had lambasted Stafford for helping to incite the riot in which the cops, in a feeding frenzy, went wild and injured two dozen students, seven of whom were seriously enough hurt to require continued hospitalization. The *News* began a fund that got Minelli and the others out of jail and pressured the court to drop charges against them, which it did.

Minelli strode out of the hearing and into the television cameras like a fighter emerging from his corner, jabbing his finger at the cameras and shouting his outrage at America, its warmongers, its pig press, and the *San Francisco Herald.* Then he marched arms upthrust into a wildly cheering crowd that awaited him and was carried on its crest beyond television's reach and onto a new and higher plane of protest's royalty. It was just after that that the boycott against the *Herald* was set in motion by Minelli, but Stafford never mentioned that as any reason why the newspaper's circulation was swirling into the toilet.

The remainder of Stafford's speech was what everyone expected, filled with the kinds of platitudes most of the staffers had heard year after year. Only the Communist threat and the dipping circulation were new, followed by a quick but unsettling comment that the *Herald* might have to make staff adjustments, which meant someone was going to get his ass canned. Since the editorial department had no union, such talk was bound to interest the Guild, which would start nosing around again as it had some years before.

The head table was occupied by Stafford, his daughter, Burns, and the paper's managing editor, Wally Wallace, whom everyone called Wally-Wally. For the first year Colfax hadn't even known that Wallace existed, until he strolled through the city room one day and Trager pointed him out. His office was on the second floor and his job was to read galley proofs of the day's top stories. If he ever actually edited anything it was unknown on rewrite. Gossip had it that the only reason Wallace was kept on was because he'd made a fortune on avocado orchards he owned in L.A. and had loaned Stafford money in the early days. Burns was really both city editor and managing editor, which fit no one's idea of editorial protocol, but who cared?

Colfax began feeling his liquor after two scotches, the ambience of the large, chandeliered room taking on a hard amber radiance and intensifying thereafter until he had reached the point where he'd had enough. At the end of his speech, Stafford awarded small statuettes of eagles and hundred-dollar checks to those he felt had accomplished outstanding work during the previous year. Colfax was one of the recipients for his reporting on the antiwar movement, specifically for identifying Jules Epstein as Communist leader of the movement in the Bay Area. Stafford always identified Minelli as Jewish and used his real name whenever talking about him, a habit Colfax had come to dislike with intensity. Despite his publisher's preference, he continued referring to Minelli as Minelli in his stories. And now, receiving the award known as the Stafford Eagle or the Staffie, fortified by the scotch, he referred to Minelli as Minelli and pointed out that he had no idea whether or not Minelli was a Communist, but doubted it.

"He's probably just a Republican with a bad stomach," Colfax said, which got a big laugh and a lot of applause, much to Stafford's obvious discomfort. Ellen laughed and clapped too. Colfax was feeling comfortable around the *Herald* staffers now. Booze was the link between them, a series of lunches, afternoons, and nights awash in the camaraderie of clinking glasses and downed liquor. Drunk one night, he had tried to undress Sally Bell, but she'd just grabbed his crotch and led him to another table. The Three-Oh crowd voted it the Class Act of the Week and bought her drinks for the rest of an entire evening. Corona McGee said he was a pig and wouldn't talk to him for a week.

Chip Dawson arrived back at the banquet room near the end of the dinner to join in on the coffee and dessert. Aware of his own hairtrigger temper, he had disappeared for the two hours of the speech and the subsequent ceremonies because they always somehow pissed him off and raised the possibility of a midsession brawl. On his return, he sat next to Colfax, who tensed at his presence but found Dawson to be soft-spoken and courtly in this, the beginning phase of his drinking. In the course of their conversation, Colfax mentioned that he had begun on the *Edenville Messenger,* which sparked Dawson's attention.

"Did you know the whole town was burning?" he asked.

This took Colfax by surprise. "What do you mean, burning?"

"It was just on the radio. The northern part of the state is as dry as Adam's ass and they had a lightning strike that set the whole place on fire."

Colfax thought about his father living at the edge of the forest just west of the town where the mountains of the Coast Range rise.

"What part of the place is burning?"

"How the hell should I know?" Dawson, a drink before him, was edging heavy-eyed into his middle phase. Trager, sitting across from them, saw it and said, "Oh-oh," loud enough for those around them to hear, but Colfax wasn't interested. He only knew he had to go to Edenville and rose quickly from his chair. He expressed his concern to Burns, who told him to go and not worry about anything else.

"I'll walk you out," Ellen said.

On the way she said she hoped his father was all right. Colfax shrugged. His thoughts were on his father. The old man had no phone, so there was no way to tell unless he actually went there. His house was out of everyone's reach, isolated among the redwoods, and no one from the sheriff's office cared enough about him to check. Many wished to hell he would burn and save everyone a lot of grief. Granger Colfax was not deeply loved in Edenville.

At the door Ellen touched his arm and said she'd like to talk to him sometime about the paper and Minelli. She handed him a piece of paper. "I have an apartment in Berkeley. That's my phone number."

Before he could reply, she had turned and walked away. Colfax watched her, tantalized by the slow sway of her hips and the way the light material of her dress clung to the indentations of her body. He shook his head as though to shake away the notions that filled his his mind. Others had lusted after Ellen Stafford before him and had ended up covering Little League baseball in the suburbs. Stafford did not take kindly to reporters pursuing his daughter. He had something better in mind for her than romance with an ink-stained rewrite man. Any reporter who thought otherwise was quickly swept out of town. That knowledge had kept Colfax's own erotic notions in check. His career mattered. He would not bat it aside for easy pussy.

The drive from San Francisco to Edenville took four hours up 101, past places like Pepperwood and Shively and then eastward along the Van Duzen River into the mountains. Once he reached Bridgeport, Colfax veered south on a two-lane county road for another forty-five minutes through redwood groves that seemed as old as rainfall and past working cattle ranches that had been passed on from family to family for three or four generations. There was a cathedral quality to the big trees that had a relaxing effect on Colfax. Emerging from the groves into the open country made him feel as though he were stepping into a world reinvigorated by their presence. Though weary from drinking earlier in the evening, from the lack of sleep, and from the long drive, Colfax emerged oddly refreshed.

As he topped a foothill that allowed a clear view of Edenville twenty miles away, Colfax could see flames lighting up the predawn sky and could smell the smoke that wafted toward him on a wind the locals called a sunriser. He figured it was mostly pine and chaparral burning because the redwoods didn't fire up that easily. It had been almost fifteen years since the last big fire, and the tangled underbrush that lay at the foot of the big trees was explosively dry.

Closing the distance, he could hear the faint roar of the fire like the muffled hum of an approaching tank. He could make out the Forest Service trucks and Bridgeport units called to help fight it. He could see as the sky lightened that much of one forest was involved in the fire, but it wasn't close to his old man's home, which was situated on a hillside opposite the burning acreage. There was a danger, of course, there always was, but the path of fires was usually north to south and the Colfax home was west of it. Planes dropping fire-retardant chemicals began making their sorties with the first light and their high buzzing added to the mixture of sound. Flatbed trucks rumbled past carrying county jail prisoners released to fight the blaze.

The town area of Edenville was as it had always been, a string of small businesses along the main route and up the slopes of the surrounding hills: a general store, the hardware store, Ben Zachary's feed place, a movie house, the Standard station, a clinic, and a combination bar and coffee shop called Eden's Cup. For any serious buying you went to Bridgeport or ordered from catalogs. Except for the retirees, most of the men worked in the lumber mills over the hill.

The last building in the downtown section was that of the *Edenville Messenger.* It was a two-story wooden structure with the fading name of the newspaper in Old English lettering across the top. Colfax had good memories of the place and its editor Henry Dustin, a peculiar guy in some ways but not against giving a young man a chance. Henry had worked with Gerald Burns once in Denver but left town after writing a Pulitzer-class story about the bloody murder of a mother and her three children. He had known the family and their deaths impacted upon him with an explosion of emotion he couldn't cope with and he vowed never to write another murder story. He ended up working at the *Messenger* and later, after he was willed the whole paper by the guy who owned it, turned it into one of the best small newspapers in the West.

Colfax felt his tension building as he drove toward the house he'd grown up in. He parked down the road just to stare at the place. It sat up among the trees, as alone and isolated as the old man himself, its front porch looking out across a meadow toward another clump of redwoods on the other side and a toward stream beyond that. He remembered Granger Colfax sitting on the porch for hours, tilting back on a wooden chair and smoking cigarettes, a reformed drunk who'd given it up for black coffee and Lucky Strikes. The house, a sprawling wooden place, was in need of repairs, but Colfax figured the old man just didn't care anymore and would let the house slowly rot away, the way he was probably rotting away inside from emphysema.

Walking toward the house, Colfax felt a shudder vibrate through him as much from inner dread as from the early morning chill. The weariness of the night lay on him heavier than ever now, leaving him vulnerable to the memories tumbling through his head. A glance toward the stream reminded him of the place where his mother had been last seen on a morning in September, walking up a path she loved, her "concentration place" she called it, a winding trail through the trees that seemed to go on forever. Colfax was ten when she'd disappeared. He remembered her as beautiful and laughing and could still feel the kiss on his cheek she had left him with. Were there tears in her eyes? Colfax thought there might have been, but he couldn't be sure now after all these years. He only knew she had turned from him and walked into the woods and was never seen again.

She'd hated Edenville and more than once had taken off to live in Eureka, but Granger had always brought her back, scowling and arguing in a kind of low rumble, but never raising his hand to her. He'd gone looking for her the last time too, but this time without success. He sat silently on the porch after that, staring off to the woods but never talking about her, burying any emotion deep inside himself.

A mechanic living down the hill who'd never like Granger in the first place flat-out accused him of murdering his wife and they'd gotten into the kind of fight never seen around town before or since. They rolled out the door of Eden's Cup and smashed each other bloody on the main street for half an hour. Granger Colfax ended the brawl with a rock against the mechanic's skull, killing him instantly. The old man did time for involuntary manslaughter but was out in less than two years, still in a silent rage, refusing to move in spite of the glares he got from others in town.

Pushing open the unlocked front door, Colfax found his father sitting in the semidarkness of the kitchen, drinking coffee and smoking a cigarette. Granger looked up when the door opened and for a moment almost expressed an emotion of surprise but then quickly buried it.

"Hello, William," he said.

"Hello, Granger." He never could call him father. In some ways, the man had almost always seemed a stranger.

"What're you doing here?"

His tone was as unrevealing as the mountains around them, bearing neither warmth nor hostility. Colfax poured coffee from a pot on the stove and sat on a chair opposite his father. Deep wrinkles that Colfax hadn't noticed before lined the old man's face and his graying hair had thinned noticeably, but there was nothing in his manner that even hinted at weakness. He sat erect in the chair and there was strength in the sinewy structure of his frame. Only a slight cough marred the picture of a man growing old without giving up anything.

"I heard about the fire," Colfax said.

Granger nodded. "It's burning itself out."

There had seemed so much Colfax had wanted to say driving through the night toward Edenville, but now that he was here it felt impossible to convey anything. So they sat in silence drinking coffee, the old man looking up occasionally to size up his son.

"You been drinking?" he finally asked.

The question surprised Colfax. "A little," he said, feeling uncomfortable.

"It ain't the best thing," Granger said. "You don't want to turn out like me."

Colfax stared at him. It was the first time his father had ever admitted his life had been less than satisfactory. It was, by Granger's standard, an admission of awesome proportions. Colfax didn't know what to say.

"Things are going okay," he offered at last.

"I know. I'm just saying you don't want to depend on the bottle too much."

Colfax suddenly felt small, like a little boy taking advice. It was a moment he'd never shared with his father while growing up, and it felt . . . well . . . different. Maybe even warm. The moment challenged him to respond.

"You don't drink anymore at all?" he asked.

The old man shook his head no. "That's one thing prison does for you," he said. "It breaks up bad habits." Pause. "Some of them anyhow."

Colfax couldn't believe it. Humor? From Granger? The old man even smiled slightly. Colfax shook his head in wonderment. The distance that had always been between them had, within the short framework of this meeting, shortened. Colfax had never been able to figure the old man out, but there had never seemed that much figuring to do. He was always simply what he was, a lumberjack without frills, and Colfax guessed he had never really tried to pierce his father's hard veneer. But now it was different. Now Granger's guard was down, affording a glimpse into his mechanisms. Colfax wasn't sure he knew how to handle it, but in a shadow of his mind a question emerged that he had always wanted to ask and he asked it now without preamble or diplomacy.

"What happened to Mother?"

It was a question Colfax had asked as a child. Always the response was, "Don't know."

This time Colfax expected more.

Granger didn't disappoint him. "You asking did I kill her, like everyone said?" It was the first time it had ever been mentioned between them.

"I guess I am."

The old man nodded and thought about it. Then he said, his voice lowered with sadness, "She just went away, son."

He had never called him son before and the single word overshadowed Granger's response. Later, as he analyzed it, Colfax would try to figure out what it meant. Had his mother, by "going away," died or had she just left them? Maybe she was out there somewhere living a new life. Did she remember him? Did she think about him at all?

"You look like you ain't slept for days. Your room is still there."

"You're right. I'm beat."

He rose from his chair. "Well," he said, "see you in a couple of hours." There was an awkward moment when Colfax wondered if he should hug him and sensed the same hesitation in his father. Then he said, "Call me if we're burning down."

On the way down the hall toward his old room he saw a manila file folder on a table near Granger's room and opened it. Inside, some yellowed with age, were clippings of Colfax's story from the *Messenger* and new ones from the *Herald*. Colfax studied them for a moment and then placed them back in the folder.

Later, as he lay on a bed surrounded by memories, he thought about his mother and decided she'd just gotten tired of it all and left. Gone away, like Granger said. Gone away from the mountains. Gone away from the forest. Gone away from the silent man she'd married who was forever committed to a life of mediocrity. Maybe Laura had felt the same way about him, and war's separation had given her time to make a decision to find someone better; to find something better. But still . . .

Colfax fell asleep wondering how his mother could just walk away like that and leave him alone in the mountains with a man like Granger, creating in him a loneliness that could never be filled, a longing that would never go away. But each time he thought about her, it was Laura's face he saw, and the words resonating in his fading consciousness were for both of them.

How could she have done that to him?

CHAPTER
SEVEN

B ack in San Francisco, Colfax collapsed on the bed without undressing or turning on the light. There was illumination enough from the streetlight directly outside his bedroom window, glowing through the closed shade as though the shade itself were a movie screen. The drive back from Edenville had been exhausting, as much from the turmoil of his thoughts as from the hours on the road. The fire had burned itself out and his father had sat as implacably as ever on the front porch, watching him drive away. Colfax had the feeling that he might never see Granger again and wondered if he should have made an effort to close the gap between them. The thought troubled him as he began to doze off . . . until he became aware of movement in the room. Colfax opened his eyes quickly and sat up, his body tingling with the intensity of a silent alarm, the way it had on the Mekong Delta, just before the explosion and the shattering impact on his leg. But then, at least, he could reach for a weapon, vowing even in pain that they would not take him without a last, violent show of defiance. He would not die in the mud like a whimpering dog or allow them to drag him away to their goddamn bamboo prisons.

There were no weapons next to him now, and as a form in the darkness emerged from a corner of the room, Colfax reacted with the instincts of the warrior he had been. He bolted upward from the bed and thrust himself hard against the moving shadow, finding the bulk of a man under him as they slammed to the floor, and then finding a throat in hands made powerful by the energy of adrenaline pumping through him.

Later, recalling the moment, Colfax knew that if the man had not shouted his name a microsecond before his hands tightened on the shadow's throat, he might have killed him. The survival instinct had been so strongly ingrained in him during a year of combat training and in the fires of war that, swept up in the emotion of peril, he probably wouldn't have hesitated in surviving at the expense of the man whose life he held, quite literally, in his hands.

"Colfax!"

His name was said in strangled desperation and Colfax instantly released his grip, recognizing the bulk that lay beneath him was the FBI agent Bruno Hagen.

"Jesus, Hagen, what in the hell are you doing here?"

Colfax helped him to his feet. Hagen coughed and rubbed his throat, unable to speak, as Colfax switched on a light, trying to make amends by awkwardly straightening Hagen's suit jacket until he was pushed away.

"I could have killed you," Colfax said. He stared at Hagen as though he weren't quite real but a training device he had somehow mishandled.

Hagen sat heavily at the foot of the bed. His coughing had stopped, but he continued rubbing his throat, wincing at the pain. Finally he looked directly at Colfax, cleared his throat, and said in a voice that cracked, "I was trying to warn you."

"Warn me about what?"

Hagen coughed again once or twice, cleared his throat again, and then rose slowly, still feeling the effects of the attack. He walked to the window and peered around a corner of the shade.

"He's gone."

"Who's gone?" When Hagen, returning to sit on the bed, didn't answer immediately, Colfax leaned closer to him. "Hagen, what in the hell is going on here? You break into my apartment, skulk around like a goddamn ghost, then begin babbling in riddles. I'm tired, my leg hurts, and if you don't start talking I'm going to finish killing you."

Hagen shook off the final effects of the attack. "I should have shot you." He lit a cigar and blew a cloud of smoke into the shadows that still enveloped the small kitchen off the bedroom.

Colfax shook his head. "If I don't kill you, those damned cigars will."

"You're being stalked," Hagen said.

"What're you talking about?"

Hagen pulled a piece of folded paper from a pocket, unfolded it, and read it. As he did, Colfax caught a glimpse of his gun tucked into a shoulder hoster. He *could* have shot him but didn't. Perhaps, Colfax reasoned, FBI agents are trained better than Marines.

"The guy's name is Theodore Strickland," Hagen said, his voice stronger. "We got it off the registration of the bug he drives. Goes to U.C., lives in Mill Valley. All that mean anything to you? He's been following you around town for about a week. Camped out in front while you were gone. Obviously knows where you live."

The name meant nothing to Colfax. "What's he look like?"

"Tall, thin, edgy, like a rabbit cornered by a coyote. Sandy hair. Maybe queer."

"You've got a thing about queers. Maybe you ought to see somebody about that."

"You know him or not?"

"Tall, thin, nervous. There's gotta be five hundred thousand tall, thin, nervous guys in the city."

"His pop's a big-time Republican lawyer, his mother a Junior Leaguer. She does charity balls and all that shit. The kid's got no rap sheet that we know of and no subversive affiliations." He stuffed the paper back in his pocket. "Maybe he just likes your cute ass."

Colfax sighed wearily. "Sure," he said. "Sure." Then, pushing Hagen toward the door, "My cute ass is tired and needs rest. By the way, how did you know this guy was following me?"

"Because I was following you," Hagen said matter-of-factly. "The chief of chiefs doesn't like it when one of his boys is murdered. We think you know more than you're saying." He shrugged. "So we follow you. It's our way."

Colfax shoved him out the door, undressed, and lay on the bed, thinking about the description Hagen had given him. It had been two years, but he thought he knew who Strickland was. He could see him bursting into Minelli's apartment, his face lined with anguish. And he could hear him saying, as if he were in that very room, *"It isn't right!"*

He thought he knew what that meant and wondered what Strickland could want with him.

A growing perception of him as the *Herald*'s golden boy was a troubling idea to Colfax. He was nobody's housecat and never had been. It had begun with his first story, a byline on day one, and had continued to this day through a whole series of pieces, lately most of them on the front page. He knew that good-natured needling by other staffers concealed a resentment that he, for some reason, was being pushed beyond them. He had become a star without earning his stardom.

It was on Colfax's mind when he was summoned to Stafford's office shortly after a raging argument with Paul Lowin. Loud debates were not unusual in the city room. Noise was always at a high level. But this argument was different. It had teeth. Lowin had proposed to Burns that he profile a growing discontentment within the student movement at U.C. and Stanford. The city editor had made it clear that it was Colfax's beat. Period. Lowin had confronted Colfax in a rage and the two men came close to fistfighting. It was prevented only when Burns stepped between them without saying a word. Lowin sulked to his desk, his hatred of Colfax a heavy reality in the city room.

"Don't worry about him," Corona McGee said in a tone meant to reassure him. "You're nobody until Crazy Paul hates your ass. This too shall pass."

The summons to see Stafford came so quickly after the argument that Colfax wondered whether Stafford had the whole place bugged, then dismissed the idea as paranoia. His main concern was his appearance. He'd been called out early to cover an explosion at a Bank of America and had worked it well past dawn without time to go to his apartment and clean up. He had tried to borrow a razor, but none existed in the city room. He was wearing the brown corduroy suit that had become his uniform, which would have been all right, except there was only a T-shirt under that. Burns offered to lend him a tie to go with the T-shirt, but Colfax shrugged and declined, though the temptation to accept had existed for a fleeting moment.

Entering Stafford's office, he found the publisher standing by a window behind his massive desk looking down on the street three stories below. For a moment, neither man spoke; then, in a voice that seemed detached, almost distant, Stafford said, "My dear father once looked down on this very same scene. That's strange to think of. It's odd that generation after generation can look at the same mountain. We come and we go, but the mountain never changes."

He turned slowly to face Colfax, who was momentarily shocked by Stafford's haggard look. There was a darkness under his eyes and a sagging appearance to his face. He slumped slightly.

"Oh, cities change, of course," the publisher said, "but not mountains, not the ocean." He paused, looking directly at Colfax. "I wonder what my dear father saw when he looked down on the street. Model-T Fords? Hoop skirts? Derbies? Men wore derbies at one time. There were manners once, Mr. Colfax. There was civility."

Colfax had no idea how to respond. He had come determined to end his role as the golden boy, but Stafford's strange, drifting, almost philosophical observations had caught him off guard and he was uncertain how he should handle the moment.

"You wanted to see me?" Colfax said at last.

Stafford sat behind his desk, the palms of both hands flat on the working surface. He was looking directly at Colfax but not seeing him. Colfax waited for him to speak. Stafford's stare was locked in place. Then suddenly, as though awakening from a dream, he snapped into focus.

"I admire your work, Mr. Colfax. Your stories have been clean and nicely written. Do you have any kind of social life?"

Once more, he was caught flat-footed. "I'm not sure I know what you mean, Mr. Stafford."

"Do you have a wife or a girlfriend? Do you belong to any organizations?"

"No to all of them."

Stafford regained strength as he spoke. The distant, melancholy tone of his voice was slowly giving way to the bolder stentorian tone that was his hallmark. His body seemed to fill and surge forward.

"The reason I ask is that there is an organization to which I belong that is interested in you as a possible new member."

Stafford let that sink in. He was being obviously circumspect and Colfax knew why. He played the same game, allowing the silence to remain between them without reacting.

"This is a patriotic organization," Stafford said, perceiving the reporter's suspicions. "Many of us in the Bay Area are members. Men of honor and worth."

"What's it called?" Colfax asked, trying to appear both interested and hesitant.

Stafford measured him carefully. "It's an organization that prefers to remain, well, unknown, Mr. Colfax."

Before he could stop himself, the words blurted from Colfax's lips. "A secret society?"

Colfax would have preferred a more cautious approach to the subject, meticulously drawing Stafford out until the publisher himself confirmed Colfax's suspicions that this "patriotic organization" was indeed a secret society. His mind raced with the possibilities, but he dared think no further than that.

Stafford weighed the question. "Secret?" He forced a laugh. It was unconvincing. "To the extent that we ask not to be publicized, I suppose you could say it's secret. This just isn't the right time. We are involved in a work that requires discretion."

"I have to say, sir, I'm really not interested in belonging to a secret society. It just isn't my thing."

Silence followed. The conversation was obviously over. Stafford busied himself opening mail for a moment and then said, "You have missed an opportunity. But the decision is yours. That will be that." Colfax nodded and turned to leave the room. Stafford's voice stopped him. "Mr. Colfax," he said, "I trust I won't see you in such a ragged state again."

Colfax responded with a nod, and the tension in the brief gesture was apparent. Stafford looked up from his make-work to watch him go, coping with the disappointment he was feeling. Everything seemed wrong. The world was out of whack, his newspaper was in trouble, and his head ached. He rubbed his brow and silently cursed the mess his father had left him with, dying at the start of a revolution, abandoning him to shuffle for himself. Stafford longed for the way it had been. The old man had a way of handling life, of roaring at the world around him, and of dispatching enemies without a trace of blood. Now he was alone and Stafford wondered vaguely as the headache intensified if he was up to guarding the legacy that had been bequeathed him.

Firings began the following spring, preceded by rumors that whispered through the city room and down the halls to photos, sports, society, the specialists, the art department, the library. No one spoke them aloud, afraid that by acknowledging them they'd come true. Newspaper city rooms thrive on a hunger for information however it is acquired. Someone confides, someone whispers, someone hears, and the word spreads. Superstition festers even as cynicism prevails, creating a climate of uncertainty that hovers like tule fog.

When the firings actually began, Sam Perkins was the first to go. It didn't surprise Colfax. Of all of those he had met on his first day, Perkins had seemed the most unlike everyone else. A nondrinker, suspicious of meat, and terrified of germs, he was an anomaly among the often disheveled heavy drinkers who peopled the city room. Buttoned down and immaculately clean, Perkins alone took Stafford's admonition to heart that his staffers must wear suits to work. He was the butt of jokes and of imitators, backing away at a cough or sneeze, spraying his phone with disinfectant each morning, opening the men's room door with his elbows to avoid touching the knob. Milton Travis, hurrying out to a story with cameras slung around his neck, never failed to pause and fake a sneeze in Perkins's direction, earning a hissing, "Asshole," from the assistant city editor, as the photographer lumbered yowling with laughter out the back door.

And yet there was sadness the day he became the first victim of Stafford's economy wave. Colfax sensed the shift of attitude as he walked in the door that afternoon from a press conference called by Wallace Korchek, whose anger toward the growing number of student demonstrations was becoming increasingly shrill. Vito Minelli was almost always his target as the stern-faced Oakland police chief, always in full uniform, faced the cameras and the notebooks to denounce what he called the attack on America. Colfax heard Stafford in Korchek and Korchek in Stafford, as though they had crawled under each other's skin and looked out at the ominous world of Reds and fellow travelers with a patriot's eyes.

It fell to Gerald Burns to tell Perkins that his job had been eliminated. The city editor's pain was apparent to all who discussed it later at the Three-Oh. His words were few, his displeasure great. How much Burns had protested the firing would never be known, because he would never say, but some who had on occasion heard the city editor argue with Stafford knew that he could be both convincing and determined. That he rarely won was more a testament to the publisher's own adamant leadership than to his editor's style.

Perkins never uttered a word but took the envelope offered by Burns and simply left the building after fourteen years at the *Herald*, never to return, leaving an uneasy emptiness with the absence of a man who served, if only as a foil, to round out the city room. The envelope contained his vacation pay and two weeks' salary, far less than would have been allowed under a Guild shop. The lack of generosity did not go unnoticed. Sally Bell was the first to leap on it, cursing Stafford between cigarettes, never minding who was listening.

"The son of a bitch will get us all," she roared across the city room. "What the hell protection do we have? He lifts a finger and another body hits the deck. Jesus Christ . . ." She blinked several times and turned away. A deep and grieving silence followed.

The book critic, Colin Stern, was next. Tall and arrogant, he strode into Stafford's office after getting the word from Burns, bristling with the indignation of damaged royalty. He emerged twenty minutes later looking as though he had just been pistol-whipped.

"Well," he said as he passed Burns, "that did no good whatsoever."

"I didn't expect it to," Burns said. "I'm sorry."

"Yes . . . I am too."

Stern had few friends in the city room but nevertheless came to symbolize with Perkins what was to be known as the First Two. During passing days, their fate would become the major source of conversation and all would wonder who next would face the guillotine. It left Colfax to ponder what he would do if the guillotine fell on him. A return to Edenville was out of the question. That was his past, as Laura was his past, a watercolor painting on a penthouse wall. The city was in his blood now. He would deal with his future later.

"We've got to talk to the Hammer," Chip Dawson said that afternoon over drinks at the Three-Oh. His temper made him vulnerable. Stafford disliked Dawson's heavy drinking and wild fights, feeling the man brought disgrace down on the *Herald*. He was kept only because Burns valued his flawless reporting and even Dawson, drinking modestly this night, knew that might not be enough to save him.

"If anyone knows we've even talked to him there'll be a mass slaughter," Barry Adams said. "They'll think the nigger did it."

Adams was the only black man on the staff, hired when racial quotas were being discussed among California publishers. He came to the *Herald* from the *Cleveland Plain Dealer,* a tense and angry man who, it was said, had secretly joined Minelli's People's Army and was Minelli's pipeline into the *Herald*. Confronted by Burns, Adams denied it vehemently, and since there was no real way to prove it, nothing was done.

The staff greeted his presence with the same mixture of friendship and suspicion with which they greeted anyone, and after about a year Adams blended into the tapestry that comprised the newspaper's editorial department. He was neither good nor bad and was never assigned major stories to cover. Only Milton Travis refused to have much to do with Adams and the issue was never pressed. They avoided each other, establishing by that avoidance an uneasy peace between them.

"Who's this Hammer?" Colfax said as they gathered at the Three-Oh.

"The Guild coordinator for this area," Gwen Ballard said. She was beginning to show renewed interest in Colfax and leaned toward him as she spoke so that her knees touched his. "The man's like a trained dog. Whenever he smells blood, he moves in."

"At the moment," Trager said, "he no doubt smells the blood of Perkins and Stern."

"I'll call him if you want," Adams said.

For a moment those at the table remained silent. Danny Doe, listening behind the bar, waited with them for a response, excited by the action being formed.

"Jesus," Gwen said, "do we go to the wall over Perkins and Stern? Such assholes, both of them."

"It's the principle of the whole goddamn thing," Sally Bell said. "The era of benevolent family employee associations is past. If Stafford thinks he's losing money, any of us could have our asses canned."

"We'd go one by one," Gwen said, "on a paper we thought would last forever."

"Nothing lasts forever," Trager said.

Adams joined in. "There'd just be Stafford and"—he gestured toward Colfax—"the Golden Boy."

He threw the words casually into the conversation and almost instantly regretted having said them. It was in the open at last.

"What does that mean?" Colfax said, the color in his face rising.

"Jesus," Trager said. He shook his head in a gesture meant to rebuke.

"I'm sorry," Adams said, "that was an asshole thing to say. I didn't mean it."

"It *was* an asshole thing to say," Gwen agreed. "But we're all a little tense. Let's ease up a bit."

She gently grabbed Colfax's leg in a friendly tug, but when she took her hand away she let it slide across his crotch. Trapped between anger and arousal, Colfax waved for another drink.

"I'm nobody's 'Golden Boy,' " he said, staring hard at Barry Adams. "I was assigned a job and I'm doing it."

"And doing it well," Trager said quickly. The others agreed.

Silence simmered in the room.

"You want to bust me one it's okay," Adams finally said, lifting his chin to be struck. "We have iron jaws."

His anger melting, Colfax reached across the table to push Adams's jaw with his fist. "Take that," he said.

Relieved that the moment had passed, the others laughed.

"I really am sorry," Adams said. "It's the callow youth in me gets out of hand."

Colfax shrugged. "So what about this Hammer? Is that his name or his description?"

"Both," Sally Bell said. "His name's Cliff Hammer. He hates anyone with big money, especially publishers, and would love to take another try at organizing the *Herald*."

"I think he may have a shot at it this time," Gwen said.

Another moment of silence. Then Trager turned to Adams, who was still feeling contrite over his outburst, and said, "Call him."

But before Adams could reply, Colfax held up a finger. "Let the Golden Boy do it," he said, mocking the term. But he couldn't shake the feeling that this was not far removed from the start of a combat patrol into a dense and tangled jungle.

. . .

Gwen's car was in the shop, so Colfax drove her to her apartment in the Sunset District of mixed homes and flats. They said little to each other, but he could feel a pressure building in him. The booze and the heavy aroma of her perfume created a density of emotions so thick they filled him. He pulled the car to a stop in front of her place, but before the car door opened, he was on her, kissing her hard, his tongue in her mouth, his hand between her legs, burning with the heat that came from her, pulling aside the lingerie that separated them, pushing his finger deep into the moisture. Her startled whispers to wait were muted by his mouth as he pulled her panties away and groped harder at her with an energy, almost a fury, that caught her off guard. She felt a rage in Colfax she had never felt in any man and it both frightened and aroused her. He pushed her legs wide apart and in the awkward confines of the front seat entered her, heaving and thrusting until she responded with a rhythmic circular motion of her hips, inviting him to go deeper, now grabbing at him as though reaching for a meteor in cosmic orbit.

It had not entered Colfax's mind to do this. He considered Gwen something of a joke even when she was rubbing against him at the Three-Oh. It was a game she played and he doubted that, contrary to gossip, she'd slept with anyone at the paper, much less every new man. He might have intended to play that game, he didn't know, but he had never anticipated this. He was on her and in her with such explosiveness that there was no time for the inner man to sort it out, to put this night into proper perspective. His orgasm came with a burst of power beyond his ability to contain, suddenly and abruptly draining him and leaving him feeling awkward and embarrassed. As quickly as it had begun, it was over.

They dressed silently, both trying to catch their breath from the violent collision of their bodies. Then, as she opened the car door, Gwen leaned over, kissed him, and said, "Thank you."

Colfax watched her hurry up the stairs to her apartment and vanish inside the closing door. *Thank you?* He sensed a loneliness in the phrase, an acknowledgment of special attention she'd never had before. It made Colfax uncomfortable. The whole thing was too wham-bam, too filled with violence, and he wondered as he sat in the car staring at Gwen's closed door if something had pursued him from across the ocean and released a demon in him whose existence he hadn't suspected. He drove home feeling a little afraid of himself.

Gunfire shattered the window of Vito Minelli's apartment just before dawn, adding new peril to the already dangerous animosity between the Bay Area's students and the Establishment they were fighting. The media fell into that category and the *Herald* was the symbol of all the media, the pig press. Never a month passed that students weren't parading in front of its tower at least twice, chanting and distributing flyers intended to fuel a spreading boycott. But for isolated incidents, they were left to picket unmolested, the hatred of the watching cops tempered by public outcries against police brutality in other confrontations.

Burns had telephoned at four A.M. with news about the attack on Minelli, and Colfax had gone quickly to the scene. He found Minelli, unhurt, standing before the lights and television cameras, raging against the fascist pigs who were out to kill him, vowing that the people's work would never be abandoned until there was peace in the world and equality over the land. Colfax took no notes. Over the past three years, he had heard the tirades before and waited patiently on the sidelines for the electronic media and other print reporters to finish their work. He noticed that blood ran from a cut on Minelli's forehead and wondered whether Minelli had cut himself for effect. It was part of his wounded warrior image.

Morning came as the others were leaving. It reached up over the Berkeley hills and lit the eastern face of Minelli's apartment, its single window shattered, bullet holes in the surrounding wood. Three police investigators were going about their work in the background, inside and outside of the apartment, as Colfax approached Minelli. The meeting was brief. Minelli had no real idea who had sent bullets flying into his apartment as he lay sleeping on the floor. He was certain, however, that whoever did it were agents of the right wing who, like night riders of the Ku Klux Klan, had singled him out as the nigger in their midst that ought to be eliminated.

"You're making yourself a pretty obvious target," Colfax said, half watching a detective search the shrubbery in front of the building.

"So we should dump the First Amendment because some asshole owns a gun?" Minelli demanded.

"The First Amendment isn't made of steel. It's a dangerous time." For all of his rejection of Minelli, a dozen interviews and what seemed like hundreds of witnessed demonstrations had created a bond between the two men.

Minelli nodded toward the bullet holes. "You're telling me?"

Back at the office, still slapped together and unshaved, Colfax wrote a dozen paragraphs on the attack at Minelli's apartment. It would be the banner line for the *Herald*'s first street edition, then slowly sink to the bottom of page one as the day progressed. The story reignited Stafford's passions, prompting an editorial that stopped just short of promising that the student Communists would be the objects of renewed violence, a tooth for a tooth, if they continued their rabble-rousing ways. The shooting alone would have increased the tempo of the demonstrations; the editorial set them ablaze. The boycott against the *Herald* gained strength as the newspaper was reestablished as a target.

As Colfax was finishing the shooting piece, the six A.M. staff was coming to work. Sally Bell saw Colfax standing to give his story one last read and went directly to him.

"You get to Hammer yet?" she asked.

"That's my today job." It was actually one of his today jobs. High on his list was to check out Strickland. The man was following him for a reason and somehow Colfax doubted that the reason was to do him violence.

"You'd better hurry," Sally Bell said. "Three more are getting the axe today."

He didn't question her source. It was always good. When he asked who, she named the half-blind night copy editor they called the Bat; a rewrite man named Eddie Pearl, a strange little guy with an expertise in transportation who wouldn't, or couldn't, stop talking about buses and the need for trains; and, surprisingly, Wally Wallace, the managing editor.

Colfax couldn't believe what he'd heard. "They're canning the M.E.?"

Burns looked up from the city desk as Sally cautioned Colfax to lower his voice. "All three will get the word this afternoon."

"How in the hell are a blind copy reader, an aging editor, and an obsessive-compulsive fucking train expert going to make a living outside of here?"

She shrugged. "That's never a consideration when this kind of shit goes down." She began to walk away, then turned back. "Call Hammer."

Colfax left the building relieved to be away from it, sucking in the cool air of the city as though it were an elixir. As he rounded the corner toward the garage, he glanced across the street. Standing alone and staring directly at him was Ted Strickland. Colfax hesitated for a moment to make certain that this was the man who had busted into Minelli's apartment the night Colfax had first confronted him. When there was no doubt in his mind, he slowly changed direction and headed directly for him. Strickland made no effort to run.

CHAPTER EIGHT

V iolence was the nature of the time, infecting the globe like a great plague. World leaders fell to bombs and gunfire, rioters and revolutionaries dismantled old values, and hatred marched hand in hand with righteousness across the face of cultures in transition.

It permeated the city room of the *Herald* like a microcosm of the world. Paul Lowin, his .38 never far away, fired at the landlord who tried to raise his rent, called him a capitalist pig, and chased him down the street. Dragged away like a common thug, Lowin was jailed for assault with a deadly weapon and held on fifty thousand dollars' bail, which he didn't have. Someone called Burns, who got Lowin out of the slammer, took his gun away, and bargained the charge down to drunk and disorderly. The judge was a friend. His one order: Have the crazy-ass reporter move to another apartment building.

Tension similarly heightened the conflict between the *Herald*'s two most prominent women. Gwen joined the Women's Liberation Movement, selecting from its multiplicity of causes the one that irritated Sally, a traditionalist, the most: a woman's right to multiple orgasms.

"What the hell is that?" Sally had demanded. "What *right?* It's not like the goddamn First Amendment. There is no *right* to multiple orgasms, you loon-box! You ever think of anything that isn't between your legs?"

"Of course you wouldn't think of multiple orgasms because you never have *any*," Gwen replied with a toss of her head. "When you have one and need another, you'll know what I mean."

"Up yours!"

"Gladly."

Colfax had been getting ready to leave, half listening to the banter with mixed amusement and incredulity. When the women realized it and looked to him as though seeking some kind of resolution, he gestured his reluctance to take any part in the debate, preferring instead to leave the question of a woman's orgasms to them. He had other things on his mind.

As he left, he caught a glimpse of Paul Lowin moving toward them. He would offer his opinion of multiple orgasms from a Maoist point of view. The right of the masses to perform.

Outside, crossing the street to confront Strickland, Colfax was overcome with the feeling that there was peril here, but he couldn't define what that peril might be. For his part, Strickland, wearing God's smile, simply waited for the limping reporter to reach him, certain now of what had to be done, one step at a time as the Lord had instructed him. The voice on the secret wind whispered to Strickland, guiding, leading, cautioning.

It was what he had learned in the three years since the FBI bombing, that prayer offers answers and that messages are whispered from God through the forces of wind and sea and the tapping of rain on the roof. It had whispered of this day and what had to be done to cleanse his own soul and to save it from fire.

"Mr. Strickland," Colfax said, "I'm William Colfax."

Colfax extended his hand. Strickland made no effort to clasp it.

"I know," he said.

Colfax was uncomfortable with the man's demeanor. The smile bothered him. There was an aura of detachment to Strickland, as though he belonged in another place at another time and was uncertain what he was doing on that street corner at that moment.

"You've been following me," Colfax said.

Strickland nodded, focusing. "I have information on the FBI bombing," he said.

"I thought you might. Shall we go somewhere to talk?"

Strickland chose the place. It was a point of land called Nathan's Cliff that looked out past the Golden Gate to the ocean beyond. The narrow road they'd taken dead-ended at the point. There were no homes in the area and the drop to the churning waves below the sheer cliff was at least 150 feet. Turning a car around under these conditions would be hazardous. Colfax felt as he had on his first combat patrol, choked by a sense of dread that could neither be denied nor lessened.

Strickland refused to be tape-recorded. Colfax wrote furiously in a notebook as the man talked, relating in detail events of the night that the FBI building had been bombed. Vito Minelli, as Colfax had suspected, was behind it all, even to the point of building the pipe bomb that had killed Leonard Rose. Strickland had a precise memory of names and times and waited patiently for Colfax to take them all down.

When they were finished, Colfax studied the man sitting next to him and said, "Why are you telling me all this? You know you're indicting yourself."

Strickland made no effort to avoid the reporter's hard gaze. He said, "I am a messenger of God."

Colfax sagged. The credibility of all the man had told him now seemed to be in jeopardy. How often had he heard a nut defend his madness by blaming God? That was the essence of Strickland's smile and Colfax should have recognized the inward glow of self-deterioration that marked a slippage from reality.

"God told you to confess?"

"God told me to do the right thing," Strickland said. "The Lord Jesus speaks to us all to act in righteousness in His name's sake."

Colfax nodded. "Would you swear to all of this in court?" he asked, holding up his notebook.

"We'll see," Strickland said. He left the car and began walking down the hillside.

Colfax shouted after him, "I'll need a signed document!"

Strickland made no effort to respond but continued on down the slope and then over a rise until he could be seen no longer. Colfax turned the car around carefully and with great effort, glad to leave the melancholy point and wondering exactly what he should do with what he had.

Back in the office, Gerald Burns, said, "Write it and we'll see." Colfax did just that and then waited for word to come from Stafford on whether or not the story would run. The *Herald* was not a careless newspaper, but the publisher was in a peculiar frame of mind and his decisions at best were erratic.

Colfax had telephoned Minelli for a response to Strickland's charge and had placed his angry denial high in the piece, but, as Trager warned, that probably wasn't enough to hold off a libel judgment should it come to that. There was no outside confirmation of Strickland's charge and a responsible journal would have handled it with care, if at all. Colfax agreed and so did Burns. "God," the city editor said, "is not a reliable backup source," and took the story into Stafford, recommending further checking.

Stafford read the story with a growing sense of vindication. As he suspected, it was a conspiracy perpetrated by Minelli and his filthy Communist subversives. Thank God Strickland had come forward! He could barely contain himself and shoved past his secretary into the city room, passing Colfax on his way to the city desk and thrusting the story at a startled Burns.

"Run it," the publisher thundered. "Run every goddamn word of it!"

"It's libelous and unsubstantiated," Burns said quietly, but Stafford was striding back toward his office. The conversation was ended.

Colfax was surprised when he realized that Ellen Stafford's Berkeley apartment was on the same street as Minelli's. As he walked up the pathway toward the old brick building, he turned to look at Minelli's place across the street and a few houses down. He stood for a moment thinking about him, wondering how the story about Strickland's confession would affect him.

It was not a story that Colfax had been happy to do and he wished he could have somehow placed more doubt in it. On the one hand he felt Strickland was probably telling the truth; on the other he saw him as, at best, an addled witness to the events in which he had willingly participated. It was only later that he learned Gerald Burns had confronted Stafford and again cautioned him that the piece was libelous, but the publisher would not be moved. So it would run all editions the following day.

What was done was done. Colfax's more immediate concern was his decision to visit the apartment of Ellen Stafford. Simultaneously lured by her sexuality and warned by his better judgment, he had decided to at least hear what she had to say. Hadn't she once suggested they discuss the paper? What harm could come of it? He paused at the foot of the stairs, still convincing himself, unaware that Ellen had come to the doorway.

"Are you coming in or what?"

She stood looking out at him. Staring back, Colfax realized again how strikingly beautiful she was, almost luminous in the sunlight that shone directly on her.

"Did you know that Minelli lives down the block?" he asked, filling the moment with talk as he approached her.

"I didn't, but I do now. Wednesday night sounded like World War II."

Her apartment was small and comfortable, its fireplace and dark oak paneling giving it the air of an expensive men's club, its living room patterned by filtered light streaming through venetian blinds. Books were piled on a desk and on a dining room table, adding a studious level to the ambience. Overstuffed leather furniture made it clear that this was the home of a rich man's daughter.

"Nice, huh?" she said, noticing Colfax's admiring sweep of the room.

"Very nice," he said, slumping heavily into one of the two chairs. He suddenly felt exhausted, realizing how little he'd slept in the past several days. They drank white wine together and made small talk with Ellen curled up on a couch, her legs tucked under her, her feet bare, still aglow in the filtered light. Even in jeans and sweatshirt her allure was obvious.

When the small talk was over she said, "You met with my dad?"

"It was a strange session," Colfax said.

"And?"

Colfax told her what he remembered of the meeting and what he suspected.

"You think my father belongs to some kind of nut right-wing group?" Her tone was both incredulous and indignant.

Colfax shrugged. "I just don't know. What I *suspect* is that he belongs to something like that, yeah."

"Like the John Birch Society." It was a statement, not a question.

Colfax shrugged again.

"You shrug a lot," Ellen said.

It caught him off guard. "I guess I do."

"Well, that's okay."

He sensed she was playing with him, touching her upper thigh in a manner that seemed unconscious but wasn't. She looked straight at him as she did it. Colfax thought he knew women. This was a message. But then maybe it wasn't. There was always that possibility. Women were natural teasers. Sex had nothing to do with it. He quickly returned to the subject at hand. Teasing wasn't what he wanted from the boss's daughter. Or was it?

Asked what she knew, Ellen told him about endless telephone calls her father seemed to be making, his endless pacing, and at least one meeting she knew of with Wallace Korchek, the Oakland police chief. It made sense to Colfax. Korchek was a known Red-hater, a violent man who had shaped his department into a band of thugs.

"I can't believe my dad would have any part of that kind of thing," Ellen said, pouring them more wine. "He's always been . . . well . . . gentle in his ways. I know he sounds gruff, but"—she snuggled down on the couch again—"he isn't."

Colfax wanted to say he thought Stafford was losing it, maybe having a nervous breakdown under the strain, but knew he was talking to the publisher's daughter and kept his own counsel. Then he remembered Stafford's blank stare. It had lasted only for seconds but was obviously more than simply an effort to define him. For that moment, it seemed, Stafford had gone comatose with his eyes wide open.

"Does your father have any history of epilepsy?" he asked.

When Ellen asked why, he told her of the moment. She had noticed it on another occasion, but when she mentioned it to her father he had brushed her off.

"Has he ever had medical problems?" Colfax asked.

Ellen shook her head no.

"Your mother . . . she isn't still alive?"

No one in the city room knew exactly what had happened to Geraldine Stafford. Burns might have known, but on the one occasion Colfax had asked about her, he sidestepped the question.

"She died several years ago," Ellen said, uneasy with the drift of the conversation.

"She was ill?"

"Why are you asking about my mother?" she suddenly demanded.

Colfax backed off. "I'm sorry, I just wondered. It's none of my business."

Ellen softened. "She killed herself." There was a catch in her voice. "She was a deeply troubled lady. So gentle and so haunted." A long pause. "My father kept sleeping pills in a drawer next to their bed. One night, she used them. . . ."

Silence.

"I had no business prying."

"He misses her every day of his life. So do I. She was caring and loving. She was the one who calmed him, who reassured him."

Colfax wanted to take her in his arms and comfort her. Instead he rose from the chair. "I've got a long drive. Thanks for the wine and the conversation. . . ."

Ellen was studying him. "You look exhausted," she said.

"I am exhausted. Driving across the bay is going to be a real adventure."

He turned the doorknob. "Would you like to rest awhile here?" she asked.

There it was again. Colfax tried to define her expression. He wanted desperately to know what she meant. In the microseconds that he stood by the door, he pondered her eyes, her body language, the tone of her voice, and found no underlying invitation beyond that offered.

"That probably wouldn't be a good idea," he said.

"You wouldn't be the first guy to flop on my couch," she said. "I'm not suggesting a love-fest, just a nap."

Colfax laughed in spite of himself. "Well," he said, "not much sleep, the wine . . ."

"You nap, I've got cramming to do," she said, settling at the nearby desk, her back to him, smoothly contoured under the sweatshirt, enticing with its radiated warmth.

Colfax sighed, took off his jacket and shoes, and lay on the couch, looking at her and remembering Laura. He still missed Laura in ways he couldn't explain. She was his first love, and, like all new lovers, they were linked by a fragile thread. It was broken when he was shipped off to Vietnam and she went on to a life of her own. Without heat, his passion faded, but there remained a memory of Laura that lay in a corner of his mind like a half-remembered dream.

His story on Strickland's confession was printed over the masthead that bore the paper's name. It filled the top half of page one, complete with a photograph of Minelli and a Stafford editorial that wove both God and anti-Communism into a web of vitrole that exceeded anything he had written before. "The stooges of terror," he called the students, "thugs and bombers." Both Burns and Colfax read it and winced.

The picture was a masterpiece of slanted photojournalism, selected carefully from a stack of Minelli photographs to show him at his ugliest and his most violent, an evil sprite out to defile heaven and blown up to accentuate all of those negative properties. Viewing the picture, how could anyone possibly deny the man's guilt?

Once more Colfax was embarrassed by the combined presentation and tried to convince himself that it wasn't his fault, that he was only doing his job, that all of this would pass someday and he could get on to become the kind of journalist he imagined himself to be. Response to the piece was almost instantaneous. A storefront Berkeley lawyer named Harry Gold, whose main source of income came from defending left-wing causes, delivered a demand for retraction within two hours after the first editions of the *Herald* hit the streets. Stafford tore it up. The *Herald* would not retract. Even sooner than Gold's letter came an enraged telephone call to Colfax from Bruno Hagen.

"What in the hell are you trying to do to me?" he roared into the phone. "They're threatening to send me to Omaha, for Christ's sake! You know what happens in Omaha? Not a goddamn thing! It's Siberia! *It's worse than Siberia!*"

The call had been patched through to the Three-Oh, where Colfax sat alone over a bloody Mary. It was not yet noon, but he had been at the office since six and for the morning crew it was lunchtime. The paper's heavy drinkers were fond of pointing out that somewhere in the world it was always the cocktail hour. Generally, he avoided joining them, but today he felt the need and a bloody Mary sounded good.

"The man came to me, I wrote the story, they ran it," Colfax said wearily. "That's not doing anything to you, Bruno. That's just called newspapering."

"Bullshit! I'm the agent on this case! I spotted Strickland tailing you! It sure as hell is doing something to me when a guy who helped kill a federal agent—a friend—spills his guts and then disappears! That not only makes me look like an asshole, but it allows a suspect to get away!"

Colfax knew Hagen was right. In the rush of events, it hadn't occurred to him to call the agent.

"Rose was your friend?" he asked lamely.

"More than a friend! We came to the Bureau together. We played cards together. I knew his wife . . . hell, I was in love with his wife!" Hagen allowed himself a moment to allow his anger to simmer, then continued in a calmer tone. "What your story did, Colfax, was to point the finger without substantiation. We've been investigating Minelli for a month. We *know* he's involved, but we don't have the stuff to file against him. Now he's on guard and we may never nail the son of a bitch."

"I know all that," Colfax said, waving at Patty for another Bloody Mary. "I had no choice. And I had no idea Strickland would take off."

"That fucking publisher of yours is ready for the looney bin. It was his idea to go with the story, right?"

"That's right."

Hagen sighed. "Do you have any idea where your God-loving friend might be? He's a material witness and we need him. We've got half a dozen agents looking for him and we're just about convinced he's been taken by angels to some goddamn heavenly hideaway."

"The last I saw of him was at Nathan's Cliff, going down a hillside headed for town."

"If he contacts you again, for Christ's sake give me a call. We've got to get him."

"I'll do that, Bruno. Now you do something for me by answering a question. What do you know about a secret society in town? Some kind of right-wing group?"

"The Leonard Rose Brigade. Your boss is a charter member. We're looking into it."

"What's it for?"

"Who knows? Vengeance. Patriotism. Folk dancing. Group picnics. That's what we're trying to find out."

"Who else is in it?"

"I wouldn't tell you if I knew."

"Fuck you."

"Love to the missus," Hagen said cheerfully, and hung up. It was a sign-off he often used. *Love to the missus.* Colfax laughed out loud. Danny Doe heard him from behind the bar and smiled, always willing to join in on whatever a *Herald* staffer did, then had Patty bring Colfax another drink, on the house. His resolve gone, Colfax went at the third Bloody Mary without hesitation, determined not to go back to the office that afternoon or to work at all. Life was weighing heavily upon him, and by the time he finished the third drink he felt oddly like crying.

CHAPTER
NINE

G wen Ballard was awake when the door to her apartment rang at three in the morning. It seemed at first a part of her dream, a slow dissolve from fantasy to reality, from a misty day at the ocean to . . . what? She sat up and listened to be certain that it wasn't the dream. The bell sounded again, a segment of the tune "Eleanor Rigby." It was Rod's idea when they were still living together a lifetime ago. She could hardly remember his last name. Rod . . . Rod Abramson. A street poet with no future, but at least he was there.

"Who is it?"

"Gerald Burns."

She had scooped a robe off the bed and tightened it around her now over the patterned woolen pajamas she wore. Even though the city was unseasonably warm, she felt a chill go through her. Dear God, she said to herself, don't let it be . . .

"Gwen?"

"Yes . . . yes . . ."

She opened the door without even looking through the peephole, freeing the deadbolt with a sense of dread that made her hand shake. When the bell first chimed she thought it might be Colfax and for a heartbeat fed his voice into what she quickly realized was that of the city editor's. She heard what she had wanted to hear, but reality wouldn't allow it to remain.

Burns appeared uncharacteristically disheveled and there was the strong smell of bourbon on his breath. Both were unusual. No matter what the circumstance, he was always neatly dressed, even color-coordinated. His long-suffering wife never would have allowed him from the house in a open-collared shirt. And he drank vodka, not bourbon. The departures from habit were significant to Gwen.

"You're up early," she said with a weak stab at conversation. "I'll make coffee."

She left him standing in the small living room staring after her.

"You could have called," she said across the distance that separated them.

"Gwen . . ."

". . . I'm in the book."

He followed her into the kitchen, turned her around, and put his arms around her in an almost fatherly gesture. Everything within him hurt. He could feel a tightness in his chest that he had never felt before, a response to the helplessness that increasingly was absorbing and threatening to overwhelm him.

"You know why I'm here," he said.

She nodded, her head tight against his shoulder. Burns doubted that she was crying, but he couldn't tell. She held perfectly still. He had known since the previous afternoon that Gwen was being fired. When he argued her case with Stafford, he was summarily dismissed with a wave of the hand. "We shouldn't have kept her this long," the publisher had said. "We don't need women like that at my family's newspaper."

Whatever compassion Stafford had felt for his staff had vanished in the turmoil racing around the tower. Burns had seen it diminish in direct proportion to the *Herald*'s falling circulation. The newspaper had been wounded by the boycott and was bleeding badly. Stafford's cuts were more than economic. They were acts of vengeance against the only group of people he could control.

"Am I fired?" Gwen finally asked.

Burns sighed deeply and held her at arm's length. "The coffee's ready," he said. "Let's talk."

They sat across from each other in the small living room and he told her how he felt about Stafford and how she was lucky to be leaving a failing newspaper. He had nailed down a job for her at the *Daily News* and she could start anytime she'd like. Meanwhile—he handed her an envelope—he had gotten her a month's severance pay to ease the pain.

"It's going to seem so strange," she said, her voice oddly remote.

"I know."

"But . . . what the hell." She managed a faint smile. "What choice do I have?"

Burns tried to return her smile. It didn't work. He liked her. He knew she wasn't a slut. He knew the sex thing was an act or a game and he knew she took a whimsical delight in the reputation. But he also knew that Stafford had never liked her, despite the efficiency of her work and the quick, clear quality of her prose. He wondered vaguely if she had ever turned Stafford down, but it was not for him to ask.

Burns hugged her again as he stood in the doorway, ready to leave. There was the faintest hint of dawn in the air, a gathering of colors below the horizon that soon would paint the hazy sky. Morning was what he had loved most about the city when he first came here, to rise before the sun and to be there when the first, faint light diffused the night. There were no mornings in Kansas, only an almost strangling monotony of open plains which had at last driven him westward, searching for anything that wasn't flat. Newspapering was the ultimate cacophony, and San Francisco the ultimate goal. He had never looked back.

As Burns walked down the stairs toward his car, he wondered if he would be next in line to face Stafford's guillotine, but it didn't seem to matter anymore. His passion for running the city room, damped by the publisher's lopsided vendetta against every social protest marching through the country, was dying at a rate faster than he ever would have imagined. He found himself longing for a dream place far from the pain he was being forced to inflict.

Gwen closed the door slowly and turned the thumb lock almost automatically. She felt strangely removed from the moment, as though she were having an out-of-body experience, looking down at herself staring dumbly at the door. Hadn't her mother claimed such an experience once when she thought she was dying? She couldn't quite remember, but it seemed that way. Her mother had been so crazy, believing in ghosts and Ouija boards and tea leaves.

The alarm clock rang at five and she turned it off quickly. Under normal circumstances she would be rising now, preparing for her shift at the *Herald*. But there was no *Herald* anymore. She threw the envelope on a table and got back into bed, squirming far down under the covers. Morning would soon come full-force over San Francisco and over the old brick tower, and then afternoon and evening, and all would find Gwen Ballard, late of the *Herald,* tucked under her blankets, eyes clamped tightly shut, trying desperately to believe it was all a dream.

Cliff Hammer was waiting in his office when Colfax and Sally Bell came at him like rhinos bursting from a forest. He was on the phone and waved them to chairs placed at angles in front of his old wooden desk. He was a bulky man in his forties with wildly uncombed black hair who smoked cigars and spit into his wastebasket, characteristics that made conversations in his office short.

"Tell the cocksuckers it goes in or we go out," he was saying into the phone in a voice as flat and dry as a desert. "The conditions are the fucking same. No shit in, no shit out."

Colfax waited impatiently as the conversation continued for another ten minutes. Sally smoked and fidgeted, coughing wildly at times, a deep, hacking cough that brought tears to her eyes. Cigarette ashes scattered on the floor. With both Hammer and Sally smoking, the room became uncomfortably dense. Colfax rose and opened a window slightly ajar, letting in the hum of traffic from Market Street four stories down.

"Close the fucking window," Hammer said, abruptly hanging up.

He wasn't a loud man, but there was a finality to his order that brooked no debate and Colfax did as he was told, the way he always had as a Goodmarine.

"It's too smoky in here," he said, defending his position even as he slammed the window shut.

Hammer ignored him and studied Sally. "Back again?" he finally said.

"He's firing everybody," she said.

"The cocksucker's crazy."

Colfax resettled himself in the fog of their smoke and wondered vaguely if the big man on the other side of the desk called everyone cocksucker. He had a drill instructor at Parris Island who called every-one "fucker." Colfax assumed it was because the man didn't want to take the time to remember names. "Hey, fucker" seemed to get results, so why go further? It wasn't until basic training was over and the D.I. shook the hand of each man in his platoon and called each by name that Colfax realized the fucker-business was just his way and had noth-ing to do with the drill instructor's ability to remember names.

"You're the pecker at that paper," Hammer said, turning to Colfax. "You go along with this?"

"You think I'd be here if I didn't?" Colfax said, allowing irritability to seep into his voice. *The pecker at the paper?* Colfax wasn't entirely certain what that meant but didn't like the sound of it.

"Gerald Burns called me last night." Hammer stood, slipped out of a dark leather jacket, and threw it in a corner. The jacket, a sport shirt, and a rumpled pair of dark slacks were all he ever wore. "He's had it up to here with the cocksucker who runs the paper."

"Burns is with us this time," Sally said. "No more kicking ass and taking names. He'll let us move ahead without any bullshit."

Even in the Corps, Colfax didn't swear that much, but he found it necessary here in order to fit it. "We've got a fucking coordinating committee ready to go," he said.

Hammer nodded. "Can you be ready in a month?"

"We can be ready in a week," Sally said.

"The sooner the fucking better," Colfax said.

Hammer spit in his wastebasket, a long trail of saliva that only broke when he brushed it with a finger. The man, Colfax felt, was a slob, but his effectiveness as the Newspaper Guild's coordinator was beyond dispute. Almost single-handedly, he had brought the *Daily News* to its knees after a three-week strike and had won a contract in Oakland that had brought the smaller *Press-Dispatch* out of the dark ages. His manner before publishers or their negotiators was abrupt and unyielding. He rarely swore in their presence and rarely raised his voice to them either, saving the harsh language for his own kind. His presence, however, was overpowering, and when he rolled up his sleeves to reveal arms as muscular and hairy as a gorilla's, you knew things were about to happen.

"I'll call the NLRB and we'll set the election for"—he flipped through a desk calendar—"September third. We'll go for what we got at the *News* and make a big fucking effort to rehire the people the cocksucker's dumped if they want to come back."

He plopped back in his chair. Only the whisper of a change in his expression indicated that he had suddenly become serious. His face otherwise seemed oddly expressionless, as though he wore a mask, behind which the real face waited.

"It won't be easy," he said.

"We don't expect it to be," Colfax replied.

Hammer pointed suddenly at him. "You've got to be the point man in this. The staff looks up to you. You're the—"

"Pecker at the paper," Colfax interrupted. "Don't call me that."

Unexpectedly, Hammer roared with laughter, an explosion that thrust Colfax and Sally back in their seats and rattled windows for miles.

"All right!" Hammer said, standing again. "Let's get the boys their union and let the cocksucker know how things stand! I'll be in touch!"

As they walked away from the old building toward a parking lot across Sixteenth Street, Colfax said, "What do you think?"

"I think you're going to be in another war," Sally said.

She began coughing again and brought a handkerchief to her mouth, glanced at it, and nervously tucked it back in her purse.

"You ought to see someone about that cold," Colfax said.

She didn't reply.

Bruno Hagen was uncomfortable with the three agents they'd assigned him for the job. They were gunslingers and he wanted none of that in this operation. It was important that they come back with a live man, not a body. He knew how they felt about the murder of a fellow agent, but this wasn't a vengeance trip. He was going after bigger game. Most of them hadn't even known Leonard Rose, but there was that feeling among them that whenever one of their own got it, the guy who did it was almost immediately a walking dead man. The three agents were young, grim, and filled with the kind of holy zeal that pulled triggers.

Hagen drove slowly through the Mission District, thinking everything over, and by the time they reached the Hotel Barkley he was ready to offer last-minute instructions. The building sat among the squalor of Skid Row's Folsom Street, distinctive by its fresh paint job, a deep ocean gray. It had been a place where tourists once came, but time and shifting demographics had eroded the neighborhood. Now it was a place where old men and drifters lived. Even so, efforts had been made to retain its early dignity, the way an old lady applies bright red lipstick in remembrance of her maidenhood.

They parked across the street and before he'd let his gunslingers out of the car, Hagen warned them that he wanted no shooting unless their lives were being threatened, and he would determine whether or not they were. He gave them a short speech on how Rose had been his best friend but there was more at stake here than getting even. They wanted the guy inside alive to get to bigger fish. When they seemed to understand that, Hagen gave the signal to follow him and they crossed the street like an army of solemn angels, led by a saint in rumpled clothes.

A few ancient retirees sitting in the lobby on worn chairs hardly looked up as the four agents entered. Nothing in life amazed or even interested them much anymore. The desk clerk, a gopher-faced man named Sammy Peck, knew they were coming and handed Hagen a key without saying a word. In exchange, Hagen slipped him a Bureau-sanctioned fifty-dollar bill in the smooth passage of a relay baton. Then the agents headed upstairs.

Motioning for silence, Hagen unlocked the door of Room 207 without making a sound, looked back at his three agents, their faces tense, their guns drawn, and nodded. Before they could respond, he had slammed the door open and they were in the room shouting, "Freeze!" and "Don't move!" as a startled young man lying on a bed in a corner of the small room sat up suddenly. Recovering from the sudden entrance of the FBI agents, he smiled a knowing smile at the artillery facing him and offered no resistance as they handcuffed him and pulled him roughly to his feet.

He was still smiling as they led him from the room. Hagen noticed his lips moving and guessed he was probably praying. The old agent was glad it was over. They had Ted Strickland now and Vito Minelli would be next. It was just a matter of time, and time was something that Bruno Hagen had plenty of.

Stafford was informed of the upcoming Guild election by the National Labor Relations Board in a document delivered by a messenger. Petitions were already circulating throughout the third floor and in the bureaus beyond and almost everyone was signing them. Even those who were essentially nonunion were putting their signatures to the sheet, responding to a question from the coordinating committee, "Who's next to be fired?" When jobs were at stake, everyone was a Guildsman.

The publisher almost immediately called Burns to his office. He seemed more confused than enraged. "Why are they doing this?" he asked his city editor in a tone softened by his confusion. "What do they want?"

Burns had been prepared to give anger for anger regardless of what it might have meant for his future at the *Herald.* He had decided that job security wasn't worth all the bullshit he and the others had been forced to endure in the last few years. Stafford's attitude threw him off guard. He felt as though he were confronting a child who'd just been suddenly set upon by a gang of bullies. Why had they done that? the small boy cried. Why had they hit him?

Instead of standing, arms on his hips in a gesture of defiance, Burns slumped into a chair. "They're doing it," he said in the measured tone of a father, "because you're firing people. They feel threatened. They want protection." He paused. When Stafford said nothing, he continued, "The only way they feel they're going to get that protection is if they belong to a union."

Stafford still said nothing and for a moment Burns felt he had lost him completely, that the publisher had drifted on to another plane of existence and was no longer a part of the conversation. But as quickly as he had left, he returned, still wearing an expression of pain and bewilderment at the turn of events.

"We've always met and worked out our problems," Stafford said, shaking his head. "My father gave them their association and we have negotiated with it in good faith. No other reporter in the city makes more money than my people."

"It isn't about money," Burns said. "It's about the changes at the *Herald* and about what seems to be a reckless reduction in the staff. People are being fired who have given us their best for most of their adult lives. There is no regard to seniority. That's what it's all about."

"Will they strike us?"

"I don't know," Burns said. "The election will be held, the Guild will be voted in, and then we negotiate."

Stafford leaned back in his chair and rubbed his eyes. "Is William Colfax behind this?"

"No one person is behind this," Burns said, but his words were lost. "It's a staff movement. Colfax just happens to be on the coordinating committee."

"I made him the most important reporter on the staff. I trusted him. He was the point man." He turned suddenly to Burns. "I felt he would understand, Gerald! He had fought for our country. He had bled for our country!"

An uneasy silence settled over the room. The lion's head above the desk seemed to dominate. Burns hated the effigy and more than once wanted to climb on the desk and tear it down. But, like everything else in his life, it remained an undone defiance, a muted shout.

"Everything has changed," Stafford said, his voice barely rising above a whisper. "Where's it going, Gerald? What's to become of us?"

Burns thought about it at home that night in the hills of the Peninsula, sitting on his patio watching the sunset and drinking a tumbler of straight vodka. He could hear his wife Helen cooking dinner. In a moment she would come outside and tell him he was drinking too much. They both were. He would sense her tipsiness and she his in a bonding of booze they had shared for thirty years. He couldn't live without her or she without him, but they both knew they were drinking themselves to death. It was their curse to be aware of slow suicide even as they were performing the ritual.

In a sense, Stafford was right. Everything was changing. But what he failed to realize was that he was an instrument of that change. Burns had wanted to tell him that but knew it would do little good. The change would eventually sweep them both away because they were a part of the old and the new was coming. The *Herald* was in decay. The presses were old, the Linotypes were old, the building was old, and even the goddamn toilet didn't work about half the time. Maybe the kids on the street were right. They were dinosaurs. Their time had come and gone.

Helen stuck her head out the door. "Dinner is almost ready," she said in the lyrical tone of a good wife. Then, "Let's cut down on the drinking, okay? We've been hitting it too much lately."

"Sure," Burns said with an air of futility. "Anything you say." The sunset was glorious. One of the best he'd ever seen.

The room over the Three-Oh was packed. Every chair was filled and some staffers stood against the wall. It was called the Alice Leandro Room, but no one knew why. It was guessed that the man who built the hotel in 1893 named it after a mistress, but there was never any proof. It was a meeting room used by the *Herald*'s Editorial Employees Association for its monthly meetings, and not a meeting passed that a male staffer, walking into the room, didn't sniff the air and say, "I still smell pussy in the room."

This time it was Trager. "I still smell pussy in the room," he said, walking through the door.

"It's mine," Rosebud Kane said. "Now sit your ass down."

"No," Corona McGee added, "yours is lilac, mine is the mint."

"Nice," Trager said. "I like it."

Colfax, Sally Bell, and Hammer sat at the head table. There was no gavel, so Colfax pounded the table with his fist to get attention. When the room had quieted, he said, "Most of you know Cliff Hammer. He's here to—"

"I know Hammer," a short man in the front row said, "and I can smell Sally, but who in the hell are you?"

"That's not Sally!" Kane shouted.

"It is too!" Barry Adams shouted back.

Laughter filled the room. Colfax pounded again. "All right, this is cutting into our drinking time, so let's get on with it." Pause. "My name's Colfax and it's Sally, all right." This time they laughed with him. Sally smiled and shrugged in a maybe-he-knows-maybe-he-doesn't gesture. "We've got business here and Hammer's going to tell us about it."

Hammer sat on the edge of the table, arms folded, and in his implacable arid voice explained how the voting process would work and what they'd be up against. Stafford had oddly made no attempt to threaten any of them and Burns had already signaled that he wouldn't interfere with the process. It looked good, but it wasn't over yet. The publisher had hired a management negotiator named Christopher Page who was used to representing the big shipping companies in battles with the waterfront unions. The ILWU was composed of the toughest sons of bitches known to man, but Page still managed to beat them down. Even though Stafford had made no outward sign of wanting to fight the Guild, his hiring of Page said it all.

Page had an office not three buildings down from the Guild and Hammer knew him well. They sometimes had a drink together to celebrate settlements in their own fights and occasionally Hammer dropped by Page's office for a drink there. Page had whips on his wall which he claimed were antique symbols of both history's cruelty and ingenuity. "The whip," he once told Hammer, "is what brought us civilization." Hammer thought instead that it was an element of the man's personality because the whip made pain last longer and left evidence of its brutality.

"We've never had to fight Page," Hammer told the Herald staffers, "but we know how he's manhandled Harry Bridges, and no one does that without being good. Better than good. The cocksucker is Attila the Hun."

"I don't believe Attila ever used whips." The voice belonged to their theater critic Harold Palmer, a tall, lean man with an affected English accent. He was from Jersey, not London, but decided that the accent authenticated his ranking in the theater. "Attila lived in the fifth century. The whip was invented much later." The brief lecture was delivered without smiling, as though there were an urgency for straightening the record before proceeding.

"No shit, Palmer," someone said, and roaring laughter followed.

Palmer stood tall and aloof from it, not responding to the mockery. He as much as expected that from the lumpen proletariat who, ignorant of just about everything, wanted to hear nothing that was either wise or learned.

"Come to think of it," a police reporter named Chick Turner said, sniffing, "I believe that's Palmer in the air!"

The meeting went on for another two hours, with a final vote to endorse the Guild and to give the coordinating committee authority to call a strike if a pay-scale settlement couldn't be reached. Issues were debated in both humor and anger, with threats following laughter, and laughter after threats. At the end, they adjourned to the Three-Oh and worked themselves into a fighting mood. The fashion editor, a hard-drinking Texan named Liz Curry, made a sign that said FUCK YOU and paraded up and down in front of the Herald Building until warned by a cop to go back to the bar or to jail. She chose the bar.

Hammer took off as soon as the happy cocksuckers, as he called them, voted informally to endorse the Guild, swearing they'd vote to unionize in the coming NLRB election that their petitions had authorized. Then they raised glasses in somber witness.

Colfax sat next to Sally, who was looking uncharacteristically somber.

"You okay?" he asked.

She shrugged, lit a cigarette, coughed at the first inhale, and then almost instantly squished it out.

The place was filled, a situation that elated Danny Doe. The waitress Patty was running herself ragged serving drinks and Doe had put another bartender on to handle the extra business. He hadn't seen a turnout like this since the Giants won the World Series. The level of noise was even louder than it had been back then. Doe turned the music up, creating a plateau of cacophony intended to prolong the party. Party meant money and the cash register was jingling.

"I've got to get tests," Sally said. "This damned cough . . ."

"They've got tests for everything now," Colfax said, trying to be light. "They can take care of things." A sense of foreboding stirred.

"Yeah," Sally said. Silence. "I miss Gwen."

"I miss her too," Colfax said.

"You talk to her at all?"

"I was planning on maybe dropping by tonight."

"That son of a bitch," Sally said, referring to Stafford.

Then she began coughing again and Colfax, peering at her through the noise and the dim lights of the Three-Oh, looked for the subtle signs of her mortality.

CHAPTER
TEN

The firebombing of the *Daily Californian* occurred sometime after midnight on a Sunday two weeks after the Strickland story appeared. The old wooden building exploded into flames and was a roaring inferno by the time the first fire truck pulled up. The sky was lit with glowing splashes of intermingling colors intensified by the night's blackness, hypnotizing a crowd awakened by the roar and the sirens. No one was on the campus when a Molotov cocktail was tossed through a window into the editorial section of the university's tabloid-sized newspaper. A crude, handwritten note was found condemning its leftist policies. It was unsigned.

Colfax beat Minelli to the scene by fifteen minutes. Rosebud Kane had stayed home, leaving the chaos of revolution to him. He and Minelli spotted each other through faint tendrils of smoke still rising from the building but never spoke. When Colfax started to approach him, Minelli made a gesture of disgust and walked away shaking his head. They had known each other for more than three years now and a tie existed between them, however Colfax tried to avoid it. This wasn't unique. Relationships form under dire circumstances. It was said that Sally Bell had fallen in love with a convict whose days on San Quentin's death row she had covered for eight years. When he was finally executed, she had refused to cover it and had not reported for work for two weeks.

Bruno Hagen arrived late in the morning. He wandered through the ashes of the burned-out building, hands deep in his pockets, looking. He touched nothing but seemed to see everything. An arson specialist from the Berkeley Police Department followed in silence like a well-trained dog, not stopping to piss or sniff.

When he had finished, Hagen inspected the note, which had been saved in a plastic bag to preserve possible fingerprints, asked where it had been found, nodded silently, and then joined Colfax.

"Does it strike you as odd," he said as they walked toward the student cafeteria, "that whoever bombed that place would leave a note?"

Colfax shrugged. "They did it in the first place to get attention."

Hagen said nothing while they walked, he with a slow, almost shuffling gait, Colfax with his slight limp. They made an odd couple, moving across a wide expanse of lawn, past students hurrying to class and the bearded and beaded hangers-on lounging against trees. Hagen glanced at the hangers-on registering their faces in his memory, but said nothing of their presence.

Colfax waited for him to elaborate on his thought, but when Hagen remained silent for several minutes it annoyed him. "What're you getting at?"

"Well, I can see militants wanting credit for what they've done," Hagen finally said. "That goes with the territory. But you don't usually get a note from the right-wing nuts. They just do it, that's all. Boom."

"You're saying they're being set up?"

"I'm just wondering why they'd do that."

Hagen stopped suddenly to solidify his thinking and then, as he began walking again, veered off.

Colfax called after him, "I thought we were going for coffee."

"I've got to talk to your friend Strickland. No time for coffee." He spoke without looking back.

"Can I get a shot at him?"

"Call me."

Colfax stood for a moment and watched as Hagen crossed the lawn and then vanished in the crowd of students coming through Sather Gate. He sure as hell didn't look like any FBI agent Colfax had ever seen. A rumpled appearance cast him more in the role of someone's demented uncle who had wandered out of the house and was meandering aimlessly through the city streets, smelling of tobacco and urine. Someone would find him and take him home or lock him up for the night in a psycho ward for his own safety.

The thought amused Colfax. He was still thinking about it when one of the men leaning against a tree pushed himself up and approached him. He was tall and gaunt with more hair than Colfax had ever seen on anyone. There was a deep and searing hostility in his eyes. Colfax braced himself as the man faced him.

"You're the reporter Colfax."

"That's right."

He seemed vaguely familiar to Colfax, a face from a crowd of revolutionaries he'd seen either here or in front of the *Herald.* Without a revolution, Colfax guessed, guys like him would end up on Skid Row or in a drunk tank somewhere. They weren't students, they weren't leaders, they weren't even committed to anything. They were men and sometimes women who drifted in and out of life, surviving by instinct, like half-starved dogs in a constant search for moral nourishment.

"And you were in Vietnam." His voice bore the turgid lisp of a junkie.

Colfax nodded, keeping a wary distance. "Get to the point."

"How could a guy who's been there love that fucking war?"

"Who said I loved it?"

"You *write* that way!"

"Bullshit," Colfax said, and began moving on.

The man grabbed at him with surprising strength, spinning Colfax backward on his bad leg. The leg crumpled and he fell to the ground, feeling awkward and embarrassed for the heartbeat that he sat on the dew-dampened lawn. Almost instantly he was on his feet again and the man who'd shoved him was lying on his back, not sure if he'd been slugged or pushed.

"Now fuck off," Colfax said, towering over him, looking down. He stood there for a moment, decided that the man's aggressive instincts had been damped, and then limped off past those who had stopped to stare. Someone shouted, "Asshole!" but he ignored it. Colfax felt suddenly and for the first time that he was in enemy territory and he wanted to get away. It would take very little, he knew, for the incident to gather a crowd, and the crowds on campus these days were meaner than cobras.

He was thinking about what Hagen had said as he drove down Telegraph and turned sharply to head around toward Minelli's place. Minelli would have a comment, no doubt about it. His walking away from the bombing with a wave of disgust had been stage-managing. There was a crowd. Minelli knew how to play to it. His level of activity had risen since his involvement in the FBI bombing had been revealed in the *Herald.* But without evidence to support Strickland's charge, there had been no arrest and Minelli was riding high as innocent victim of the pig press. The *Herald* had been mob-picketed a second time, this time in even greater numbers than the first, but no arrests were made. By now the world was watching the confrontation between Stafford's newspaper and the campus radicals, and the law enforcers were well aware of the scrutiny.

Minelli understood the importance of singling out an enemy as the focus of student rage. "You need a dog to kick," he'd told Colfax in one of those odd, edgy, off-the-record meetings that flesh out a reporter's background knowledge. "They want to hear the dog howl. They want to hear him yelping and see him running down the street, his tail between his legs."

"The old man won't yelp," Colfax had said, "and he won't run."

"Just watch."

For now, Stafford roared and shook his fist at the students whenever they appeared chanting and shouting in front of the *Herald,* a defiance greeted once by a thin plastic bag thrown from the crowd, breaking against his chest, and drenching him in a fluid that proved to be urine. For a moment, realizing what it was, it seemed he might charge into the crowd, but instead he stared in a rage deeper than midnight and turned without a word to march back into the tower.

As Colfax moved deeper into the cauldron that was the Berkeley student movement, he discovered a new force edging into the spotlight that until then Minelli alone had occupied. He was Maxwell Callahan, the tall, red-haired, bad-tempered son of an equally rowdy Berkeley city councilman who had once petitioned for the city to negotiate a separate peace with North Vietnam. It was a proposal that brought him international notoriety and the condemnation of the President himself, who accused the elder Callahan of undermining the nation's war effort. The councilman laughed and gave him the finger in a photograph printed on front pages across the nation.

Maxwell Callahan had come out of nowhere, riding the coattails of his father's name to an almost instant position of prominence among the campus radicals jockeying for leadership in the growing revolution. By now the antiwar movement had mushroomed to include the civil rights and feminist movements, adding sex and cultural muscle to what had become the spearhead of a national drive. Minelli found himself suddenly under fire by the new leaders for creating a cult of personality that made him more important than the revolutions and for emphasizing his personal vendetta against the *Herald*. It was said that many of Minelli's people were joining forces with Callahan, whose voice was rising over the clamor of the debate. Colfax had heard rumors that Minelli was planning a major event that would unequivocably establish him as a protest leader of national significance. Fearing the worst, most Bay Area Police departments were on standing alert. The Berkeley radicals were being watched carefully.

Colfax reached Minelli's place in twenty minutes. It was early morning and he had guessed correctly that Minelli would be home. As he approached his door, Colfax heard voices, one of them a woman's, and figured that Minelli probably had an overnight guest.

He hesitated at first, wondering if he should go somewhere and telephone Minelli that he was coming, but decided not to. This wasn't a question of manners but of pursuit. He was a reporter, Minelli was his quest. Push, push, push, Burns liked to say, and push he would. Colfax opened the door after a quick, perfunctory rap and very quickly wished he hadn't. Minelli was still tucked into his sleeping bag on the floor, the flap of the bag turned back to expose his bare chest. Next to him, her legs curled under her, wearing shorts and a halter that barely concealed her breasts, sat Ellen Stafford.

Rumors surfaced that Wallace Korchek was somehow involved with a growing number of incidents directed at the campus radicals and culminating in the fire at the *Daily Cal.* His reputation as a violent man had achieved mythic status, as had his politics. Twice his name had been mentioned as a possible Republican candidate for governor to tap into a growing fear that the Communists were at the door. The hard-ass Oakland chief waved off reporters' questions on the possibility. He hated the press almost as much as he hated the student rebels. He also understood the value of silence as much as he understood the inflating process of notice. He was not displeased at rumors that said he was in direct control of a secret army composed of Bay Area policemen who had, among other activities, burned down the student newspaper office. This was good stuff, a call to rally around him when Armageddon came. But he worried that Jeremy Stafford, hearing the rumors, would bolt and run. That he didn't want. His was the only newspaper that Korchek could count on. He needed Jeremy Stafford.

In the distance Korchek could see Stafford's black limo winding up the hill toward him. They had agreed to meet at a place where they could be alone and Korchek had suggested a ridge above Wildcat Canyon that looked out across the vast rural expanses of Contra Costa County, all green and hilly and just now becoming a bedroom community for the sprawling Eastbay. Stafford had also heard the rumors and was clearly worried. His voice lacked the bombast that had often come through during their previous conversations. He had asked for this meeting away from prying eyes.

Stafford stepped slowly from the limo, looking like a man who hadn't slept in a week. Korchek thought he could detect the smell of liquor on the publisher's breath and wondered if he was coming unraveled. If so, dealing with him under such uncertain circumstances could be risky.

"You've had problems," Korchek said as the two men walked a few feet from their cars out of earshot of their drivers.

"It's a mess," Stafford said, uncharacteristically candid. "There is no honor anymore, Chief, no gentlemanly agreements, no handshakes that characterized our fathers' time." He shook his head in dismay, looking into a warm wind that was blowing up off the Moraga Plateau.

Korchek wasn't quite sure what Stafford was referring to but assumed it was the talk generally of a man under siege, as the publisher certainly was.

"All the more reason to stand together," the chief said, waiting.

Stafford was silent for long moments, staring off to the distance as though he were locked into it. Korchek cocked his head so he could see the publisher's face, uncertain whether the man had even heard him. Almost immediately, Stafford turned to face him.

"I want your assurance, Chief, despite certain rumors I have heard, that you are not involved in violence against the students. I value your friendship, but I will not be associated with violence."

In other circumstances, Korchek would have laughed in his face, but the *Herald* was a powerful ally in their struggle against international Communism and he had to play his hand carefully.

He spoke slowly and deliberately: "I have been a policeman most of my adult life, Jeremy, sworn to uphold the law even when I don't agree with it, and I will never break that vow for any reason. You have my word."

The publisher seemed relieved. Had he listened carefully to the chief's words he would have been aware that Korchek had avoided any mention of violence, for the chief felt that any response to revolution was protection, not violence, and upholding the law meant upholding the Constitution in the face of those who would destroy it. Barry Goldwater had said it for them all: Extremism in defense of liberty was no vice. And this was, without doubt, a defense of liberty.

"Then we are united in our cause," Stafford said, extending his hand. Korchek clasped it firmly and for a moment thought he saw tears of gratitude forming in Stafford's eyes, as though he and he alone were all that the publisher had left in a growing clamor for his hide. The notion made the chief uncomfortable and he loosened his hand from Stafford's emotional grip.

"I have something for you, Jeremy."

They walked back to the Korchek's car. The chief reached in and brought out a small leather walletlike holder and handed it to Stafford. The publisher opened it. Inside was a departmental badge similar to the one the chief himself carried, gleaming silver edged in fourteen-carat gold.

"The City Council has authorized me to honor those who have honored our society by giving them one of these badges," the chief said. "Yours is the first, Jeremy."

Now there was no doubt that Stafford's eyes were tear-filled. He shook his head in gratitude, unable to speak, and finally responded by clutching the chief's hand again with both of his own. His lips formed the words *Thank you,* but no sound emerged, so filled was he with the moment. Then, without any further attempt at speaking, he turned and hurried to his limo, which almost instantly began its descent down the winding road that led to civilization.

Korchek watched it go as he had watched it arrive, uncertain just how Stafford would fit into the scheme of things, unmoved by the publisher's emotional response to their meeting. He would use Stafford as he must and discard him if he had to and meanwhile do whatever had to be done. He climbed back into the unmarked police car. A young plainclothes officer at the wheel turned as Korchek slid into the backseat. He was in his mid-twenties with a face as smooth and fair as young boy's and eyes that were a deep and secret blue.

"Shall we return to the office, chief?"

Korchek observed him carefully, then smiled and reached out to gently massage the nape of the man's neck in an almost loving fashion. "Let's stop by the house first, Jason. I have some . . . business to take care of."

The man touched the chief's hand and returned the smile with a sweetness that showed he understood exactly what that business might be.

Colfax's intent by barging in the door was essentially to embarrass Minelli, whom he figured would be atop one of his witless groupies, but seeing Ellen severely altered the situation. It was he who found himself uncomfortably out of place, staring like a guilty child at the woman, who stared back, stunned by the abruptness of his entry. Minelli was also surprised but recovered quickly and seemed to instantly revel in the awkward position Colfax found himself in.

"Come right in," Minelli said, unable to conceal the satisfaction in his voice. "You of course know Ellen. . . ."

Had he followed his instincts, Colfax would have spun on his heels and removed himself immediately from the room. He would not have said a word to anyone about what he had seen and would have gone about his work as though nothing had occurred. It would not have changed anything about his standing at the *Herald*, which was already in peril anyhow. What Ellen did was none of his business. Colfax could understand Minelli's lure. He had seen women drawn to the man almost hypnotically, sucking up the power he radiated like an airborne aphrodisiac. They were supplicants worshiping a strong, sometimes ruthless leader who could also charm the pants off a nun if he was so inclined. Ellen, Colfax decided in the micromoment that he stared at her, was simply another nun.

"I should have knocked," Colfax said when he found his voice.

"Probably," Minelli said, rising from the sleeping bag. He was completely naked and bore himself as though the situation were nothing new to Ellen, slipping into old Levi's, a T-shirt, and sneakers in a manner that was both deliberate and achingly casual.

Ellen glanced at his nudity and then quickly looked away, leaving Colfax to wonder whether her gesture was due to familiarity with Minelli's body or embarrassment at Minelli's nudity.

"I'd better leave," Ellen said, without trying to explain.

For a moment, Colfax felt an overpowering need to charge forward and do physical damage to them both, but for what reason? Ellen was not his to claim and Minelli's morality not his to fashion. And yet, Colfax felt the rush of unreasonable jealousy pulse through him as he saw them together. He struggled to subdue it and in the end simply held his ground and said nothing.

Ellen moved quickly, her breasts brushing his arm, and she squeezed by him through the doorway. Colfax made no move to step aside but now locked his gaze on Minelli, who, in turn, studied the reporter.

"Surprise, surprise," Minelli finally said. "It's funny how close neighbors can get." There was mockery to his tone, but without Ellen in the room Colfax was unmoved by it.

"Cut the shit," he said. "I'm here to ask a few questions, then I'm gone."

"Ask away."

Before Colfax could begin, Minelli informed him that a libel suit was being filed almost at that very moment that named Stafford, the *Herald,* Colfax, and several John Does. It was based on Strickland's accusations that Minelli had masterminded the FBI bombing, contained in the story Colfax had written and Stafford had forced into the paper.

"I hated naming my old pal," Minelli said sourly, "but you know how lawyers are." He smiled. "It's such a lousy world."

"I don't give a shit what you do. I'm a reporter, not a priest or, thank God, a lawyer. We'll meet in court when the time comes. Meanwhile . . ."

Colfax questioned Minelli closely on his knowledge of the firebombing and asked directly whether he had anything to do with it. This was what he did best, asking the questions others skirted, hardened by four years in big-city journalism, able to brush aside personal feelings for the sake of getting answers. He knew that Burns would want the answers. That was motivation enough.

"Why in the hell would I bomb a newspaper that backs us all the way?" Minelli demanded. "If the fucking *Herald* is ever blown up, okay, sure, come around, I did it, you bet."

Colfax relayed the suspicions of Bruno Hagen, and Minelli responded with a fuck-you gesture directed toward the FBI. He had nothing to do with the firebombing. Period.

"Print whatever shit you want," he said sourly, "we'll sue again. The movement can use the money. Now, if you'll excuse me, I've got phone calls to make. . . ."

Ellen's presence had escalated their relationship to a new and bitter level. The revolution Minelli led was one of self-glorification and Colfax could understand why opposition to his leadership was gaining strength.

His final question to Minelli was intended to loosen information on a rumored move that would ultimately establish him as a kind of king of protest, but Minelli gave nothing away and at the end angrily asked Colfax to leave.

"Why should I tell you shit?" he demanded. "You spend your days sucking up to a fascist pig and then expect me to embrace you as a brother-in-arms? I thought you were beginning to learn something about who we were and what this whole fucking thing was about. This is a no-shit revolution that will establish a new order of doing things, but you don't get it, do you? If you did, you'd walk away from that prick-shaped tower and never go back. Trust me, it's over for all of you. We'll be your judges someday even as you have been ours." He laughed suddenly. "I say all that and all that's going through your head is whether or not I fucked Ellen Stafford. Is she the fantasy cunt in your life?"

The question followed Colfax out the door and into the bright sunlight. He winced against the glare as he walked up the few steps to the street. Minelli had accomplished what he had probably set out to do when Colfax unexpectedly barged in, which was to create turmoil in his head. And yet, there was serenity too as there almost always is when a certainty establishes itself in one's mind. He had defined at last what Minelli was and had with equal clarity relieved himself of any thoughts he might have had about Ellen. His fantasy cunt? Not a bad way to put it, Colfax thought, limping down the street toward his car. She had been a kind of fantasy, he guessed, though it wasn't her vagina he'd been thinking about. It was her in a gentler, more romantic way. Only his dedication to career had kept him from pursuing the fantasy. Well, so much for that. It was all bullshit anyhow. He'd never intended this to happen in the first place, to become involved in anyone's life, especially a publisher's daughter. He had always seen himself as the distant reporter, the one who observed and then fashioned those observations into words the world would notice. This was too close, too suffocating, too—

Colfax heard his name being called and looked across the street. Ellen was gesturing for him to come over. He ignored her and continued on toward his car. She called again in a more determined way, but still he continued ahead, not looking toward her. Then, after a brief silence, he heard her footsteps behind him and knew he couldn't escape the inevitable confrontation. He slowed and waited for her to reach him.

"I want to explain," she said.

Colfax looked at her in a way he never had before, with the scrutiny of meeting someone for the first time.

"You owe me nothing," he said flatly, without anger or hostility.

"I know that," she said. There was the blood of patricians in her veins. She would not be cowed by him. "But I'm going to explain anyhow. Would you come back to my place for coffee?"

"I've had coffee," Colfax said.

She nodded. "All right, we can talk here. I went to see Minelli because I have been asked to write a term paper on something entitled

'The Campus Revolutions in America' for a history class in contemporary social movements. The professor is a dedicated liberal who takes delight in embarrassing me, my father, and our newspaper. He knows what's going on between Minelli and the *Herald* and asked specifically for me to build my paper around Minelli. Today was my first interview. It was no more than that."

Colfax felt he ought to care, but he didn't. There was no trust in him anymore. He was alone in the city. He always had been, but Ellen seemed at least someone he could talk to and if there were fleeting thoughts of romance or a sexual liaison they had dissipated. He was free now of even the most remote attachments, free of the left, free of the right, free of the middle. It was as he had been in combat, a single unit, an individual, a one, surrounded by chaos but never abandoning his oneness.

"Aren't you even going to say anything?" Ellen asked.

"There's nothing to say."

She nodded. "Okay, then I guess I'll see you later." Her voice had lost its resonance and was that of a small girl.

"Right," he said, "later," and continued toward his car.

"By the way," Ellen said after him, "have you been listening to the radio?"

"No. Why?"

"You've been awarded a Pulitzer Prize for local reporting. Congratulations."

She ran back to her apartment, leaving Colfax to stare after her and to absorb as best he could the news she had brought. It was April 1969. In four years he had gone from cub to . . . to what? Colfax wasn't sure. He should have been elated. He should have danced down the street. He should have been singing. But for reasons he couldn't understand, Colfax felt strangely subdued. He almost felt guilty.

The party began as soon as he reached the office. Bottles of champagne were being passed around, along with the girls from classified who had come up to join the celebration. Their appearance in numbers was generally limited to Christmas, when they visited each of the *Herald*'s departments to sing the worst carols Colfax had ever heard. Editorial was their last stop, where hard liquor was always available in quantity on Christmas Eve, and the classified girls were always willing to join in on the drinking and whatever followed. To the best of anyone's knowledge no one had ever been raped, but as Corona McGee pointed out, rape had never been necessary.

Colfax edged into the party still stunned by news of the Pulitzer and was instantly leaped upon by the copygirl Jill, who kissed him full on the lips, both legs wrapped around his waist. Colfax had to fight free of her to breathe and to accept the congratulations of others who were surrounding him. The specialists had come out of the back offices to shake his hand, and all seemed genuinely pleased that his coverage of the revolution had won him journalism's highest honor. Paul Lowin glanced up but never left his desk, burrowing deep into the clacking of his Remington, its muted staccato lost in the greater noise of the room.

"Are you sure?" Colfax asked Burns, who responded with a slight smile and a nod. "I can't believe it." Jill was still clinging to his arm, a glass of champagne in her free hand that someone seemed to always fill. "I didn't even know I'd been nominated."

He felt childlike and ill at ease, like a sixth-grader who'd just won an essay contest. It was happening too fast. Only Corona McGee seemed to understand his discomfort, watching him from across the noisy city room, gesturing, palms down, for him to relax, to stay cool.

"Now you know," Burns said. "Glory in the reward of good work." He began walking away, then turned. "By the way, Stafford asked to see you when you got in." He pointed to Jill. "Without her wrapped around you."

The publisher was at his desk facing the window and turned in the swivel chair when Colfax entered. For a moment he simply studied the reporter and then finally said, "Congratulations," without conviction, at the same time gesturing for Colfax to sit.

The office seemed unusually quiet to Colfax, as though a new stillness had descended over it, enclosing the place in an almost funereal suffocation. Stafford was a part of the stillness, his muted voice an integral slice of the quiet, dropped to an octave that was barely audible. Colfax had to lean forward to hear.

"What are your plans?" Stafford asked.

The question surprised Colfax. "My plans?" He shrugged. "To continue doing what I'm doing."

"There will undoubtedly be other offers."

Colfax didn't know what to say. He guessed there would be, but he felt committed to the *Herald* the way he'd felt committed to his dying platoon in the fire of combat. You just don't run away from an outfit in peril.

"I have no interest in other offers," he said.

"You might want to consider them," the publisher said.

Now Colfax was confused. Was he being fired on the day he'd won a Pulitzer?

"I don't understand, Mr. Stafford. Are you telling me my days here are numbered?"

"This newspaper has never had a need for unions," Stafford said, finding some of the lion's roar in his voice. "And there is no need for one now."

So that's what this was all about.

"That's not up to me to say," Colfax replied evenly. He wanted to get the hell out of there. Too much was happening: the prize, the party, Ellen . . . His composure was a thin façade over the turmoil in his head. "The staff will vote," he finally said.

"You brought this on!"

"I was asked to look into the possibility and I did."

The lion's head over the desk looked down in open hostility, an attitude that was a part of the stillness. Stafford said nothing for what seemed an eternity. There was silence in the room. Not even a clock ticked, and the double-paned window that looked out on Mission Street shielded the office from any traffic noise.

Finally Colfax said, "Is that all?"

"I never thought you would betray me." Stafford's voice was almost a whisper. Having said that, he turned once more toward the window.

Colfax found himself overwhelmed with pity. A man he had once viewed as awesome had become suddenly pathetic. Stafford had misjudged him as a soldier come back from the war ready to fight in a new one against a vague army of enemies, but that was simply not Colfax's nature. Duty was his nature as the moment defined that duty, committing him at the *Herald* to report the news in terms that were both fair and compelling. He could do nothing less.

"You just had me figured wrong, sir," he said, leaving the publisher to ponder his meaning.

The first face he saw as he reentered the city room was Gwen Ballard's. She hurried to him and hugged him gently. "They let me back in the building long enough to say I'm desperately happy for you. So are a lot of admirers at the *News*. You have fans."

"I was going to come by—"

"No, don't. It's okay. I think I'm going to like it over there. New challenges intrigue me." She winked and rubbed against him in the parody of herself she had perfected so well. Colfax laughed and held her in his arms, burying himself in her softness and in the faint essence of her perfume. He liked her. That wasn't to say he lusted after her again, only that there was a quality to her he had failed to notice before. She had grown in the moment of her firing and radiated a warmth that came from deep inside.

"I owe you," Colfax said, not quite knowing what he meant.

Ballard shrugged and smiled. "Let's have a drink," she said.

Three television stations shot footage of Colfax. Telephone calls came from across the country, as much from those interested in the burgeoning violence of the student antiwar movement as in the Vietnam veteran who'd been covering it. Prizes create experts quicker than either knowledge or experience, Colfax discovered. He tried to explain that to a reporter from AP, but it didn't seem to matter, so he assumed the mantle and wore it uneasily.

As the party was about to move to the Three-Oh, Burns took Colfax aside. The city editor had drunk very little and had advised half the rewrite staff to follow his lead. Pulitzer or no, there was still a newspaper to put out and someone had to stick around to do it. They could join the party later. Then he motioned Colfax to follow him, leading the way into an empty back office where he kept a bottle. He poured a drink for each of them, made a toasting gesture, and emptied his glass. Colfax did the same, subduing a wince. The liquor burned.

"What did Stafford say?" Burns finally asked.

"I'm not sure," Colfax said. "I think he wants me to leave."

"He doesn't know what he wants," Burns said with surprising candor. "His old man made this newspaper. He gave it pride and honor, and now his son is seeing the whole thing unravel. He can't deal with it. Did you know he had a breakdown once?"

Colfax shook his head no, feeling slightly out of focus. This was heady stuff, the prize and then the invitation to Burns's inner sanctum.

"It was just after his wife died."

"She killed herself," Colfax said, displaying his inside knowledge.

"It was messy. He's never gotten over that and every once in a while he comes undone. Ride with it for a while." He paused. "We don't want you to leave."

Colfax nodded in an exaggerated manner. Liquor did that to him, expanding every move he made. He wondered vaguely if he'd live through the day.

"I don't think I'm going anyplace," he said, "except across the street."

"Then," the city editor said, "go!"

Gwen Ballard took one arm and Jill the other as Colfax passed through the city room headed to the place of their party, not knowing that Jeremy Lincoln Stafford III was looking down on them from his third-floor window as they crossed Mission. Feelings of rage and betrayal burned in his chest.

The party lasted until well after two A.M. Danny Doe turned off the lights, but no one seemed to care. They drank in the dark. Gwen had gone home early, leaving Colfax to be fondled by Jill, who finally ended up in his bed, the moans of their mutual delight adding to the drunken ecstasy that surrounded them.

The next day, two more staff members were fired, the librarian in the newspaper's morgue and a police reporter with five children. They were given no notice and no severance. Wrapped in gloom and fear, the editorial staff of the *Herald* voted overwhelmingly to join the Newspaper Guild.

CHAPTER
ELEVEN

S ally Bell had not been a part of the celebration and, unlike most
of the others, was able to rise early and be at the doctor's office
at nine. The tests had all been taken and she waited patiently in the
lobby of his office for him to call her in with the results. At exactly 9:22
on a morning dark with a gathering storm, the receptionist put down
the intercom phone and said, "Doctor will see you now," in a manner so prissy and self-righteous it made Sally cringe in spite of her
growing fear.

She had secretly known what horror had inhabited her lungs, but
a portion of her head held out determinedly for pneumonia or tuber-
culosis or even some kind of mysterious fungus brought back from
Vietnam by a cousin she'd slept with one drunken night to ease his
ache for a woman. Realizing in the morning what he'd done, he immediately left her apartment, too ashamed to even say good-bye, and
had never contacted her again. Sally watched from her bed as he
hurried out the door, wondering if he even knew what she had done
for him.

The doctor, a cancer specialist, was a large, bearlike man with a
fatherly attitude. His name was Bob Montana, which seemed to fit
both his girth and his manner. Sally had liked him from the beginning
and never ceased liking him as he discussed possibilities with her and

took her through the X rays and tests that would determine her malady. It had all taken the longest two weeks of her life and had now come down to this strange, surreal moment, this gap in time in which she and she alone existed. As Sally entered his office, she immediately noticed two X rays placed against a lit panel on a wall. Seeing them and seeing him, his expression uncharacteristically glum, told her what she had to know.

He put one arm around her shoulder, feeling the tremble of her body, and directed her attention to the X rays. Everything inside of her was sinking, drifting downward into depths she had never before known. She heard Montana's voice as though he were speaking from a great distance. He pointed out shadows on the film and told her what she had suspected, what both her mind and her body had whispered, that she had cancer of both lungs. The shadows were like clouds on the backlit pictures of her lungs, at once innocent and ominous, light enough to seem innocuous but dark enough to take her life. He did not say she would die, only that there was nothing they could do.

"What about an operation?" she asked, barely able to articulate the words.

He simply shook his head no and then asked if there was anyone he could call for her.

"How long do I have?" she asked, ignoring the question. There was no one either of them could call because Sally had no one.

"It's the worst kind of cancer, Sally. It spreads quickly."

"Days? Weeks? Months?"

"Three months at most. At some point it would be best to enter a hospital. They can make you comfortable. I can arrange that when you're ready."

"When I'm ready?" She was on the verge of tears. Her whole body shook. "How will I know when I'm ready? When the pain is too much for me to take? When I can't walk or breathe or rise from my bed? When is ready?"

She didn't want to hear the answer but instead left his office quickly and found herself on Market Street, forging blindly ahead, filled with pain and wonder, unaware of the rain beginning to fall or the people rushing by her caught by the sudden downpour, covering their heads with folded newspapers to avoid being drenched, cursing this brief, wet affirmation of life. She pushed into the crowds and then through them, robotic in her motions, all of her senses turned inward to the being that was ceasing to be even as she plunged toward the distance.

A police reporter for years, she had seen death up close many times and once, as a child lay dying in the street after being hit by a car, she had leaned in close and whispered, "It will be better." A patrolman heard her and asked what she'd meant. Sally had shrugged. She didn't know what she'd meant. They were words to simply comfort . . . or were they? As she walked through the heart of the city going nowhere, she wondered now if it would be better where she was going or whether there would be a nothingness beyond comprehension, a sudden ceasing to be that no one could adequately explain.

In her apartment, a jumble of books and newspapers and notebooks and old photographs, Sally slumped on a couch, more alone than she had ever been, and knew she had to deal with her dying. She had to tell someone. She had to make plans. And she had to speak to a person who would be able to discuss with her if where she was going would really be better. . . .

The third power failure in a year darkened the *Herald*'s city room at four in the afternoon. The lights went out, the police scanners went dead, the Linotype machines fell silent. Stafford charged from his office like a rogue bull, strode through the city room and down the back stairs, ominously silent.

"There'll be the remains of dead electricians found in the morning," Corona McGee said, wincing as he slammed the door. She had made her way down a dim hallway from her office to the city room.

"I thought they fixed the damned thing," Colfax said. An unfinished story sat in his Remington.

"They've fixed it a hundred times," Trager said. "Nothing is working right anymore. We're rotting away."

"You may be rotting away," Barry Adams said, "but I'm not. I'm going to get the hell out of here first chance I get. Fuck this place."

There was an eerie tone to the half-light, a flatness that seeped in through the dusty windows, flooding the room in the kind of glow that illuminates dreams.

"Trager's right," Corona said. "The presses are old, the Linotypes are old, the whole goddamn building is old. Why doesn't it surprise me that the electrical system is old too?"

"How did it get this way?" Colfax asked. "What happened?"

No one addressed the question. Instead, they stood in silence until the power returned with a mixture of hums, clicks, and voices. The memory of the dimness remained. There was a strong feeling of hopelessness in the air.

Max Callahan was sometimes known to affect a slow Southern drawl, though the likelihood was he had never been in the South. He did it, his antagonists felt, to prolong the agony of his diatribes, to stretch his messages to maddening lengths, thereby confusing his enemies and weakening their resolve. He made it clear that he was not to be interrupted, not by threat or facial expression, but by simply continuing to talk over whoever else was speaking, as though his challenger were not speaking at all. Oddly, the slow, drawling speeches often suddenly exploded into raging temper tantrums, the roar of an idling race-car engine suddenly come to life, the real Callahan leaping through the mask.

Minelli knew this and played his cards carefully in a meeting with Callahan on his father's boat, a thirty-two footer docked at the Berkeley Marina. The boat was named *Spider,* a nickname given the elder Callahan when he played basketball at U.C. They met at night to avoid detection, gathering in the cramped hold of the boat, Minelli on his own and Callahan accompanied by two of his lieutenants, a hostile nonstudent named Roscoe, known for his violent confrontations with police, and a woman, Leary, who had renamed herself after acid king Timothy Leary, with whom she was said to have enjoyed a sexual liaison.

The boat was rocking gently in the incoming tide, causing a queasy feeling in Minelli's stomach. Adding to that was the feeling he had been "summoned" by Callahan, and, thinking about it later, he cursed himself for accepting the meeting in the first place. Walking out now, however, was unthinkable. Word would spread quickly that Minelli was unwilling to unite the antiwar effort, which was the stated purpose of what Callahan called a one-front war against war.

"The truth is," Callahan was saying, tapping a pencil on a table as he spoke, fixing the slow rhythms of his speech, "we've got to do something to reignite ourselves and I'm suggesting that there is strength in union. While your efforts have been noble, Vito, the results are diminishing—"

"How in God's name can you—"

"—and we ought to unite under one leader to reestablish the might of our commitment. The whole world is looking toward us, Vito, to lead the way and we're not doing that in any—"

"What the world is seeing, Callahan, is—"

"—degree that is getting us any closer to shaking things up in Washington. I'm not talking about killing anybody. Doing in FBI agents just isn't the way to go. I'm not saying that was your idea, but whoever's it was has turned us into violent people and that's not what we're supposed to be."

By the time he had finished, Minelli's temper had approached critical mass and was on the verge of exploding, but he knew instinctively that a whisper often gained more attention than a roar and kept his voice so low the others had to lean forward to hear.

"The People's Army has always been open to anyone who wants to join," he said carefully. "To say our results are 'diminishing' is just plain bullshit, Max. There were twelve thousand of us at the *Herald* a week ago."

"There were fifty thousand on the streets of Georgetown a week ago," Callahan drawled. "That's something we've got to discuss," he continued, talking over an effort by Minelli to retake the floor. "We're not at war with the *Herald*. It's a convenient target, sure, but to gather all of our efforts to put Stafford out of business ought not to be our goal, Vito."

Minelli didn't like the way Callahan said Vito, as though he were mocking the name by letting it linger a beat too long on his tongue. *Vitoah*. He made no response at first to Callahan's comment. The sound in the room was the slapping of waves against the *Spider*'s hull, emphasizing the stillness in the hold. Minelli let the silence build, utilizing it the way a comic buys time by twirling a cigar in his fingers or drawing on it slowly before delivering a line.

Finally he said, "Let's cut the bullshit, Callahan. Mine is an established movement and you want a piece of the action."

"Yours is a dying movement, Vito, and to save it we want to merge our efforts."

"With you as the new leader."

"I think it will take that," Callahan said slowly. "The prominence of your position is not, of course, lost on us and you will occupy an important place in the new army. That's what we'll call it, by the way. The New Army of the People."

"Fuck you, Max."

Minelli rose, glaring at the three. Callahan nodded in acknowledgment of the refusal, then gestured to the man called Roscoe, who stood and left the cabin. For a moment, Minelli felt in danger.

"What's going on?" he demanded.

"I want to show you something," Callahan said. The casualness of his tone didn't indicate peril. Reading Minelli's trapped-rat expression, he added, "You're not a prisoner here, Vito. This is an effort to unite, not destroy." Roscoe returned and stood at the top of the stairs. Callahan smiled at his presence. His drawl intensified, his delivery slowed to a crawl. "And I feel that uniting might be something necessary to save not only your movement, Vito, but you."

Two men came slowly down the stairs and into the cramped hold.

Minelli recognized them instantly. Their names were Lawson and Steele, and they had helped build and set the bomb that had killed Leonard Rose.

Outside the boat, in a nondescript sedan at the far end of the dock, parked among other cars left by boaters who were out to sea, Bruno Hagen sat in darkness, resisting the strong urge to light a cigar. He held it in his mouth unlit and watched as Minelli left the boat. Hagen slumped down behind the wheel as low as his paunch would allow. From what he could see in the semidarkness, Minelli seemed shaken by whatever had transpired inside.

Hagen was tempted to follow him again, but instead instinct told him to wait and the instinct paid off. A man he recognized as Max Callahan finally emerged, followed by Roscoe, the woman Hagen knew as Timothy Leary's whore, and the two men from the car. When they drove off in one vehicle, Hagen followed. There was a tightness in his stomach. Something was brewing among the shit-makers and it figured to be no good for anyone.

Gwen Ballard was surprised when the *News* city editor asked her to handle what he called the War Games, meaning the antiwar movement in the Bay Area. She would directly confront Colfax on the beat and didn't like the idea, but felt she had no choice. Two weeks on the job wasn't long enough to start turning down assignments when you needed work. The *News* wasn't as "family" as the *Herald* had been in its better days. The city editor, Ross Frasier, was younger than Gerald Burns and probably, Gwen felt, less perceptive. He seemed more a parody of city editors than a real one, always in a kind of sweat, shirt collar open, tie askew, his voice booming across the city room, his stride a blur, compared to Burns's quieter and more measured ways. She missed the *Herald*'s wit and its madness, even its psychotic leadership, and would have traded her job here for her old one at half the pay.

Gwen had just finished setting up an interview with Oakland Police Chief Wallace Korchek and was half out of her chair when her phone rang. She had been after Korchek since her second day at the *News*, following the paper's exclusive that revealed existence of a Leonard Rose Brigade. At first reluctant, he had suddenly agreed to be interviewed that afternoon and Gwen's head was filled with him. For a moment she thought of not answering the phone, but finally couldn't resist it. Later, she would view her action with mixed feelings, glad in a way that she had picked up the receiver but regretting the news it brought. The call was from Sally Bell. She was dying.

The business of winning requires a certain attitude and Colfax wasn't sure he was up to it. A Pulitzer had not been on his agenda this soon. Henry Dustin had refused a prize for the *Edenville Messenger* when Colfax was working there. "Pulitzers," he'd said, "are not for the living. They're for headstones, the culmination of a life's work. We ain't dead yet." Colfax already felt a sense of isolation from others on the *Herald* and this would only deepen the divide. Burns had submitted his stories with Stafford's approval, a position the publisher no doubt regretted. Colfax had no idea that his work had been in contention; the rumor mill had not picked it up or, if it had, chose not to share it with him.

"The world is yours now," Burns had said to him in a tone of voice difficult for Colfax to isolate. Mockery? Elation? Sadness? Perhaps all three. Increasingly, the city editor had become a mystery to him, hiding behind the slight smile of noncommitment, doling himself out in pieces when there was work to be done but otherwise content to dwell behind an enigmatic shield. Only at home after several drinks did Burns allow himself to seep through. He was a creature of the telephone and would call any time of night to discuss a story or a rumor. Sometimes he'd call Colfax, the soft, slurring voice emerging from the shadows of insomnia.

"Don't mind Stafford," he said to him on one of those nights. "Things have happened to him. Sad things. Bad things. That happens to all of us, kid. You were hurt. You know."

You didn't interrupt Burns or ask questions. You listened. You tried to find the point that was his aim. You tried to find lights that illuminated who he was. This was no stick figure, no cardboard facade of a man.

"Be good to yourself," he said. "Forgive yourself." Then he hung up.

Colfax was thinking of him this Saturday night as he sat at his desk in the city room. The place was empty except for the Bat hunched over at the slot, a circular desk which in the daytime was occupied by a dozen copyreaders. Pressure from an institute for the blind had forced Stafford to rehire his night copy editor. With nothing to edit at the moment, the Bat read paperback novels printed in large type especially for the nearly blind, but even so his face was almost pressed up against the pages of the books. He said nothing when Colfax entered from the rear elevator, but that wasn't unusual. The Bat rarely spoke, as though near blindness had also robbed him of the power of speech. Somehow, however, he seemed always aware of who was in the city room, directing telephone calls as necessary or yelling in a strange, reedy voice at the writer whose copy he might be editing. To find an error was the Bat's only purpose in life and it was said that Burns sometimes let a grammatical mistake pass by so the Bat would have something to gloat over.

Colfax struggled in the night's silence as he worked on a story about Max Callahan, trying to place the newest campus radical in the context of what was happening on the street. Winning a Pulitzer was interfering with the flow of his writing and Colfax found himself too inclined toward "importance," a position that seemed to require more insight than observation. Three times now he had jerked copy paper from his typewriter and tossed it into a basket, cursing himself for allowing importance and *prose* to influence an easier style.

As Colfax started on his story the fourth time, determined to restore the flow, the Bat's voice crossed the city room. "For you!" He was holding a telephone high without looking up. "Line four." Colfax hooked his headset on, punched line four, and leaned back, ready to spend a few moments listening to Burns reveal a little of himself. He wasn't prepared for the woman's voice that said simply, "Hi."

For a moment Colfax said nothing, confused by the intrusion on his expectation. He waited, looking straight ahead toward the faint glow of the city that refracted on the dusty windows, listening to traffic noises three stories below.

"I wanted to congratulate you," the voice said, coming from someplace distant, someplace far away in his memory. He still said nothing. "Your father gave me your numbers." There was hesitancy, uncertainty. "I tried your place first. . . ."

The voice drifted off, waiting.

"Laura?"

Colfax said the one word, the name, as though he could hardly breathe. It was unlike him to suffocate so grandly on a name, to be hurled into total bewilderment by a voice.

"I . . . I wasn't sure I should call . . . or that you wanted to hear from me. . . ."

"I can't believe it's you."

Colfax forced himself back from the strange, cloudy area he had inhabited moments before. He sat up straighter.

"Is this a bad time?" she asked suddenly, on the verge of ending the conversation.

"No . . . no . . . I was just, you know, working on a story. It's not due."

"A Pulitzer! That's really something."

"Are you in the city?"

"No, I live in Santa Barbara now."

"How are you, Laura?"

It was an empty question. He wanted to say how much he had thought about her and how much he had missed her voice and her laugh. He wanted to know why she had drifted away from him, why she had left him with an unfulfilled dream thousands of miles away. He wanted to tell her of the terrible loneliness he felt when he came home from the war. But it was too late for all that now. It didn't matter anymore. Time had damped the fires of his passion. There were no embers left. Their conversation was flat, perfunctory.

". . . I'm doing okay. Going for a masters, working part-time . . ."

". . . I didn't even know I was nominated, much less that I'd won . . ."

Their awkwardness drifted into silence and then good-bye. What had been was over. They both knew that now. Colfax was suddenly overcome with a deep and powerful sense of freedom.

Stafford had felt strangely light-headed that morning, as though he were floating. He noticed it first as he reached for the telephone at his bedside to call Burns. It was a call he made every morning precisely at six for a rundown from his city editor on major events of that day. As his hand moved toward the phone it veered to the left. When he closed his hand, he closed it on air even though his eyes said it was closing on the telephone itself. It was an odd sensation, one that Stafford couldn't recall feeling before, but then nothing was the same now as it had been. He pulled back from the phone and fixed it into focus. That took effort, and it was while exerting the effort that he felt the floating effect. It wasn't unpleasant, just disorienting. If he closed his eyes it seemed to go away.

Burns would recall that the publisher's speech was slurred when they spoke that morning, though he seemed alert during the story rundown. The city editor knew his boss didn't drink and wondered if it could be something more serious. Staff members had mentioned "lapses" in Stafford's conversation, but nothing was ever said about it to the publisher. One did not intrude easily into the man's personal life. He had shielded it from anyone since his wife's death as though within the circle of his protection dwelt anything he ever held dear and he didn't want it violated.

Stafford rose uneasily from bed and sat for a moment at the edge. Nothing spun, nothing seemed out of the ordinary, so he brushed off the brief floating effect, dressed, ate hurriedly, and prepared for a visit from Vincent Benet, an adviser to the mayor and chief troubleshooter for the city. He pronounced his name *Ben-ay*. Stafford had met him before and took an almost immediate dislike to the slick, handsome man who spoke in an accent intended to be French. Stafford was certain his real name was Garcia or something and was Mexican, not French. *Ben-ay,* hell.

Benet rang the doorbell precisely at ten, appearing appropriately scrubbed, buttoned down, and effusive. Stafford let him in and poured them coffee, wondering what the man wanted. His phone call had sounded mysterious and important. Stafford would have turned down the meeting but was curious. What could the city possibly want of him?

Benet arrived at no point quickly, playing the oily diplomat until Stafford insisted that he was a busy man and Benet should get to the point quickly or leave with the point unmade. Thus pressed, the "mayor's pig," as he was known to the *Herald*'s reporters, leaned in toward where the publisher was sitting across from him.

"Mr. Stafford," he said, minimizing his accent, "we're concerned about what appears to be a serious, er, rift between the *Herald* and certain other citizens of San Francisco. The mayor has asked me to say that we're worried about the divisiveness inherent in the various confrontations that have occurred and especially about the violence that these confrontations increasingly involve. We're wondering if we could act as negotiators and arrange a meeting, or meetings, between you and this Mr. Minelli who seems to be the leader of the—"

"Let me understand you, Mr. Benet," Stafford interrupted, his tone heavy with growing anger. "You are asking the publisher of the *San Francisco Herald* to meet with a raggedy-ass Communist agitator who is bent on destroying the structure of our government? A treasonous, murderous gutternsipe who would like to see us all under Russian rule? That will never happen, Mr. Benet!"

Benet nodded. His expression, fixed in noncommittal repose, never seemed to change. Reporters theorized that it was composed of a special, pliable plastic and that behind it was the real Benet with a face not dissimilar to that of a pirate's with a slash across one cheek and perhaps one eye covered with a black patch.

"Let me say this, Mr. Stafford. Our interest is not simply a question of détente between two seriously antagonistic factions. We are not enamored of Vito Minelli. We are concerned about the future of a San Francisco tradition, which is to say the *Herald.*"

"The future of the *Herald* is my concern, Mr. Benet, not yours, not the mayor's, and not the whole goddamn board of supervisors!"

Stafford's voice rose and his face reddened as he addressed what he now considered an adversary. The veins on his neck bulged as though they might burst. His eyes burned with a terrible rage, glowing in the half-light of a gray morning that seeped into the ornate living room.

"Mr. Stafford, please," Benet was saying in his most unctuous manner, "we would never presume to intrude on the private business of an institution this city has admired for a hundred years! Nothing could be further from our minds!"

"Then state your case, goddamn it!"

"Simply put, Mr. Stafford, we don't want the *Herald* to cease operations. We know that circulation has dropped alarmingly, that advertising has diminished, and that you are in the process of cutting back. We want to offer our assistance before the problems become, shall we say, unsolvable."

Was he hearing this correctly? Was this pipsqueak of a man, this mayor's pig, telling him his newspaper was in jeopardy of failing? Was this a threat? Stafford grasped for an explanation, but a fuzziness had overcome the moment and all he could feel was the heat of his own fury coursing through his whole body. Benet would recount later how the publisher had stared at him in a strange and terrible way and had suddenly leaped from the couch where he sat and strode across the room toward him with an intent that seemed at best murderous.

"Mr. Stafford!"

Shouted into the room, Benet's voice had lost any trace of a French accent and was rough-edged and panicky. The urgency slammed into Stafford's head like a physical blow and he stopped halfway across the room, confused by the sound and by the purpose of his own movements. He felt again as if he were floating and heard himself say to his startled visitor, "Please leave, Mr. Benet," and then sat heavily on the chair nearest him.

Benet didn't wait to assess the situation but instead moved instantly out the door without another word.

Left alone, Stafford sat staring out the window at the fog that had risen up from the Golden Gate and was disappearing into the growing sunlight. He turned his head to make certain he could. He raised one arm. He touched his face and then his head. Something was happening to him, but he couldn't tell what. He wanted to call Ellen or Gerald Burns or his driver, but he couldn't muster the will to do so. And in that moment of total isolation, cut off from even his own reality, the publisher of one of the oldest newspaper in the West lowered his head and cried loudly.

Vito Minelli watched the release of Strickland with a sense of foreboding. The man was locked into pursuing his vision of redemption to who knew what end. It was because of that madness, that beatific stare toward the unknown, that Strickland was released without being charged with any crime. His father had seen to that. Position counted before the courts. But because he was a material witness, Strickland was ordered to stay in town. The FBI had questions. But psychiatrists wanted him first.

As Minelli watched the proceedings on television, he was taken by the silent hostility of the crowd that had gathered outside the Federal Building. Its members seemed frozen in a fixed expression of hatred, blurred into a solid front by the panning camera. They believed that what Strickland had said, and what Colfax had reported, was true, and their animosity was palpable beyond the screen. It wasn't Strickland they necessarily hated, Minelli knew. It was him. He, Vito Minelli, was the instigator of death, the killer of two decent people, the leader of wolves that tore at a living carcass. Never before had Minelli felt this much hatred directed at him. Rage, yes, but rage was satisfying, something he could control. Hatred, silent and pervasive, was different. And now FBI agents would be dogging his every move. For the first time in his life, Minelli felt uncomfortably enclosed and surrounded.

He watched Strickland's parents lead him like a child toward a waiting car and beyond the crowd he could see Colfax watching and taking notes. But most importantly, Minelli could see his own destiny etched in the single, overpowering emotion of the crowd.

In an upper room of the Herald Tower, Cliff Hammer and Christopher Page sat on opposite sides of a long table, waiting. Hammer puffed hard on a cigar and Page tapped impatiently with a pencil on the tabletop.

"The cocksucker isn't coming," Hammer finally said, blowing smoke toward the ceiling. It lingered for a moment in the small room, then disappeared in a puff from an unseen breeze.

"Give him time," Page said.

Page was a tight, balding man with an edgy manner and an iron commitment to the American profit motive. Unions were the enemy and he a general in the fight against them. Twenty years earlier he had martialed a scab army to fight the oil workers across the bay in a strike at the big Standard Oil refinery that left three men dead.

"I've waited long enough," Hammer said, shifting his weight on the chair in preparation for rising. The two men were direct opposites: Hammer loosely composed and slightly disheveled, Page scrubbed clean, flawlessly attired, and tightly controlled.

"I'll try him again," Page said. He dialed the phone on the table. It rang several times at Stafford's home without being answered.

"I don't understand it," Page said.

Hammer rose. "I understand it. The cocksucker is telling me that he's not interested in talking."

As he stood, Hammer's bulk seemed to fill the room. He hovered over the table, hands resting flatly upon it, fixing Page in a hard gaze.

"You tell the cocksucker for me," he said, "that the last offer is the final offer. I am going to recommend a strike on midnight Friday the twenty-second. No more of these bullshit just-us-three meetings. We tried it, Page, and it doesn't work. Negotiations have gone on longer than they should have. We've been patient, we've been fair. If Stafford wants to meet again, it will be with the whole unit and he'd better come with an offer on the table that's one hell of a lot better than what he's come up with so far."

"You know he won't meet with the whole unit."

Hammer stood and faced Page, staring directly and ominously into his eyes. The *Herald* negotiator was not intimidated. He had been here before back in the days when dockworkers made their points with grappling hooks and Teamsters cracked heads with tire irons.

"Midnight the twenty-second," Hammer said over his shoulder as he left the room.

Page nodded to no one in particular. Hammer's footsteps vanished into silence down the corridor outside the room. It wasn't a nod of acquiescence but of understanding. The *Herald* could ill afford a strike. Hammer was aware of that. He was kicking a sick dog and enjoying it. Page snapped his briefcase shut, turned out the lights of the room, and made sure the door was locked. As he headed toward the elevator he wondered what had become of Stafford and worried that the publisher, whose sanity he hadn't fully trusted since his wife's death, might have gone off the deep end.

After each bout of coughing, Sally Bell had difficulty catching her breath, sucking it in quickly as though it were the last she would ever take. An oxygen tank lay unused on the floor by her bed, a symbol of dependency that even now Sally could not abide. Gwen Ballard sat across from her in Sally's small Mission District apartment. Colfax sat on a box of books in a corner. It was as if she had never actually moved into the place, though she had occupied it for more than six years. It was a part of Sally's transitory nature not to totally settle or unpack but to leave doors open for movement; to allow escape exits.

"Can I do anything?"

Colfax asked the question as Sally gasped for air. He instantly regretted it. There was, of course, nothing he could do.

"You can clean my fucking lungs," Sally said, wiping the cough-induced tears from her eyes. "It's a funny thing. I didn't cough this much until he told me I was dying. What is it in us that curls up and dies when we're told we're supposed to?"

"Maybe you should convince yourself you're not dying," Gwen said.

"I'm not good at the power of positive thinking."

She stood, smothering down a cough as she did, and brought a bottle and three glasses from a cabinet, pouring whiskey for each of them, squinting from an angle to make certain they all had equal amounts.

"At least," she said, suppressing a dry laugh, "I can die drunk."

Colfax clicked glasses with the two women and drank deeply. The whiskey, a cheap brand Sally preferred, burned going down, but it was small pain compared to what he was feeling now for her. He couldn't help but view her as a dead person, wondering how she would look stretched out in a coffin, the fire gone from her eyes, the glowing energy blinked out.

Gwen had called him shortly after she'd heard from Sally, not wanting to face her alone. He in turn had informed Gerald Burns. Sally Bell was dying. Mortality hovered over the city room like a dark cloud. Chip Dawson instantly left a story half done and walked to the Three-Oh, where he drank quickly. Barry Adams doused his cigarette and swore he'd never smoke another. Burns greeted the news with an almost imperceptible nod, hiding whatever feeling might have been building in him.

It didn't seem possible. A world without Sally in it was simply not acceptable. Colfax realized on his way to Sally's apartment how much a part of his world she had become. She had mastered the techique of being both an observer and participant, shifting from distance to near-ness with the agility of a magician. Colfax felt close to Sally Bell, closer than he had ever dared admit until now.

He had come to Sally's apartment because Gwen wanted him to. Would he have come alone, sitting awkwardly across from a dying woman, a colleague, a friend, not knowing what to say, at a loss to offer anything that would ease her terror? He wasn't sure.

"What's out there?" Sally asked, filling their glasses again. "Darkness? Oblivion? Heaven?"

"A glory beyond belief," Gwen said.

It surprised Colfax. He wouldn't have suspected that Ballard would have that kind of faith and wondered if she was saying it for Sally's sake or if her actions concealed a hidden belief in God and the hereafter.

"I wonder," Sally said.

"There's so much we don't know," Colfax said, lacking anything better to offer.

He was echoing the words of a Navy chaplain who had accompanied them on the raid where he was wounded. The man—what was his name?—sat by him on the soggy ground to comfort him. Afraid that Colfax might be dying, he talked about heaven and then, as if to doubt his own words, added, "There's so much we don't know. . . ."

The doorbell rang. Gwen motioned Sally to stay where she was and opened it. Rosebud Kane came in and wordlessly embraced Sally, holding her head against her breast. Sally made no effort to resist. The two toughest women on the staff of the *Herald* hugged like children.

"I'm fucked," Sally said in resignation as they pulled apart.

"I know," Kane replied, making no effort to gloss over the truth that existed in the room. Seeing the whiskey, she found a glass and poured a double shot. Then she filled the glasses of the others. It was a wake before death. Colfax couldn't help but feel privileged. He had been admitted into a special company, a circle of friends linked by a single, overriding reality. A spiritual connection had been made at this terrible moment. He was a part of them now.

"I'm thinking maybe I don't want to go through all this," Sally said. "Maybe they can do something about the pain, but not . . . not the—"

A fit of coughing ended the sentence and again she had to gasp for breath. They knew what she meant. The emotional anguish of dying, of thinking about it, of being denied a choice, was probably more painful than any physical discomfort. To have your lungs fill, to slowly be denied intake of the very air around them . . . that would be the hardest part.

The coughing continued in what seemed an interminable sequence separated only by brief moments. Kane brought her water and wet washclothes and stayed next to her during the deep explosions of the cancer's hacking voice, then finally turned to Gwen and Colfax.

"You'd better leave," she said. "I'll take care of her."

They stood. Gwen embraced Sally quickly. Colfax touched her face the way he had touched the face of his mother the last time he ever saw her.

Outside of the apartment they paused for a moment and faced one another. "She's going to kill herself," Gwen said.

Colfax nodded. "Yes. I know."

He kissed Gwen softly. There were tears in her eyes. As he drove away, he watched Sally's apartment in the rearview mirror as it disappeared in the growing distance behind him, becoming smaller and smaller as he moved away until it was only a blur and then it was gone.

CHAPTER TWELVE

T he music of Trager's harp lingered above them like feathers in the wind and then drifted out over the bay with the last of Sally Bell's ashes. He played "Danny Boy" because, as Colfax had discovered over the past three years, it was the only piece Trager played well. That it fit the mood there was no doubt, bringing to the cold, foggy morning a sense of loneliness and grief befitting the final moments of a newspaper legend. Even the most cynical among them bowed their heads as Gwen Ballard shook the canister bearing the ashes into the breeze, which carried them away from the point of land jutting out over the crashing surf below.

If there were traces of memory in Trager from his long-ago love affair with Sally, he displayed none of them, his craggy face concealing whatever emotion churned inside him. The music, this single song, encompassed all that the old copy chief was or had ever been. His history was entwined in its loneliness, its pain, and its melancholy, all offered now in a eulogy to a woman he once loved.

No clergy was present, the religion editor, Carter Blake, having been sent out of town to cover an Episcopal convention in Portland, and no one thought to prepare last words to say on Sally's behalf before they adjourned to the Three-Oh for the wake. Finally, the most unlikely among them, Chip Dawson, already half drunk and in the mean phase of inebriation, stepped forward and said, "God bless you, you sweet son of a bitch." A mumbled, "Amen," from the dozen men and women journalists followed, although some seemed reluctant to add a religious tone to a decidedly unreligious event.

An awkward silence followed until Trager filled it with another rendition of "Danny Boy," which somehow signaled the end. It wasn't until they were leaving that Gwen Ballard noticed Stafford's limo just in time to catch a glimpse of the publisher's face in the rear seat as the tinted window went up. He had apparently come unnoticed at the last minute, the limo rolling up to a place behind them from where he could witness the last of Sally's ashes being given to the wind. "He looks like shit," Gwen said, and Trager, hauling his harp off the hill, said, "He is shit."

"He's getting out," Rosebud Kane said, as the back door of the limo opened and Stafford emerged, leaning unsteadily against the car. Ellen, dressed in dark clothes and appearing somber, stepped out a moment later and hooked her arm through her father's as though lending physical support to his shaky stance.

Colfax stared transfixed by the publisher's appearance, a slightly hunched and uncertain figure who glanced at them in an expression of bewilderment and then faced the bay. As the mourners stopped to watch, Stafford's voice suddenly boomed over them, the baleful roar of a human lion.

"Our father who art in heaven . . ."

There was an unreal nature to the moment, a painting with sound captured on a broad canvas of fog and water, words strewn through the air like birds startled into flight. Colfax exchanged glances with Ellen, whose expression was a mixture of pride and embarrassment laced with a plea to him that did not go unnoticed.

". . . for thine is the kingdom and the power and the glory forever and ever . . ."

As quickly as they had emerged from the limo, they returned to it. A moment before the door closed, Ellen looked again at Colfax, who, for reasons he couldn't quite understand, nodded. No one had noticed the exchange and when the limo moved off, Kane said, "The fucker is crazy!"

"Maybe we all are," Colfax said.

They adjourned to the Three-Oh, where Danny Doe served free drinks and where they turned glass after glass over in Sally Bell's memory, told stories of her escapades, and laughed until they cried: Sally kicking the shit out of a cop because he refused to give her the name of a shooting suspect. Sally posing as a corpse to get into a secret conference of homicide detectives at the morgue. Sally stowing away in an ambulance to interview the victim of a serial rapist. No one mentioned the irony of her nickname, Suicide Sally, and the manner in which she took her life or the likelihood that Rosebud Kane had obtained the poison that allowed her to slip peacefully into her dreams. Her doctor, a decent, caring man, asked no questions and signed her death certificate, listing natural causes as the reason for her last breath, gently kissing her forehead as he left the cluttered apartment that had been her home.

The wake lasted until well after dark. Trager played "Danny Boy" on the harp another dozen times. No one complained.

The sexuality of grief is a compelling beacon, drawing to its light and heat those of a caring nature who embrace the bereaved with both mind and body. There is a oneness to compassion, a warmth to the proximity of naked souls and naked bodies entwined in each other, consoling one another, asking nothing but the purity of their giving. Thus, there was no doubt in Colfax's mind that he would make love to Ellen when she appeared at his apartment that late afternoon. She sensed it too, allowing herself to be enfolded in his arms as she entered, as an element of both compassion and eroticism.

She was clearly upset but not just about the death of Sally Bell.

"I don't know what to do about my father," she said, the moment their embrace had ended. "He's sick, very sick, but won't do anything about it. You heard him this morning. That was *not* Jeremy Stafford."

She had been summoned from a sociology class three days earlier by Gerald Burns. The city editor had gone to Stafford's home to check on him when he had failed to attend a negotiations meeting and had not answered the phone. He had found the publisher conscious and aware of his presence but in a state of bewilderment. Stafford had refused to allow Burns to call for medical help, instead offering a rambling explanation about his general health and the stress he had been under from the Communists and those of a treasonous bent within his own perimeter.

"We must be careful, Gerald," he had said in a conspiratorial tone, leaning closer to the city editor, his words slightly slurred. "I am ordering new precautions to be taken on the third floor. We must be alert."

By the time Ellen reached their home her father seemed to be in control of his faculties. The slurring had disappeared, although she noticed a droopiness to his right eyelid and a sag to the right corner of his mouth. Once more he refused to see anyone or to even discuss his physical condition with his daughter.

"I called a doctor father's had for years," Ellen was saying. "He thinks he may have had a stroke."

Colfax had poured them each a drink and they sipped it still standing facing each other, allowing the chemistry of their sexuality to sizzle in the emerging twilight. There was no illumination in the apartment other than the dim reminder of day that seeped in through the single window in the front room, a flat light that was slowly losing the last golden substance of a fading afternoon.

"Any chance of the doctor just, you know, dropping by to see him?"

Ellen shook her head. Colfax could see she was on the verge of tears but was managing to control them. After a pause she said, "It's a series of small strokes that leave him confused and sometimes a little odd. You saw him this morning. Everyone must have gotten a big laugh out of that."

"No one was laughing, Ellen."

"I don't know what to do. . . ."

She put a hand over her mouth as though to stifle the sobs that were already pulsing through her body, spilling the contents of her glass on the floor. Colfax took the drink gently from her hand and put both their glasses on a coffee table. Then he put his arms around her and softly rubbed her back. One hand slipped under the loose blouse she wore and the physiology of their longing united. Continuing to caress her back, he moved his fingertips under her bra, unsnapping it, and then down inside the waistband of her denims. He could feel the beginning curve of her, the heat of her, and continued downward.

Her sobs had ceased and now Ellen's breathing was deeper and faster as Colfax's hands moved down farther into her denims, rubbing, caressing, seeking, until they descended into her panties and lower, his fingertips touching between her legs, teasing.

They kissed deeply, breaking only to allow Colfax to slip the blouse over her head, and resumed kissing as he slid off the remainder of her clothing, letting his hand slide lower, claiming the warmth and softness there as his own. They both undressed him and then stood together naked in the room, his hardness pressed against her, loving, touching, kissing, sighing gales into the dark and quiet room, at last merging as one on the carpeting.

Colfax took her without the rage that had consumed him with Gwen. This was a gentle lovemaking, neither a whore's feast nor a demand met, and they couldn't get enough of each other, she spreading to meet his orgasm and responding with hers and then taking him in her mouth until he hardened again and filled her with himself. Later, he slid down her body to put his tongue in her in a commitment that needed no words. Their bond had been complete.

It was only after Ellen had left his apartment that Colfax lay naked in the darkness and wondered where the fire would take him. It wasn't what he'd intended—or was it? He recalled his first view of her, so shiny in the tawdry encompassment of the city room, and wondered if that first glance had set him on a course from which there was no deviation. Had this union been predestined? That was too metaphysical for him, like the predictions of witches who saw things others couldn't.

But still . . . Ellen was so like Laura, or that vision of Laura he once held; a vision now dimming like faces in a fog. But Ellen was more. She was the boss's daughter, and that placed her on a different plane. The complexity of the situation was too much. Colfax closed his eyes and wished in a way he couldn't explain that he was back in Edenville.

The Guild's strike against the *Herald* came off as planned, a boisterous condemnation of the past that perfectly fit the mood of the staff. Word of Stafford's peculiar behavior and possible illness had reached Cliff Hammer, but it was not in Hammer's makeup to allow sympathy or compassion to intrude on his schedule. The last of many deadlines to negotiate had come and gone and the editorial staff of the *Herald* had, for the first time in the hundred-year history of the paper, hit the bricks. Every member of the staff picketed the first day, carrying signs that said the *Herald* was unfair, pacing back and forth in front of the building and on the side that held the loading dock.

The Teamsters had agreed earlier to respect the picket line, glad that the paper's editorial staff had at last seen the light and voted to unionize. No one, however, harrassed the few who did cross their human barriers, including Gerald Burns as a member of management and Ellen Stafford who had come to help out. She had dropped out of her classes at U.C. the preceding week to take care of her father and now was a familiar sight on the third floor. It was clear she held no animosity toward those who picketed and stopped long enough to tell Hammer that she hoped negotiations could continue. She would talk to her father. As she passed Colfax, she smiled directly at him, a gesture that was not lost on the others.

Alone in his apartment, Vito Minelli watched the picketing on live television and checked his watch. Something had gone seriously wrong. The device he had smuggled into the *Herald*'s pressroom had been scheduled to go off almost twelve hours earlier and now, as the clock neared noon, Minelli wondered if he had set the timing device wrong. Without expert help, he had been forced to create the bomb himself and sneak it into an unguarded, unlocked entryway off an alley in back of the newspaper. He had set the device to explode at midnight under one of the old presses. It would have been between shifts then, with no one anywhere near where the bomb, much smaller than the one at the Federal Building, would go off.

Noon came and went without an explosion. Minelli cursed the hour and his own incompetence. This was to have been his statement, a declaration written in fire and smoke, clearly his but untraceable, the perfect affirmation of his commitment. Instead, the device lay inert in a dark corner of the *Herald*'s basement, like a serpent waiting to strike. Any attempt to retrieve it could be dangerous to him, but he couldn't allow the bomb to remain where it was and explode when the press-room was full. This wasn't a killing mission. This was a roar, a fist in the face of Callahan, a reminder of who was in charge. But now, as he considered it with growing depression, visualizing the inert bomb, a shadow of doubt began to darken his confidence.

The city room of the *Herald* was empty but for Burns, Ellen, and the few department editors not covered by the Guild. They sat at the desks on Rewrite Row and the uneven clatter of their typewriters filled a small corner of the silence that existed in the large room. The newspaper had never missed a day of publication in its century-long history and Ellen Stafford did not intend to see the record broken because of a strike. Downstairs, printers and pressman who had crossed the picket line waited for the copy that would help them produce a skeletal issue of the newspaper. There would be only street-rack distribution, but it would at least be a signal of determination that the *Herald* would not be shut down for any reason.

Ellen had tried to seek guidance from her father, but he waved her off, standing instead by the window of their living room, transfixed by a view of the bay as though somehow communicating with the panorama that lay almost at his feet. She had shouted at him once in frustration and he had turned and said, "It's okay, Ellie," and then turned back to the view and to his detachment. Time and again he had returned to her with his usual bombast only to then retreat into silence, leaving her unsure of his condition and, in a way, of hers.

At the office, she had tried sitting at his desk under the hostile glare of the lion's head and hated it. There was a repressiveness about the room, a darkness that seemed to possess her, and she couldn't wait to get out, instead seating herself at a desk facing Burns, ready to do her part in filling four pages of the *Herald.* They did telephone work, contacting the beats normally covered by their reporters, rewrote wire copy, used filler material from the syndicates, and even retooled yesterday's *Daily News.* It would be a sham and a fake, but at least it would be a newspaper.

Ellen was trying to write the story of a murder in the city's Tenderloin when Burns, answering his ringing telephone, said suddenly, "Where?" It was the tone of his voice that caught her attention, a single shot fired into the room. Others sensed his urgency and all typing suddenly stopped. They listened. Burns began to say, "If this is a . . ." but stopped. The other party had obviously hung up. He sat for a moment looking over the top of his rimless glasses at Ellen and glancing at the others.

"We've got another bomb threat," he said, his voice resuming its softer qualities.

No one spoke for a moment. This was probably the *Herald*'s twenty-fifth bomb threat in the past three years of its battle with the radical left. The threats had been taken seriously at first, but then were eventually treated as jokes due to their frequency and to the fact that no bomb was ever found. Many suspected that the newspaper's editorial cartoonist, Billy "the Bug" Kent, a wry, talented instrument of the political left who gloried in chaos, had made at least some of threats, enjoying not only the calamity he caused but the party atmosphere that resulted. The building had been abandoned every time and the staff had adjourned to the Three-Oh to mix with the girls from the classified advertising section, who were not unwilling to join whatever party that seemed at hand.

No one knew exactly why they called him the Bug, although if you looked at Kent in a certain light his pinched expression and large eyes did contain some of the qualities that might be observed in an enlarged photograph of a fly. He signed his cartoons with the small image of a bug and seemed to take delight in the nickname, assuming it had something to do with the way he bugged the city's right wing. His cartoons were pretty much left alone even though they contradicted the *Herald*'s conservative stance, depicting leaders of the Republican party in hideous ways. Only when he almost artistically worked the face of Richard Nixon into the shape of a horse's ass was his judgment questioned and his cartoon rejected. The Bug mailed it personally to everyone he could think of and the distribution, though not immense, was satisfactory.

"What do we do?" Ellen asked.

"We abandon ship," Burns replied with a sigh.

"Was it real, you think?" the sports editor asked.

Burns thought for a moment and then finally said, "It was real."

Now feeling the responsibility of her position, Ellen dialed the switchboard and said simply, "Abandon the building." Security was alerted and word went to every department almost instantaneously. Soon those who had crossed the picket line were streaming out from the tower, past the staff members, who viewed them with bewilderment.

Ellen stopped by Hammer. "We've had a bomb threat," she said. "Burns thinks it's the real thing." Colfax had moved in and was listening. "I suggest you move everyone away from the building."

Even as she spoke they could hear sirens in the distance, growing louder as the bomb truck and squad cars merged on the *Herald*. A crowd gathered across the street, mildly resisting efforts to disperse. Burns relayed the message he had received that the bomb had been planted under one of the two presses in the basement. The bomb squad, in shrapnel-proof suits and masks, headed for the basement.

"What is this?" a police captain asked, approaching Burns. Clearly he didn't believe a bomb existed. "Another pain in the ass from the Bug? Party time? A TNT holiday?"

"Not this time, Mark." It was axiomatic that Burns knew every cop in town. "This was no nut call."

Traffic had been stopped in every direction two blocks away and cars already within the perimeter around the *Herald* had been siphoned off. Crowds moved slowly away at the police commands, curiosity keeping them from moving more swiftly. Those who had abandoned the building and those on the picket line mingled in front of the tower, feeling that they occupied special positions and therefore were immune to the orders to move. That is, until a member of the bomb squad stuck his head out of a doorway and shouted to the captain, "We've got a live one!"

Police Sergeant Morris Wilson leaned over the bomb without touching it. It was a makeshift device approximately eighteen inches in length and three inches in diameter, composed of a lead pipe, a cheap timing device, lamp wiring, and caps at both ends. He lifted the heavy plastic face mask that somewhat obscured his view to take a closer look.

Wilson had seen these devices before and knew how unpredictable they could be. His stomach bore the scars of one that had exploded unexpectedly and had blown him out of a room. Amazingly, he had suffered only surface wounds. The bomb-maker, a high school physics major, had used insufficient firepower to kill. The boy, Wilson would observe sourly as they carted him off to emergency, needed better training if he planned on becoming a career terrorist.

"Everybody out," he shouted to the others who stood behind him. They obeyed instantly, knowing the wrath of their sergeant, an ex-paratrooper with a temper as explosive as the bombs he disarmed. Alone in the pressroom, he lowered his face mask again. If this was what he thought it was, an unsophisticated time bomb without tricks built in, he could simply clip the wires attaching the timer to the bomb and render it harmless. From the tool kit around his belt, Wilson took a pair of needle-nosed wire cutters, knelt before the bomb, and put his face as close to it as he could without touching it.

Still he studied it, noticing that the caps on either end were composed of a heavy plastic similar to those used in the bombing of the FBI building years earlier. They had called him in on that one to search through the debris and he had found enough of the bomb to put it together. Wilson missed nothing. Even after the FBI experts had gone through it he was still finding pieces of the puzzle. One of the pieces was a plastic cap that would have fit perfectly over an end of that bomb and which fit perfectly over the end of this one.

Now he reached down with the wire cutters. The immensity of his concentration began to clear his mind, and he wondered as he considered the damage this piece of shit could cause why anyone would do a thing like this in the name of peace.

Ellen wasn't quite sure what she ought to be doing. Most of the staff had adjourned to the Three-Oh even though they had been advised to evacuate the entire area. Colfax sensed her uncertainty and beckoned her to follow. "You're not an enemy," he said, "just a momentary adversary." They crossed the street together, following the flow into the dank interior of the bar.

"Why does this place always smell like pussy?" Milton Travis demanded as he entered the door, two cameras slung like bandoliers over his shoulders. As he said it, he noticed Ellen and winced, immediately sorry he had repeated an old joke in such important company.

Colfax rolled his eyes upward and for a moment no one spoke. Ellen glanced at him, uncertain how to respond or whether she should respond at all. It was Trager who broke the ice.

"Welcome to the sewer," he said, settling in a chair with his harp. "It's not much, but it beats drinking in a doorway from a bottle in a paper bag."

"Just barely," Corona McGee added.

"Please don't play 'Danny Boy,' " Colfax begged in mock supplication, glad that the awkward moment had passed.

Trager took offense. "I wasn't going to," he said indignantly.

"And this ain't no sewer," Danny Doe said, equaling his indignation.

The barmaid Patty was on duty and took orders with her usual inattention to detail. The scotch might contain 7UP instead of soda. The martini might be vodka instead of gin. They understood, however, that she was an imperfect human being and accepted her mistakes without complaint. Sometimes Danny Doe realized the errors when she gave him the orders and corrected them behind the bar without saying anything. And he watched with amusement as those at the table first tasted and then rearranged the misdelivered drinks so that they ended up with their proper owners. Ellen ordered a soft drink and tried to remain unnoticed.

It was as the first round came that a muffled *thrump* rattled the windows of the Three-Oh. It seemed to come from deep within something, an explosion contained in a tight complex.

"What the hell was that?" Rosebud Kane asked, pushing open the door to look across the street.

Colfax listened for screams that might follow. None came. A gunnery sergeant had explained it properly. He called it the boom-scream syndrome. "Unless there's a scream after the boom," he'd said, "don't even look up. It's just a fart in the wind."

"Nothing," Colfax said. "Just a fart in the wind."

The lid of the steel bomb vault had been closed and bolted shut within the enclosure of the heavily armored bomb truck seconds before the device exploded. Wilson was the only one inside the truck and, despite containment of the bomb, felt the sudden sharp pressure of the explosion.

It left his ears ringing and his eyes stinging, a condition he referred to as "the loops" when talking to his men. Had the bomb exploded moments earlier, it could have killed him. He had treated it with respect even after cutting the wires that connected it to the timer, because he knew that bombs built by amateurs often assume a life of their own, exploding when they shouldn't or, conversely, lying inert when they ought to blow.

The rear door of the truck was jerked open by his men as the bomb exploded and Wilson was helped out in clouds of dark smoke. Although shaken by the event, he pushed away the helping hands, lifted his face mask and breathed in the clean, damp air of the city. Then he faced the squad members who had gathered around him. He looked at each face, buying time, and said in a voice both sad and instructional, "Look what we do to each other, boys."

Picketing was called off for the day as a Guild token of goodwill and the staff was allowed to return to work. Television cameras had never left the scene and now documented the staff filing back into the Herald Building. Colfax was the last to enter and turned slightly at the doorway to look back at the camera, his expression grim. In his apartment, Minelli felt Colfax had been looking directly at him and knew precisely who had planted the bomb. The FBI would know it too and would tighten the circle around him. They had questioned him a dozen times before and now they would question him a hundred times again. Damn Strickland! Damn Colfax!

Minelli felt himself being forced to the outer fringes of the revolution. Spurred by an expansion of the war into Cambodia and Laos by American troops and bombers, the peace movement had been fueled with new energy. They had forced Lyndon Johnson to retire and now they were after Richard Nixon. A million war protesters marched on Washington in a display of solidarity never before seen. In San Francisco Maxwell Callahan, his strength growing, led a suddenly enlarged army into City Hall demanding that San Francisco officially oppose the war. Student radicals filled the supervisors' chambers and the adjacent offices, including the mayor's. But here Minelli sat, hunted and wanted, a rebel increasingly abandoned by his cause. He stared at the images on the television screen and wondered what to do.

CHAPTER
THIRTEEN

T he strike at the *Herald* was called off after the bomb threat. The explosion had abruptly altered the attitude of its staff members. Hammer sensed their tribal instinct and feared they might band together against their own best interests if he pressed to continue the strike. He saw the situation as a bunching together for protection against a common enemy. He would let that instinct cool for a while. Waiting wasn't something he did well, but he could wait if he had to. He agreed to new negotiations with a characteristic burst of obscenity. After a one-day walkout, the staff was back at work.

The libel hearing followed within a week. The courtroom of Judge Hyman Walker was almost empty as Colfax took a seat at the defendant's table. Already there were Ellen and the *Herald*'s lawyer, Stanley Fairchild, a dark and towering man who, at six-foot-six, dominated every room he entered. His piercing gaze, jet-black hair, and threatening manner labeled him as someone to beware of, though he was a gentle and cultured man who often brought his children to the tower to spend the day as he pondered over contracts and commitments that involved the newspaper. Now he waited patiently for Judge Walker to make his entrance, assembling in his head the arguments he would present in sustaining their case.

At the plaintiff's table Harry Gold sat alone, flipping a pencil end over end and glancing occasionally at the doorway. Shaggy and cloaked in a cloth raincoat he never seemed to remove, he was otherwise dressed in jeans, a heavy wool sweater, and sneakers, an appearance that simultaneously disarmed his opponents and annoyed the judges before whom he appeared on behalf of leftist causes and clients. And yet Gold was a brilliant litigator and a forceful speaker, and judges were ill-disposed to throw him from their court room lest they become enmeshed in a legal web that would tie them up for months and even years. Gold knew law and if his dress and his manner were unorthodox, they were tolerable.

The audience consisted of two television reporters, two female trial junkies, and the lieutenant of Max Callahan known as Roscoe. Bruno Hagen entered at the last minute, sitting alone in the back row, playing with an unlit cigar. At one point Colfax turned to study the audience and acknowledged Hagen with a nod. The FBI agent in turn blew him a kiss.

Judge Walker entered the courtroom at precisely ten A.M., interrupting the bailiff's command to "All rise" by waving everyone back into their seats. "Let's get on with it," he said in a tone that brooked no debate. "Are we all here?"

"The defendants are present, Your Honor," Fairchild said, rising. His height gave him the appearance of a gothic statue placed unceremoniously in the center of the courtroom.

Gold stood hesitantly, still looking toward the door. "I seem to be missing my client," he said.

"And where might your client be, Mr. Gold?"

"Beats the shit out of me," Gold replied.

"I see," the judge said, observing him carefully. "Well, then, we'll spend a few moments discussing language while we wait to see if Mr. Minelli might favor us with his presence. As for you, Mr. Gold, if you desire to continue using this courtroom to present your case, you will not use that word again."

"What word would that be, Judge?"

"That would be the word 'shit.' "

"Is it the word or the process that offends the court?" Gold asked.

"I have no quarrel with a regular movement of the bowels," the Judge said, "only with the manner in which it might be described."

"Then if the case—"

"Enough!" Walker interrupted slamming his gavel down. "The word is not relevant to this case. Now take off that raincoat and let's move forward. Where is Mr. Minelli?"

"Damned if I know," Gold said, ignoring the order to remove his coat.

Stanley Fairchild seemed to grow taller as he spoke. "Your Honor," he said very, very slowly, "if the plaintiff feels so uninvolved in his own legal action that he fails to appear for its preliminary presentation, I suggest that the entire reason for filing the action reflects its singular lack of commitment, importance, and relevance. I therefore move for summary dismissal."

"Not so fast," Walker said, turning to Gold. "This does not bode well for your case, Mr. Gold. The date was set three months ago and I expect an appearance by your Mr. Minelli. Libel suits are not matters to be dismissed casually, nor are they political tools to be utilized at the caprice of someone with a cause."

"I saw him last night," Gold replied, glancing again at the doorway as though he expected Vito Minelli to saunter in, unaffected by the lateness of his appearance. "He believes that the *Herald* damaged him intentionally and that—"

"I read the briefs," Walker snapped. "I am going to forgive this insult to the court once, Mr. Gold, by postponing this prelimary until ten A.M. next Tuesday. If Mr. Minelli does not show up at that time, I am dismissing your suit forthwith. Is that clear?"

Gold shrugged. "I'll do my best," he said.

Walker turned to the defense table. "I expect all of you to return on that date."

"We'll be here, Your Honor," Fairchild said.

But Walker had not waited for a response. Black robe flowing behind him, he had left the bench and disappeared into his chambers before the bailiff could acknowledge his absence. Instead the man shrugged and followed him out.

Outside the courtroom, Fairchild chided Gold. "Better start checking the opium dens," he said, looking down on the smaller man as though he were an amusing child.

"I'll start checking the graveyards where Stafford might have buried him," Gold replied, adjusting his raincoat and reshuffling a binder he carried under one arm. He headed down the wide staircase leading to the door, then stopped and turned. "Then," he said with a hard smile, "we'll come looking for you."

Bruno Hagen, standing in the courtroom doorway, listened with interest and then watched as Gold sprinted down the stairs and out the main door. He played with the unlit cigar as the others started to leave. Then, as Colfax was about to descend the stairs, Hagen called his name. When the reporter turned, he beckoned.

They drove together in Colfax's car toward Minelli's apartment. Hagen had obtained a search warrant from a judge who was a known Commie-hater and offered no resistance to the FBI agent's request. Hagen used his knowledge of the old judge's politics to obtain the warrant, even though he had neither probable cause nor Bureau approval for the request. Colfax was asked along to witness anything that might transpire.

"Why not ask another agent?" Colfax said as they drove across the Bay Bridge. He had opened both windows to blow away Hagen's cigar smoke and the wind off the bay bore an icy chill. The squawk of seagulls, riding the currents over the graceful arches, pierced the morning like animated elements of a movie.

"They get in the way."

"I may get in the way."

"If you do, I'll shoot you. I can shoot a reporter but not another agent." He puffed on the cigar. "You see that guy in court today? Behind Gold?" Colfax acknowledge that he had. "That was Harold Roscoe, one of Callahan's guys. He's a half-crazy Indian from Arizona who drifted out here when all hell busted loose on the campuses. Or campi." Hagen paused thoughtfully. "Is the plural of campus, campi?"

"In the *San Francisco* by God *Herald* it is."

Hagen nodded. "His real name is Harold Tallfeather. He took the name Roscoe from the street he lives on. What an asshole."

"So?"

"So I'm thinking that maybe your pal is in trouble with his own people."

"I already figured that. In fact, I wrote about it."

"Then I'll tell you something you didn't write about and can't write about, at least not yet. I've got to get your promise you won't. Not that a reporter's promise means shit."

"How can I promise if I don't know what it is?"

"Just promise, that's all."

"Okay, I promise. What the hell."

"The slugs from the shootup at Minelli's place? They disappeared from the police evidence files."

"How?"

"Who knows how?"

Colfax waited as Hagen relit his cigar. The car came off the bridge and swung over to the Eastshore Freeway.

"But I got hold of one before they disappeared and had it tested. The slug was a dumdum, one of those soft-nosed bullets that expands when it hits. It'll rip your insides out."

"I know what a dumdum is."

"I keep forgetting you're one of those smartshit reporters who knows everything. What you don't know is that those things are hardly used anymore except by one group of people." Hagen took a long draw and blew the smoke away. "The Oakland Police Department."

"You're saying an Oakland cop shot up Minelli's place?"

The car turned off the freeway at University and edged toward Channing Way, passing a street rally by Callahan's army that was ominously close to Minelli's apartment; a kick in Minelli's ass from the new kid on the block.

"I'm saying that's possible. Korchek is a fucking Nazi and has surrounded himself with other Nazis. His guys feed on the hatred of people like Minelli."

Colfax had guessed as much and wondered if Ellen suspected the same. She had said nothing more about her father's association with Korchek since he had become ill or crazy, whichever the case might be. Nothing seemed normal to Colfax anymore. The world was out of whack. The war he had once been a part of seemed strangely distant. Only this was real. Here. Now.

The car pulled up in front of Minelli's apartment. Colfax turned to Hagen. "Minelli wasn't in business to make friends, but you've got him sounding like he's already dead."

"That's why we're here," the agent said, easing himself out the car door.

They walked toward the apartment and as they did Hagen leaned in close to peer through the only window to the basement unit. He beckoned Colfax to do the same. What he saw through the dust streaked across the glass was an apartment in shambles.

"Good God," Colfax said, then turned to Hagen, realizing. "You knew!"

"Let's go in," Hagen said.

Inside, the chaos was even more evident. All of Minelli's meager furnishings were broken and scattered. His clothes had been jerked from a closet so hard the wooden rod had broken. Even a sink had been pulled from the wall.

"How did you know?"

Hagen pointed upward. "The fat lady told me."

"Godamn it, Hagen—"

"The landlady, Beverly Barnes. She called me. She's my friend. I like fat ladies. She came down to inspect and . . ." He gestured openly to indicate the room. "This is what she saw."

There was a graveyard feel to the room and Colfax was ill at ease standing amid the chaos that might represent Minelli's final struggle. He could imagine screams and could hear the violent sounds of impact as Minelli clung to a perilous strand of life until he could cling no more.

Hagen reentered the main room from a kitchenette, his hands in his pockets, an expression of concentration on his face. "No Minelli. No blood. Just wreckage." He lit his cigar and continued to look around. Then he said, "Why would anyone rip out a sink? You don't need to rip out a sink to drag someone off. Same with the closet. It's a trashing without purpose."

"They pay you guys to figure out things like that. So figure. I'm calling this in."

"Everything I told you stays off the record, right?"

"But not this."

"Hell, no, not this," Hagen said, studying the mess. "This is big time. This is front page."

Colfax knew where he could find a phone and crossed the street to Ellen's place. As their lovemaking had intensified, she had given him a key. Her apartment, he decided, taking a phrase from a headline writer's notebook, had become their love nest. Six weeks had passed since they had first made love and Colfax had felt himself falling deeper into the sphere of her influence. Now, in the fall of 1970, he had given up something of himself to become a part of her. Overwhelmed by her fluorescence, he continued to feel awkward in the arrangement, isolating himself even further from the rest of the staff. He was certain that the insiders knew of their relationship but remained silent. How much they gossiped among themselves Colfax had no idea. You didn't fuck with the guy who was fucking the boss's daughter.

The city room had formed into two camps, those who cheered Colfax for his conquest and those who were beginning to despise him for his sellout. In a session at the Three-Oh, Corona McGee held firmly to his side. "He's in love," she said to an angry Barry Adams, "and love is blind . . . but not so blind as to force him into the Republican Party. The man knows he's not an heir, for Christ's sake. He's just getting a little poontang."

"You don't go after front-office pussy during a goddamn labor confrontation unless you're on the other side," Adams shouted back. "He's fucking us as much as he's fucking her!"

"Shut up and drink," she said, staring morosely at her gin and tonic and wishing Colfax were with them. Everyone was edgy. Negotiations between Hammer and Page had gone nowhere and the threat of a strike continued to hang over them. Maybe Adams was right. Colfax was becoming a stranger to them. But as she waved for another round, she wondered if, in a way, they weren't all becoming strangers to each other.

Minelli was nowhere to be found and his disappearance was bigger news than anything he could have planned. So big that Jeremy Stafford returned to his desk, blustering to conceal an obvious unsteadiness but in control. No one discussed his illness. No one dared. He summoned both Burns and Colfax to face him under the lion's head and ordered Colfax to form a team that would determine exactly what had happened to Minelli.

"Find him, find his body, or find what happened to him," the publisher demanded, fighting to maintain his baritone. Clearly it was there but not easily summoned. "Leave no stone unturned. Work day and night if you must. I want it made clear that the *Herald* is every bit as concerned with his disappearance as any other citizen in the Bay Area. Now let's do it."

The meeting was over, but as they left Stafford said, "Mr. Colfax, I would like you to stay."

Burns glanced at him as he left the room, leaving Colfax standing before Stafford's desk, waiting. For a moment, the publisher simply observed him through critical eyes. Colfax had taken to wearing sport coats and slacks, even Levi's sometimes if he was going to hang around the Berkeley campus. Was that what was eating him? Colfax could only guess.

"I want you to stay away from my daughter," the publisher said.

The order caught Colfax off guard. He stared at Stafford in bewilderment, as though what he thought he'd heard wasn't said. Then, absorbing it, the inclination to deny flashed through his mind but was quickly put to rest. Denial was running, and he never ran.

"That isn't just up to me," he said. "We have feelings for each other that have nothing to do with this newspaper."

"It has to do with me," Stafford replied, "and I am this newspaper."

It was a rationale the reporter could not debate. "Have you discussed it with her?" he asked.

"That's none of your business."

At a loss on how to proceed, Colfax raised his eyebrows up and down in a gesture intended to convey a we'll-see attitude. "Is that all?" he said.

"Form the Minelli team," Stafford said by way of dismissal. "I want the situation clarified."

When Colfax left the office without another word, Stafford leaned back in his chair and covered his eyes with one hand. His head hurt and he was feeling sorry for himself. Was nothing ever easy anymore? God forgive him his entanglements.

Colfax left the building immediately, both angry and confused. Pushed to the wall, his tendency was to push back. But this was more complicated than a fistfight. On the way out, he met Corona McGee coming back from lunch and told her what Stafford had said about keeping away from Ellen.

"That's the trouble with men," she said after a moment of thought. "They walk around with their flies unzipped, all ready to go, and never think about the consequences. Pussy has its price, Colfax, and you pay it one way or another." Then she walked away.

Colfax stared after her. The anger dissipated. All that remained was confusion.

In the weeks that followed, Colfax threw himself into the search for Minelli as though he were pursuing a ghost. Rather than crush him, his confrontation with Stafford had finally energized him, challenging him to perform under duress. The confusion he had felt was gone. He would not think of Ellen, he would not discuss Stafford's admonition with her. But neither would he avoid her. Colfax knew that ultimately he must make a decision regarding his relationship with the publisher's daughter, but at the moment his concentration was centered not on his love life but on finding Minelli, dead or alive. He would form a team later. At the start, he would act alone.

The revolutionary seemed to have vanished without a trace. A Berkley police lieutenant who had helped Colfax in small ways in the past allowed him to revisit Minelli's apartment, which remained empty and sealed off as part of the police investigation. They walked together through the eerie silence of the place as the lieutenant recounted what they had learned so far, which was essentially nothing. No fingerprints, no witnesses, and no suspects.

Remembering that it was dumdum bullets that had been fired into Minelli's apartment weeks earlier, Colfax tried questioning the lieutenant on the source of the bullets. Had any effort been made to locate the missing slugs? Had detectives looked into the possibility that they might have come from an Oakland policeman's gun? The lieutenant's spirit of cooperation suddenly faded. Colfax was surprised at the quick transformation from friendly to cold.

"There is no reason to associate the earlier incident with the disappearance of Mr. Minelli," he said, his manner abruptly official. "We are investigating all aspects of the situation, but until we learn otherwise, this is being treated as a missing-person case." He could have been reading from a press release.

Colfax began to push. "But the condition of the apartment would suggest—"

"We are investigating all aspects of the case," the lieutenant interrupted. "That's all I have to say."

For the next two weeks, Colfax spent most of his time on the U.C. campus, talking to both students and nonstudents who had marched with Minelli. They knew nothing. Beyond his public efforts to bring down the *Herald,* Minelli had lived what amounted to a secret life, sharing very little of his background with those who followed him. He had emerged on campus like some kind of god borne on a lightning bolt and had disappeared just as dramatically. No one recalled him before he was suddenly leading the student revolution and no one knew him well during the period of his leadership.

Colfax paid special attention to a woman who called herself Tillie Something. He had seen her on various protest marches. She was described by others as Minelli's occasional girlfriend and lived in a commune tucked away in the Berkeley Hills. It was an isolated, non-descript house in desperate need of repair, occupied more by drifters and hippies than by revolutionaries.

Tillie was a small, pretty woman in her early twenties who seemed too straight and sane to be a part of her shabby surroundings. Her opening tirade against the *Herald,* Stafford, the police and the Establishment in general was predictable. Colfax waited her out as he had learned to do in dealing with the student radicals. Then he tried to pull from her any small detail of Minelli's life that might indicate what had happened to him. It wasn't easy. Tillie resisted every step of the way until Colfax, becoming increasingly frustrated with dead ends, decided he'd had enough.

"Goddamn it, woman," he shouted angrily, "you follow the man like an apostle trailing Jesus, you fuck him, you claim to love him, and you won't offer shit in an effort to find him? What in the hell kind of misplaced fucking adoration is that?"

The outburst took her by surprise. "Why should I tell you any-thing?" she demanded, less certain than she'd been.

Colfax leaned in close. "Because you care about him."

He let that sizzle in the tense atmosphere of her room. Then he slapped his notebook closed and quickly strode away.

Word of his father's illness reached Colfax by way of Milton Travis's car radio. They'd been searching a hillside south of the city on a psy-chic's tip that Minelli's body would be found there, carved up in some kind of satanic ritual. The order to pursue the tip came from Stafford himself and could not be ignored, though no one took it seriously. The hill overlooked the Cow Palace, a great round warehouse of a building that hosted everything from rodeos to political conventions. Other than that, the area was part of a drab freeway environment that led ultimately past Candlestick Park to the San Francisco airport.

Colfax had just about given up on this lead when Travis, who had returned to the car for another lens, called to him, holding up the microphone to the car radio that connected them with the city desk. Pressed to form what was being called the Minelli Team, Colfax had chosen the photographer as a member because he was tough, aggressive, knew cops, and never stopped digging. He was the bull of the photo staff, his bulk crashing through any barrier, and he was somehow always there when the shit was going down. But there was a downside. Travis hated blacks. Twice Colfax had to remind him to quit using racial slurs when referring to them. No more Mau Mau. No more jungle bunny. The photographer shrugged acquiescence, not wanting to be dumped from the team, but simmered with resentment at the curtailment.

Colfax took the radio receiver and heard Burns say that his father had been hospitalized in Eureka and was in serious condition. He'd better call up there. Travis offered his nearby apartment for the call and they arrived there in a burst of rubber-burning speed that had found Colfax clinging to his seat. Travis was known for this kind of driving. He never arrived second to a murder scene, and now Colfax knew why.

The floor nurse at Eureka's St. Joseph Hospital was clearly agitated. "The man just up and left," she said over the phone. "He's got pneumonia and ought to be right here, but I couldn't get him to stay." He could imagine her glaring, lips pressed tightly together, jaw set. "When a steward tried to stop him, he shoved the poor guy against a wall and threatened to choke him to death! What kind of a man is that father of yours?"

"Did he say where he was going?"

"Home! And he'll die there without treatment!"

Colfax hung up and stared into space, trying to figure out what to do.

"Call him at home," Travis said.

"He doesn't have a phone."

In the moment of silence that followed, a strange screech stabbed into the living room. It sounded someplace between the whine of a saw and a scream of pain.

"What in the hell is that?" Colfax said, staring toward a closed door.

Travis shrugged uncomfortably. "That's Kaiser." To Colfax's concern, he added, "A monkey."

It caught Colfax between amusement and disbelief. "You have a monkey? Here? In your apartment?"

"It's a vervet monkey," Travis explained, as though the type of monkey would normalize its presence in a San Francisco apartment. He opened a bedroom door and a ball of fur the size of a small cat leaped from the room and into the photographer's arms. "I named him after Henry Kaiser. One of Kaiser's engineers got him in Kenya and gave him to me."

A strong smell of urine emerged with the monkey from the back room.

"I have to keep cleaning up after him," Travis said apologetically.

"Do the others in the building know about . . . Kaiser?" Colfax asked, staring at the animal snuggled in Travis's arms.

"Sure. They don't mind."

"They don't *mind?* It's a wild animal, for Christ's sake. There's got to be some kind of city ordinance against keeping monkeys as pets."

Travis's voice became uncharacteristically soft. "Don't blow it for me, Colfax," he said. "It's all I've got." It was a different voice for Travis, empty of bombast, revealing a kind of anguish Colfax had not heard before.

Colfax shook his head, momentarily distracted from the decision he had to make. Travis sensed the moment. "You want me to drive you up there?" he asked, anxious to change the course of their conversation.

"No, no," Colfax answered quickly, then, realizing the haste of his answer, softened it. "If I go at all, I'll fly."

"Suit yourself."

"We'd better get back to the office. I've got to make arrangements." He paused. "I won't say a word about the monkey."

"Yeah, great."

Kaiser was placed screeching and chattering back into his room. Colfax watched as the big photographer patted the little animal and spoke softly to him. Well, he thought, we all need something, even if it's only a monkey.

Colfax made contact with his father that night by telephone through the efforts of the *Edenville Messenger*'s editor, Henry Dustin. He had sat alone for a long time in the *Herald*'s city room before deciding that he'd go to Edenville only if he couldn't reach Granger any other way. Colfax wasn't anxious to face the old man again. The distance between them was more than miles. Despite the slight warming that had occurred on his last trip north, Colfax could not alter the utter remoteness of his feelings toward Granger. He neither loved nor hated the man who had raised him. Where emotion should have existed, there was emptiness. Thinking about it, Colfax guessed a psychiatrist might find that he blamed Granger for the disappearance of his mother, but he would make no effort at the moment to probe his psyche. What was there, was there. The telephone call was perfunctory, not personal.

Dustin made the contact happen. He went out to the old man's place and brought him to the *Messenger.*

"He's too mean to die," the editor said over the phone, assuring Colfax that his father had made the short trip in good shape.

"You should have stayed in the hospital," Colfax said to him.

"What for?" the old man demanded. "If I'm gonna die, I'm gonna die. I don't need help for that."

Colfax envisioned him sitting upright in a chair in the *Messenger*'s office. He doubted that either age or illness had softened Granger. His voice sounded as hard as ever.

"I'm okay," the old man added. "How're you doing?"

"I'm fine. I heard you were ill and just thought I'd check in."

It occurred to Colfax that this was the same kind of awkward conversation he'd had with Laura. Was he at long last abandoning his past? Had he nothing to say anymore to those who had inhabited his yesterdays? As he had glowed with a sense of freedom when his conversation with Laura had ended, he now felt a growing sense of closure talking to his father. By the time he hung up, Colfax was certain that he owed no further allegiance to Granger. The emptiness in him would cease to exist. He placed the telephone receiver in its cradle and sat staring at the memories of the person he had once been. And by the time he left the *Herald*'s city room, he had quietly bade the memories farewell.

Bruno Hagen sat staring at the agent in charge in disbelief. "You're firing me?" he said.

The man behind his desk, a fortyish statue named Ross Houlihan, said, "Not firing but suspending you. It isn't my idea, Agent Hagen. It was the chief's."

He said it almost reverentially, the way a kiss-ass might when discussing J. Edgar Hoover. Houlihan had been named agent in charge by the grace of his juicy lips. A drab, by-the-book man, he lacked the imagination of a good cop but fit perfectly into the mold of Hoover's kind of guy, obedient to the very depths of his shallow soul.

"Fuck you," Hagen said, "I quit."

"I urge you not to act hastily," Houlihan said in the manner of a fifth-grade teacher. "A ninety-day suspension isn't the end of the world."

Hagen noticed that he didn't move his upper lip when he spoke. You couldn't trust a man who didn't move his full mouth.

"I was doing my job," he said. "I got a search warrant based on instinct and scraps of information and I was right. A violent act had been committed in the apartment."

"You acted without departmental authorization. That's in strict violation of the rules. You visited the site without backup. That too is a viol—"

"I'm not interested in the goddamn rules, Houlihan. I'm interested in finding out what the fuck is going on."

"Reconsider your options, Agent Hagen. Take the ninety days."

Hagen closed his eyes in an exaggerated fashion, then reopened them again quickly. "I've considered them," he said, rising and laying his gun and his credentials on the desk. "I still quit."

Then he left the room.

Stafford summoned management to his office. They sat under the lion's head waiting for him to shuffle through papers, watching carefully for any hint of his plans. There was Burns, Stanley Fairchild, Christopher Page, the production chief Joey Morris, the circulation manager Mel Clark, and the *Herald*'s business manager Gloria Seaton. They sat in a semicircle facing Stafford's desk.

As labor negotiator, Page wondered why he had been included. He made no policy. He had nothing to do with distribution. He should have been meeting now with Cliff Hammer, trying to prolong the strike moratorium until they could work out an agreement. He had managed to ward off a walkout now for seven months, but whatever patience Hammer had displayed was rapidly fading. Their sessions, never gentlemanly, were becoming openly hostile. Page had tried many times to convey that to Stafford in strong terms, but each time met with either vagueness or dismissal.

"I'll be brief," Stafford suddenly said, looking up from his papers. "We are ending the outer editions."

It was as though air had suddenly been sucked from the room, leaving a vacuum of silence.

"Which ones?" Clark finally asked.

"All of them," Stafford replied.

Another silence.

"That's eighty thousand home-delivereds." Clark's tone was argumentative.

"We're not depriving them of the *Herald*," Stafford said, his heavy baritone seeming to drop an octave in rebuke. "Cost is involved here." He turned to Gloria Seaton. "Am I correct in assuming the savings would be considerable?"

"I would have to do some calculating, sir, but I would say yes, they would be."

"And the press run?" Stafford asked, turning to Morris.

"It would sure as hell end overtime," the production chief replied. "Those damned presses are ready to fall apart anyhow. Are we still thinking of new equipment?"

Stafford fixed him in a glare. "Would I be shutting down zone editions to save money if I was thinking of spending money?" he demanded.

Morris retreated. "I guess not."

Page understood at last why he was there. "This will mean further staff reductions," he said. It was a statement more than a question. Stafford nodded in response. "Then we're going to drop into a whole new phase in negotiations."

"Then it must be so," Stafford said, turning to Burns. "It will be up to you, Gerald, to so inform the staff."

"If we could just reassign the people to other—"

"No one will be reassigned," the publisher interrupted.

Burns shook his head in disbelief. "You are indiscriminately firing"—he thought for a moment, calculating—"twenty-eight people? Some have worked the zones for twenty-five or thirty years! Belcher in Marin County and Hutchinson in San Mateo are damned near ready to retire!"

Stafford sensed the deep anger in his city editor and made no effort to confront him. He knew Gerald Burns. He knew what the man, if pushed beyond his limits, was capable of. Twice he had simply quit the *Herald* and had to be lured back. The second time it took months. Stafford knew he could not control the staff without Burns.

"It can't be helped," the publisher said into a room that gleamed with tension. "The city is our primary area of circulation and we will concentrate our efforts here rather than in the outer areas. The zones can be covered from the office."

He stood. The others followed, except for Burns, who continued to stare in disbelief. Only when they were gone did the city editor stand, his gaze still locked on an unrelenting Stafford. Neither man spoke. Burns simply shook his head, turned, and walked out.

He crossed to his desk without a word to anyone, though all eyes watched as he took his coat off the back of his chair and headed for the door. They had known about the meeting and now wondered at its portent. Trager began to approach but could see by Burns's expression that now wasn't the time. They had been together a long time and each knew the habits and moments of the other. As the elevator door opened, the city editor came face-to-face with Colfax. For a moment he observed the reporter without speaking and then said, "This was a hell of a paper once, William Colfax. Remember that." And then he was gone.

CHAPTER
FOURTEEN

R osebud Kane left the *Herald* without bothering to attend her own good-bye party, leaving a backroom at the Three-Oh oddly forlorn. Jill, loving a party, had decorated the room with red and white balloons and strings of crepe paper that hung now in lifeless abandonment in the almost empty room. Rosebuds placed on a half dozen tables seemed to wilt even as the remaining group sat drinking the last of the booze bought especially for the party.

"What did she say when you called?" Trager asked.

Colfax shrugged. "To quote her exactly, 'I don't want a fucking party.' "

"Rosebud never was a student of subtlety," Corona McGee said.

"I guess."

"The family's breaking up," Trager said, a note of sadness in his voice.

"And it won't be getting any bigger," Adams added. "They ain't hiring no-*body.*"

Milton Travis took a picture of them sitting there. "I'll send her a copy," he said to no one in particular. "Where's she going?"

"L.A.," Colfax said. "The land of smog and palm trees."

"It's also the land of the *L.A.* fucking *Tribune*," Corona McGee said, "the fattest newspaper in America. That's where the future is, my friends, in the city of fruits and nuts."

"We're in the wrong place at the wrong time," Jill said.

Colfax raised his glass. "Well, anyhow, to Rosebud. . . ."

They joined in hoisting their drinks high.

"And to the wrong place at the wrong time," Trager said.

Milton Travis took another picture. His flashbulb lit the room.

Burns wasted no time in gathering the zone staffs together. In desperate need of a drink, he deliberately avoided having one. It was an element of his personal ethos not to drink when an important moment was at hand. Most of the staffers were waiting for him at the restaurant where he had chosen to break the news. He would buy them drinks and buy them dinner and destroy them. How odd, he told himself, entering the private dining room he had reserved; how perfectly, insanely odd.

These were people he had personally hired, top reporters and editors assigned to the sticks because their talent was needed there. They had agreed to abandon the fast lane at his request for the sake of the paper. They trusted Burns when he told them that someday they would be returned to the city room and rewarded for their efforts beyond the limelight. Now he was about to give them their reward and hand them back their trust.

Burns waited until everyone had a drink before breaking what some already suspected. "You are victims," he said, standing at his table, "of a disaster in the making. The *Herald* is in big trouble. Why it's in trouble is, I know, obvious to all of you. As a result, Stafford has ordered that all of the bureaus in the zones be shut down and the zone sections eliminated."

He let that sink in. During the moment of silence, a woman editor asked, "And that means . . . ?"

"That means we're on our ass," a reporter answered.

Burns sighed deeply. He wondered as he stood before them if the pain he felt would ever be eased. He should have quit. He should have punched Stafford in the mouth and walked out. But then who would tell them? Who would show how sorry he was, how sad, how much he hurt? Who would drink with them during the long night of their funeral?

"I have no choice," he said. "I have to let you go. I've managed an extra two weeks for everyone beyond what you've already got coming. Your severance pay, vacations, that kind of thing. And I've already put out the word here and across the bay that you're available. I'll see that you all get work. The *News* and *Mercury* are champing at the bit to hire you. Consider yourselves lucky in a way. The *Herald* is sinking. You're getting off before it does."

They stared at him. Someone said, "Son of a bitch" under his breath. A woman's quick sob stabbed into the room. A few turned to each other, but most simply observed him in silence. It wasn't just the job. It was the *Herald* they wanted. It was Burns. A sense of place had been abruptly taken from them and for the moment at least there was a drifting quality to their lives.

"I have your envelopes," Burns said. "I'm going to sit here and hand them out as we drink and eat."

"A last supper," a reporter said.

"Sort of, I guess."

"What the hell is going on?" another asked, as though saying it again would clarify, as though saying it again would absolve them of fault.

Burns had downed his drink quickly after the announcement and ordered another round for everyone. "I wish I knew," he said.

Against the immensity of the moment, a woman began to cry. Inside, in his way, Burns cried with her.

Once Rosebud's party ended, Colfax drove Corona McGee to her apartment on Clayton. It was either that or a taxi. Like Trager, she never drove. The Haight-Ashbury had changed since the Summer of Love. The flower children were mostly gone and the streets had turned mean. Drugs had transformed the hippie paradise into an open-air market for dealers. Acid, speed, horse, grass; anything you could swallow, sniff, or shoot into your veins. Gunfire had become common.

"The guitars are all gone," ,was the way Corona put it as she unlocked the double bolts of her apartment. "There's no music anymore, if you know what I mean. Just the strangled sound of a culture going under. A kind of gurgling." She showed Colfax her work, poster art with a San Francisco slant: the bridge and the Ferry Building and Coit Tower and the Embarcadero and the cable cars and even the *Herald*'s old brick building. The strokes were bold and the characters in the paintings surreal floating figures.

"Nothing is real in them," she said by way of explanation, "but then nothing is real in the world, is it? We're all kind of floating through, Colfax. We're puffs of clouds."

They drank brandy as the night lengthened and the music from her stereo played Beethoven. The mood was softly mesmerizing. Corona leaned back and listened and stared at him.

They say dog owners begin looking like their dogs after a while. Colfax wondered as he drove through the night from Corona's place whether people who worked for the same newspaper all began thinking and acting alike after a while. He was getting as crazy as everyone else at the *Herald*. At least he was beginning to drink like everyone else. He had to cut down. He had to cut down now.

He ended up at the *Herald* for no good reason at two A.M. As he did, his head began to clear. The fog was on the outside of him now, drifting slowly across the hills on to Market Street, laying a thin, damp mist over his windshield. The city's lights shimmered in the moisture. He loved these kinds of nights. They embraced his sense of loneliness, allowing him to stand back and observe his own feelings of isolation. Laura and his father were all somehow remote figures now in the drama of his existence. Even Ellen had lost the dreamlike quality he had once attributed to her. Colfax's search for Minelli had become obsessive. As its intensity increased, he saw less and less of Ellen. He wondered if psychologically he had been cowed by Stafford's order to stay away from her. He couldn't decide.

Colfax had difficulty sometimes thinking of himself as real, as though he were a figment of his own imagination, a ribbon of the fog that surrounded him. He wasn't sure whether the feeling had begun before or after Vietnam. War does things that even a warrior can't explain. Damage is done to the soul, creating a vacuum that Colfax was attempting more and more to fill with alcohol.

The city room of the *Herald* was empty. These were the dog days of summer. The town was quiet. It was in the best tradition of newspapering that when a reporter had nothing to do and no place to go in the deepness of night he would come to the paper. Like churches, they were always open. Staffers brought their wives or their lovers or characters they'd befriended wandering the streets. It was home in ways that others could never imagine.

A police reporter named Grover once utilized the city room best by turning it into an after-hours whorehouse. He'd still be in business if Stafford hadn't caught him. The old man came in after opening night at the opera to show friends around, one of them being a U.S. senator. The men wore white ties and tails and the women elaborate gowns that glowed with money and good breeding in the messy but vaguely picturesque environs of the city room.

Grover was using several different offices, including Stafford's, to accommodate the whores and their customers, mostly sailors left over from the war, and always had a guy clean up afterward when he shut down about four A.M. Stafford's group had been at an after-opera party when, in an uncharacteristic flash of generosity, he'd offered to show them around the *Herald*. They arrived just as a naked whore emerged from the office of his secretary, pursued by a drunken and similarly naked seaman whose state of sexual excitement was obvious to all.

"My God!" Stafford had roared and, thus alerted, the place was suddenly full of half-dressed whores and sailors hightailing it toward the exits. The senator, who was a carousing old drunk himself, stayed calm, setting the tone for everyone except Stafford, who was still bellowing with red-faced rage. He made no effort to explain or apologize to anyone, figuring it was beyond any adequate explanation, but fired Grover on the spot and led his party out the door. It was the last tour he ever conducted.

Colfax sat at his desk, looked around at the emptiness for a moment, and then thumbed through papers next to his typewriter. Memos to himself written on half sheets of copy paper were crumpled and dumped into a wastebasket one by one, reminders he no longer needed or no longer cared about. He stopped at the last memo to himself and studied it. It said simply, "Bullets."

The disappearance of the bullet fragments found in Minelli's apartment when it had been sprayed with gunfire nagged at him. Evidence does not simply disappear. The Berkeley Police Department was known for its efficiency and it wasn't likely that the fragments had been either lost or misplaced. The most likely possibility was they'd been stolen. The fact that they'd come from soft-nosed bullet heads used only by Oakland cops further intrigued him. He knew that Korchek was somehow involved. Could that influence have extended to the Berkeley P.D.? Was there a massive police cover-up involved?

The search for Minelli or for his body had left little time for any deep investigation into the Leonard Rose Brigade. Each tip had led nowhere. Each body in the morgue was someone else's. Bloodhounds, rented from a kennel on the Peninsula, turned up a grave on a slope of Mount Diablo, but the remains turned out to be those of a John Doe drifter probably murdered for his wine. Colfax felt his whole effort drowning in hopelessness. But now the possibility that police had murdered Minelli posed staggering implications. They could easily have entered his apartment. He would have answered the pounding of the cops. They could have beaten him into submission and then killed him and disposed of his body in a hundred different ways. Would Stafford have known of this? Was he a part of murder?

Colfax looked unconsciously toward the publisher's door. As he sat staring, he realized more than anything that he had to know. He rose slowly, toying with the unthinkable. Only the muffled sound of Teletype machines in a glass-enclosed section of the city room broke the silence. Colfax looked around to assure himself he was alone. The Bat had gone home hours ago. The security people were downstairs. Then he walked cautiously, a cat on the prowl, toward the door, opened it silently, and stepped inside.

In the semidarkness of Stafford's office, the lion's head seemed even more ominous. The light that shone into the room from the street below threw shadows over the beast, animating its features into a terrible visage. Colfax had to make a physical effort to avoid looking at it, as though to stare would be to acknowledge its dominance in the room and to admit his own guilt at being there. He imagined himself on combat patrol, silently stalking through shadows too deep to penetrate, on a mission too vital to evade.

He opened the office's only filing cabinet, not certain what he was looking for, thumbing through the folders that had been tagged in alphabetical order. Under "Korchek" he found only a parchment of commendation from the chief to Stafford, praising the publisher's patriotic efforts. Under "Minelli" he found only letters from like-minded super-patriots extolling Stafford's editorials and offering to join him on the front lines of defense against the Jews and the Reds in their midst. It was the kind of bullshit Colfax had come to despise, the simmering hatreds of thugs wrapped in flags. He studied each file folder but never got to open any more. A light suddenly snapped on, filling the room with a brilliance so hard and abrupt that he had to blink to focus.

"What are you doing here?"

Ellen's voice was a shot fired into the suddenly illuminated room and Colfax turned to face a woman he had never seen before. This was a different Ellen, no longer sunlit but dark with anger and confusion. He felt trapped by both the woman and the lion's head, a prisoner of his own making, struggling to find a pathway out of his sudden predicament.

"I won't lie to you," he said, trying to sound reassuring but mostly at a loss for anything else to say.

"Why are you going through my father's files?" Her voice was as hard and dangerous as a bayonet.

She had come to the *Herald*, after studying half the night, to find a book left in her father's office. What she found was Colfax. He felt vulnerable and unconvincing as he tried to explain that by searching her father's files he was hoping to find something, anything, that would help him follow Stafford's order to find out what happened to Minelli. It was a rationale created at the moment and lost on Ellen.

The blood of the Staffords ran through her veins and while her femininity could cool its heat, there were times when it boiled. She faced Colfax hands on hips, her anger growing, altering any softness that had existed in their relationship. Colfax sensed the change. What had connected them had been weakening and now was severed, as though the light she had flicked on were a razor that had sliced through the remaining bond between them.

"You could have asked my father," she said.

"He wouldn't have cooperated."

"Then you fucking well find other avenues in your search for information! You had no right to come in here like a common fucking burglar and rifle through the files of the man who has hired you and placed you in a position of importance! He *trusted* you!"

"Look," he said, dropping to a tone of reason, "maybe this was a case of very bad judgment on my part, but your father may be involved in something insidious and dangerous. He thinks he's being a patriot, but—"

She sighed deeply. "Just leave."

There was both sadness and anger in her voice. She closed the file drawer and left the room, not knowing what else to do, leaving behind the heavy atmosphere of her presence. Colfax watched her go, frustrated with himself. He glanced at the lion's head as he turned off the light and said, "Fuck you."

Ellen would remember later, the way one recalls details of awesome events, that she telephoned her father at exactly three A.M. It was a

Thursday. She had watched from her car as Colfax left the building, and had returned to the publisher's office to make the call. She worried at first that it was crazy to be calling him at such an hour, but knew her father would understand. He always understood. She had to talk to him about what had happened tonight, regardless of the consequences to Colfax. He had to know. This was family. She had no choice. The phone rang three times and was answered. For a moment, she thought she had dialed the wrong number. A male voice answered and spoke, but the words were desperate gibberish. The voice rose in anguish, almost a cry, but continued to make no sense.

"Father?"

Again the cry, half muted scream and half moan, faintly like an animal's. Ellen held her breath, listening in fascination as the cry faded and the voice, low and pathetic, a suffering she had never heard before, came on again, still incoherent but modulated, and this time she realized in horror that it was her father.

The ringing of the telephone seemed a remote and muffled jangle, like a bell compressed between pillows. Stafford heard it, rather *sensed* it, in the darkness of his sleep and opened his eyes to a lighter shade of the same darkness. What he could see of his room seemed similarly remote, as though he were somehow detached and viewing it from afar. The ringing stopped and started again, and as he made an effort to sit up a sudden, excruciating pounding in his head pushed him flat on his back again, staring at the mottled patterns of shadow on the ceiling and trying to understand what was happening.

His perception of time had become engulfed in the confusion that was filling his brain. He had no idea how long he had been lying there or how long the telephone had been ringing, only that he was in a world that was not of his making, a dream world whose landscape was shifting into increasingly bizarre shapes. As he leaned on one elbow in another effort to sit up, his right arm collapsed beneath him. With the madness now came terror and Stafford hurled himself out of the bed, collapsing on the floor. As he tried to stand, his legs wouldn't hold him, and it was only with an effort born of panic that he managed to reach the telephone on his nightstand.

He heard a voice and he understood in a remote part of his brain that the voice was Ellen's, but he could make no sense of the words. He shouted into the mouthpiece in a plea for help, but the words were strange and unformed and he could not give voice to his plea. Every effort failed, as though he had suddenly found himself in a place where language simply didn't work. His shouts turned to screams and his screams to moans as he dropped the telephone at last and lay on the floor like a fallen dinosaur until a darkness greater than any he had ever experienced took him even deeper into a new and distorted world.

CHAPTER
FIFTEEN

T hree days later Ellen sat at the foot of her father's bed and studied the lines and needles of the life-support monitors on the wall behind him. It was as though his persona had been altered into a form of robotic machinery and the man lying there, his mouth half open, his eyes shut, no longer represented the person who had raised her. Haggard from worry and lack of sleep, she huddled within herself like an old woman hunched slightly forward in her chair, a tiny figure in a windowless room evenly lit with fluorescence, where there was no night or day.

She had found him unconscious on the floor and at first thought he was dead, so gray was the color of his skin and so shallow his breathing. Now on the VIP level of the U.C. Medical Center, cared for by the finest neurosurgeon available, he seemed no better in skin tone, but the heavy sound of his breathing testified at least to the fact that he was alive. A stroke had sent him reeling into a deep coma from which he might never emerge.

Ellen looked up only slightly when Colfax entered the room. Grateful for his presence, for *anyone's* presence, she was embarrassed by the need to have called him after their confrontation. But, and she realized this with some pain, there was no one else she could think of to call. Her father had no close friends, nor, as she thought about it, did she—no one who had known them all their lives and who could offer the level of comfort necessary in a crisis. So she had telephoned Colfax and only later did she reach Gerald Burns, who had already learned that his boss had been hospitalized. Others would know soon enough in a town where the mighty fell with thunderous explosions of sound.

How Burns got the news was a part of his mystique. He paid no sources and wielded no great amount of political power in the city, but tips and bits of inside information came to him the way they came to no one else. Cops tipped him, asking nothing in return. Ambulance attendants dropped off important patients and hit the phone. Taxi drivers, politicians, fifth-grade teachers, barmaids, cat burglars . . . they were all Burns's people. Trager swore that Mao Tse-tung called Burns before the Chinese entered the Korean War, and Burns never denied it.

Colfax kissed Ellen on the forehead and embraced her with one arm. She made no effort to either respond or resist. "I'm sorry," he said. She nodded. There was no mention of the confrontation in Stafford's office now in the cool enclosure of crisis. Colfax couldn't contain the feeling that he might have caused the stroke.

Moments earlier he had tracked the neurosurgeon into a corner of the physician's lounge where the man rested on an overstuffed chair with a hand over his eyes. His name was Vincent Manning. What Colfax noticed about him first was the size and strength of his hands. A small, trim man, his hands were disproportionate in size to his body. Large and muscular, they belonged to a boxer or a steelworker rather than to a man who could slice with delicate precision into the human brain. The man and the hands, Colfax decided, were the physical equivalent of a prima ballerina with big feet.

Manning had been summoned by the medical center's chief of staff, who had stood by during the entire battery of examinations and tests. This was no ordinary patient who lay inert on the examining table, but a media giant whose condition would be news throughout the country. Cornered by Colfax, Manning made no effort to conceal the condition of his star patient. He had learned all he could about Stafford's medical history and subjected the publisher to a series of tests before determining that a blood clot on the left side of the brain had felled him.

Colfax listened quietly as the surgeon explained how "little strokes" had apparently preceded the massive blockage, accounting for Stafford's erratic behavior in the preceding months. Confusion, visual disturbances, and speech impairment characterized small clots in the long, thin arteries penetrating deep into the brain. This had created a form of dementia which, while allowing Stafford to function, had often clouded his ability to reason and occasionally occluded his very sense of *being*.

Colfax went to Ellen armed with that much information but still not knowing whether or not Stafford would ever recover. Months and maybe even years of therapy would be required to bring him back. It would be up to Ellen now, the only existing relative, to run the *Herald*, and he wondered what this would mean for all of them. Stafford had kept his own private agenda and she would be stepping into secret places of his life from which she had been shielded.

Colfax stayed with her until Burns called him into the office to write the story of Stafford's illness. He touched Ellen on the shoulder. She looked up momentarily and half smiled, acknowledging the hours he had spent with her. Before he left he stood for a moment staring at the body that had once contained Jeremy Lincoln Stafford III and wondered if there was anything inside the shell of him that thought or felt or even for the smallest portion of a second regretted anything at all.

The city room of the *Herald* took the news as one more indication of the newspaper's failing fortune. There was a darkness about it, a helpless assessment of what would happen now and where they would go. Corona McGee called it Limbo Land and others took up the term. They were in a lightless place of no beginning and no ending.

Burns tried to snap them out of it by saying that they, not Stafford, ran the paper and it would go on as usual. There were shootings in Oakland and fatal crashes on the bridge; there was graft at City Hall and the mayor was still fucking a supervisor's wife and maybe her daughter too. Life was going on. But the darkness continued to loom over the *Herald* and seeped out its doors to the Three-Oh.

"Limbo Land," Burns said to Trager in private, "that's exactly where we are."

Colfax found himself drifting, as much in a twilight zone as the others, unable to restart himself. So much had happened in the five years that Colfax had been at the *Herald*. There was a suffocating feeling to the events of those years, a compression that made him yearn for days of nothingness. Sleep was difficult. Screaming nightmares of Vietnam found him bolting upright in bed, his heart throbbing, his body soaked with perspiration. The effect of the dreams often lingered throughout the entire day, leaving him listless and ill at ease.

He took Jill to dinner to relieve the pressure, but it was a joyless night. Rain fell hard over the city's North Beach area, pounding at the windows of a small Italian restaurant off Columbus. It was good to have her with him. She was nonjudgmental and asked for nothing but his presence, offering a silvery ebullience in exchange. Their words disappeared the moment they were said, pieces of nothingness that joined the sound of a lone violin inside and the murmur of rain outside. Still, Colfax failed at first to recognize the figure that had stopped outside the restaurant. The lack of recognition didn't last long. Colfax blinked away the moment and stared in disbelief at the hatless man, his hair matted by the rain, his cigar unlit, who looked directly in at him.

"Son of a bitch," Colfax said aloud, "it's Bruno Hagen!"

"Who is Bruno Hagen?"

"An FBI agent," Colfax said, both annoyed and surprised by his presence outside the restaurant window. The bastard had been following him. "An *ex*-FBI agent, that is."

"What does he want?"

"He wants me."

Colfax waved him off. Undaunted, Hagen entered the restaurant and hovered over their corner table. Reaching down, he took Jill's napkin from her lap without a word and wiped the moisture from his hair and face, then returned the damp napkin to her lap.

"You busy?" he said without preamble.

"Jill," Colfax said, "this is Bruno Hagen. Hagen, this is Jill Carter. Busy? Well, up until now, Hagen, we were enjoying a quiet evening together." Pause. "Together, just the two of us."

"I need a witness," Hagen said, ignoring Jill. "You want to come or not?"

For a moment Colfax said nothing. The violin that played in the background provided a haunting counterpoint to the moment, three people isolated by their involvement, each staring at the others.

Finally he said, "A witness to what?"

"I don't have all night. If you come, you may get something out of it. Have them box your linguine or whatever the hell that is," Hagen said, trying but failing to light the wet cigar in his mouth. He tossed it aside. "This is more important than linguine."

Jill, who had been observing them silently, finally stood. "You guys go play in the rain," she said with resignation. "I'm going home."

Colfax nodded and rose from his chair, conceding that their evening had ended. "I'm really sorry," he said. "I'll make this up to you, I swear." He reached for his wallet. "At least let me pay for a cab."

"I have money." Jill's tone was polite but edgy with disappointment and annoyance. She had expected something better from the evening. She peck-kissed Colfax. "Nice meeting you, Bruno," she said. In a moment, she was gone.

Colfax watched her leave and then turned to Hagen. "Thanks a lot," he said sourly.

"Nice ass," Hagen said.

"You quit the Bureau," Colfax said as they drove across the bridge and into Berkeley, "so why keep screwing around on this case?"

"It's not 'the case' I'm interested in," Hagen said. He was at the

wheel of his old Chevy, its rear seat loaded with newspapers, maga-
zines, and sealed Bureau directives he'd never opened. Traffic whizzed
by on both sides. Hagen stayed solidly in the center lane, as though to
leave it would place their lives in jeopardy. "Leonard Rose was a friend.
I want the son of a bitch that blew him up."

Colfax nodded. "I don't think I've got a job either."

"You get caught fucking the boss's daughter?"

"I got caught by the boss's daughter burglarizing her daddy's office."

"You find anything?"

Colfax shook his head. "I was trying to connect Stafford with
Korchek."

"The Bureau's on to Korchek. He's being watched."

"You know that?"

"Shit yes," Hagen said angrily. "I've still got contacts there. I'll tell
you something else. Your girlfriend's a Communist."

"Ellen?"

"Naw, the other one. The short one."

"Corona McGee? The midget?"

"A dwarf. Midgets are perfectly formed little people. Dwarfs have
disproportionate parts. Her disproportionate parts are the short legs."
Her relit a cigar. "I can't believe you tried to stick a dwarf."

"How is she a Communist?" Colfax asked, amused by the possibility he had been sleeping with an enemy dwarf.

"Her father was Willie McGee, an old-time Bolshevik and union
organizer in the garment industry. He was killed by company cops.
She's a chip off the old block. Worked for the union awhile, joined
some of the pink clubs, then went to work for the *Herald*. You fuck
her?"

"That's none of your business. Where are we going?"

"You'll see."

They pulled up in front of a place off Ashby. The house was small,
almost cottagelike, a square, wood-framed building with vines almost
covering the front. The smell of night-blooming jasmine filled the air,

strands of perfume drifting toward them. The yard was otherwise over-grown with weeds and crabgrass that were threatening to completely engulf a stone walkway that led to the porch.

The front door was locked, but Hagen gave it a little shove and it opened easily, swinging into darkness.

"This is breaking and entering," Colfax whispered.

"Then you ought to be familiar with it," Hagen said.

He felt around on a wall and flicked a switch. Light flooded a small living room packed with a half dozen people, both men and women. Some curled in sleeping bags on the floor, a woman lay naked on a blanket, two men snuggled on a couch too small for them. As the light went on, they reacted in different ways, staring at Colfax and Hagen with the perplexity of proselytes at a visitation. The naked woman made no effort to cover up, the dark triangle of her pubic hair demanding the eye's focus like the centerpiece of an Eisenstadt photograph. The two men on the couch unentangled themselves and sat up.

"Where's Callahan?" Hagen demanded. Colfax glanced at him, finally realizing who they were looking for.

The naked woman pointed to a back door.

"Who are you?" a man in an overstuffed chair asked. Colfax recognized him as the one who had attacked him at the U.C. campus.

"Your worst nightmare," Hagen said, heading toward a back door.

Again, a flick of a switch filled the room with light, but this time the reaction was instant. Callahan bolted up in bed, jolting awake the woman who slept next to him, rolling her off the side of the bed into a startled heap on the floor. In a cot near the door, Callahan's chief lieutenant, Harold Roscoe, dove for a shotgun leaning against a wall but was blocked by Hagen, moving like a cat, who threw him into a corner as easily as a bag of garbage.

"Don't nobody be foolish," Hagen said calmly. He sniffed the air. A heavy odor of rotting food permeated the place. "How can you live in this shit?"

Looking around, Colfax was amazed at the debris littering the bedroom. Bits of half-eaten sandwiches, apples, and a carton of sour milk lay in a corner. It had been the same in the large living room. They had entered from a perfume-scented night into a garbage dump.

"My name is Bruno Hagen and I'm here to talk to Mr. Callahan. I'm FBI. If anyone tries any kind of shit, my partner here is authorized to blow your fucking brains out, which ought not to cause too much of a mess considering who you are."

"What do you want?" Callahan was finally able to say. "My father is—"

"I know who your fucking father is," Hagen said. "This isn't between me and your daddy. It's between you and me. You man enough to handle that, Maxie?"

Callahan said nothing. The woman got up off the floor and crawled back into bed. Roscoe was nursing the place on his head that had slammed into the wall.

"Where is Vito Minelli?" Hagen demanded, staring directly at Callahan.

"How should I know?" Callahan said.

"Because you know." Colfax watched in fascination as Hagen turned a chair around so that the backside was facing Callahan and eased himself into it. He was a cannon being aimed in the direction of his enemy. "You were the last one to see him. You threatened his leadership of that raggedy-ass following he's got. And you've got an ego the size of an elephant's dick. The trouble with you dumb bastards is you don't plan your killings. You blow things up and blow people away and leave a trail of shit behind you aren't even aware of. You bury him somewhere? You burn him up?" He leaned closer and in a voice of mock incredulity whispered, "Jesus Christ, you didn't eat him? Is that him?"

He suddenly rose, thrust the chair aside with a loud bang, and dumped the contents of a paper bag on the floor. Beer bottles and molding slices of pizza fell out, entangled with a bra. Hagen held the bra up with the tips of his fingers, shook his head, and dropped it again.

"I don't understand women burning their bras," he said. "Do

you?" He looked toward Colfax, who offered a noncommittal shrug. Then suddenly, abruptly, like the lightning strike of a cobra, he turned to Callahan and in a voice that rattled windows bellowed, *"Where in the fuck is Vito Minelli?"*

The search for Vito Minelli grew colder as the days passed. Hagen remained convinced that Callahan had something to do with it, but as impressive as Hagen's performance had been that night at Callahan's pad, nothing had come of it. Six months passed. The team Colfax had formed was at a standstill. He asked Barry Adams, whom he suspected of having ties to the radical Weather Underground, to join.

The black reporter responded with a tight laugh. "You want *me* to join in helping you and the FB-fucking-I find some honky's bones to ease Stafford's rotting conscience? You got the wrong nigger, Colfax."

"A nigger isn't what I want," Colfax replied evenly. "A reporter is what I need, a pro who may know more about the radical movement than he's saying." Adams began speaking, but Colfax interrupted him. "And I don't like the word nigger. So I want you to do this, Barry. I want you to stand there and say it to me a hundred times: nigger, nigger, nigger. When you've said it that many times right into my face, then you won't be so tempted to use it in the future. Because if you do, trust me on this, I'm going to break your flat, black fucking nose."

Colfax smiled pleasantly in conclusion and waited. Adams stared at him, trying to figure out if this was real or a put-on. Then he burst into laughter.

"I haven't heard such honest talk from a white man in all my life!" he finally said, slapping Colfax on the shoulder. "Okay, no more nigger talk, but I still ain't joining your team, man. My interest is the black movement, not body-hunting, and I'm gonna concentrate on that. We've ignored it too long, baby, and as long as I'm still stringing words for the pig press, I'm gonna string 'em for us"—he paused—"black folks."

As he turned to leave, he paused once more. "You're a decent guy, Colfax. You're just like Trager said, in the wrong place at the wrong time. Leave. This motherfucking place is doomed."

Colfax assigned Jill to follow Korchek. It was her life's ambition to be a reporter and Ellen only shrugged when Colfax told her what he was doing. The distance between Colfax and Ellen had grown greater. Their relationship was proper but unheated. His feeling of uneasiness persisted and he cursed himself for ever having gotten involved with her.

"He's a fag," Jill told Colfax one evening at the Three-Oh. She had been watching and following Korchek for a month. "He's humping his chauffeur, some pretty guy named Jason Blackwell, another cop."

"You sure of that?" Colfax said, surprised.

"Well, I never saw him actually mount the guy, but I saw the way they looked at each other. And one night I tail pretty Jason and he goes to a place called the Dirty Cat, a queer joint in Polk Gulch, and I see him dancing with some guy in leather."

"Keep after him," Colfax had instructed her. "You're doing good."

A profile of rejection was emerging around the Oakland police chief. Looking into his past, Colfax had found him to be a posturing rabble-rouser at a small city college in Fresno but not on behalf of anything remotely liberal. While he wore no swastikas, some suggested that Korchek was about as close to being a Nazi as anyone could imagine. But shorn of the emotional uniform he wore, he ceased to exist. Awkward at sports and a failure with women, his ultimate rejection came from the military. An irregular heartbeat made him 4-F in the draft and left him hopelessly adrift until he joined the Oakland Police Department. Being a cop was as close as he could come to establishing any kind of military manhood.

The chief was in an eternal quest to prove his machismo and holding physical sway over others was one way to achieve that goal. His brutality was legendary when he was a street cop and later when he took over the Oakland department. Colfax knew that men who lacked confidence in their masculinity were drawn to guns and violence, the way short guys bellow to establish a presence. He had seen them in the Corps, the crazies who weren't satisfied with the innate cruelties of war but had to sate themselves with up-close rifle-butt clubbings of unarmed enemy soldiers who had the misfortune to fall in their paths.

Colfax observed Korchek later at a luncheon honoring the mayor in Oakland and studied him closely. His mannerism revealed no hint of homosexuality, only the stiff, unyielding portrait of a man who would never bend and who would show no mercy.

Ellen Stafford sat under the ominous lion's head and waited. The room had always provided comfort when she was little. She remembered bouncing on the large overstuffed chair and chiding the lion's head to stop looking at her. She remembered her mother swinging her around and her father's gruff voice admonishing them that this was an office, not a play yard, but secretly enjoying their presence in the solemnity of the place. There had been warmth to the office back then. Now Ellen found herself in a place where she had never intended to be and the once-powerful warship she suddenly found herself captaining was foundering.

The *Herald*'s negotiator was meeting at that moment with Cliff Hammer in a final effort to avoid a strike. Hammer had made clear that unless the *Herald* agreed to each and every one of the Guild's demands, he would shut the newspaper down. Ellen thought he might forgo a walkout in view of her father's stroke, but Christopher Page quickly dispelled that notion. Hammer was not one to feel sympathy for a stricken publisher. Illness was only another weakness to be exploited on behalf of his union. He shed no tears for the cocksuckers that composed management's otherwise formidable army.

Ellen knew that her father would never agree to the Guild's demands and she, as his surrogate, felt compelled to carry out his wishes. It was a difficult time. If she concentrated on it, Ellen could see her life slipping away. Her father was locked in a body that no longer worked, the *Herald*'s circulation was falling daily, and the man she thought she loved had moved out of reach. There was within her a tendency to run, as she had run from danger as a child, but she knew now that childhood's options were no longer the options of the woman who sat beneath the lion's head and waited for the telephone to ring and for Page to call. She waited for someone to shield her from the terror she was facing.

Colfax arrived in Miami in the afternoon. Heat and humidity hit him in the face like the overheated air of a Swedish sauna the moment he stepped from the door of the plane. By the time he entered the terminal's air-conditioned environment his whole body was drenched. How could anyone live in this? he wondered. He longed for the cool fog of San Francisco as he stepped out the terminal's front door and hailed a cab. It took him to an apartment in the city's grade-three section, far below the luxury enjoyed by the rich Jews who retired there, but above the poor who lived on small pensions in the clustered ghettos of the south side.

Under normal circumstances, his first trip east would have been to New York to accept the Pulitzer, but he'd decided not to go. Somehow, in view of the *Herald*'s misfortunes, the prize had diminished in importance. The newspaper was the butt of everyone's joke and the derision of those who, once supporters, had drifted away like Corona McGee's floating figures. The disappearance of Minelli, against whom Stafford's editorials had raged, seemed to sound a funeral toll for what had been a proud newspaper. But Colfax persisted in his mission to find the missing rebel, a search that was both a distraction from the *Herald*'s woes and a personal obsession. That obsession grew both from Stafford's challenge and from his own need to conclude a relationship with Minelli that had grown close.

A break came when the rebel's sometime girlfriend, Tillie Something, called him. She did care about Minelli, she told Colfax, and she did want him to be found. Toward that end she offered the fact that Minelli had often mentioned a family in Miami Beach. A mother. The information led Colfax to Vera Epstein.

She was a small, slightly hunched woman who bore her years

with difficulty. Her life seemed wrapped in disappointment. She had hoped her son Jules would be a lawyer, but he had scorned the very idea and gone the way of a troublemaker. She had counted on the company of her husband into their old age and he had died of a sudden heart attack only six months after an early retirement.

"One minute he was there," she said to Colfax in the living room of her apartment, "and the next minute he was gone." She snapped her fingers to illustrate how quickly it had occurred.

She occupied a tiny studio apartment on the second floor of an aging building. Efforts had been made to keep it up, but nothing could hide the effects of age and harsh weather on its wooden exterior. Photographs filled the living room, on shelves, atop a small television set with a rabbit-ears antenna, on a windowsill, and even on the floor in a corner. One was a picture of Minelli at about ten, his hair neatly cut and parted on the left, smiling uncertainly for the camera.

Colfax had tracked her down through voting registration records. It had not been difficult once he knew where to begin. She lived alone in a building that seemed to overflow with old ladies just getting by. He had paid for the trip himself. To ask the *Herald* to finance it would have been out of the question. He took a week's vacation and headed east in an effort to find the man that the whole country knew as the missing Vito Minelli. He could have phoned, but disembodied voices, as Burns called them, were never as real as a face-to-face meeting. His quest had become personal by now. Plane fare was a small price to pay for the satisfaction he might receive.

"I don't know where he is, as God is my witness," Vera Epstein said, as she brought them coffee from a kitchenette. The chair Colfax sat in was worn, its cushion sinking deep into itself, forcing him lower than what he would have preferred. Doilies crocheted by Vera helped cover some of the furniture's wear, but not all of it.

"I never thought I would live this way," she said, drinking her coffee. "We had such a nice home. Did Jules ever tell you about our home? No? Well, he's a funny boy. The trouble began when he was, what, thirteen? After his brother Jacob passed on."

"I didn't know he had a brother."

"Such a good boy Jacob was. Jules was so jealous of him. Envious is the word."

"What did Jacob die of?"

"It was cancer. So terrible. Such a bright boy, Mr. Colfax. Jules felt guilty because he thought he killed him with hatred. Maybe that's when the trouble started."

"What trouble was that?"

Colfax had tried to coax her to the point of Minelli's disappearance but had discovered earlier in their conversation that she would not be rushed. He could see in her where Minelli had inherited his single-mindedness. Projecting Minelli into the future, he would even look like his mother someday . . . if he was still alive.

"Why are you asking me questions? The television says he's probably dead. My son is dead."

"I'm not sure he is."

"You're not sure, they're not sure, nobody's sure."

For a moment they drank their coffee in silence. A hot wind blew in gusts through an open window, moving the worn lace curtains that otherwise hung limp.

"This is hurricane weather," Vera said. "The devil is breathing into this godforsaken place."

"What was Vito . . . Jules's trouble you were talking about?"

"He never told you?"

Colfax shook his head no.

"He was crazy. All that dope made him sick in the head. Up until then he was my darling. Then he turned on us. I found him one night standing by our bed looking down at us. His eyes were crazy. I screamed and he ran. Right out the door. Down the street. The police found him two weeks later naked at the zoo! He thought he was a monkey or something, I don't know. . . ."

Colfax listened as she told about years of psychiatrists and periods of incarceration for her son. Three times they had to have him placed in a mental home because of his erratic behavior. They were afraid he would kill them. This was a Minelli Colfax hadn't known, the part of him kept locked away in the dark corners. But this much he did know: Minelli was good at disappearing. He had run from his parents, from his friends, from a parole office, and now from a revolution. Where would he show up next? Colfax wondered. In a shallow grave somewhere or with a new name in the middle of another uprising?

Ellen was waiting in a private lounge of the hospital when Colfax arrived. It was a room reserved for VIPs, complete with a small bar, a refrigerator, and hot coffee. Heavy leather couches and chairs made the room seem smaller and closer than it was. A dark maroon wallpaper added to the cloistered effect.

Colfax was surprised to see she was smoking. She frowned as she inhaled and squinted at the smoke that curled up from the cigarette toward her eyes. It was a habit acquired under tension and she was awkward at it. Colfax couldn't help thinking of Sally Bell as he watched her blow the smoke out hard to avoid inhaling. He thought about Sally the way he thought about the men he knew in Vietnam, as players in a drama that lacked any kind of reality. The memory, once clear, was fading.

"How's your father?"

"He's doing okay, I guess." She paused, searching for words. Then, abruptly: "I want you to forget about Minelli. We're not running this." As she said it, she held up Colfax's interview with Vera Epstein. The words whistled past Colfax's ear. She allowed no time for response. "I need you more in the city room than out in the field looking for someone who is probably dead. It's history. Forget it."

He spoke softly but firmly. "No way." The response was instinctive.

"What?"

"I'm not going to just let it go. Spike the interview. That's your perogative. But I'm not giving up on the search. If I have to, I'll do it on my own time." He leaned forward. "This isn't just a family thing, Ellen. This is newspapering in its best sense. I may be a beginner here, but I know what matters."

Ellen sat staring at him through tendrils of smoke that drifted toward the ceiling, uncertain how to respond.

"Let me tell you what I think," Colfax said, breaking the silence. "Minelli may have just taken off, true. But the fact remains his place was shot up by guns that may have been fired by cops. That means that maybe, just maybe, some of those right-wing nuts could have done him in and buried him somewhere. They're crazy and possibly violent men who consider themselves super-patriots and hate anyone they think is threatening their beliefs. Your father's editorials were filled with the kind of crap they espouse and were an embarrassment to anyone in his right mind. I won't be a part of that. I'm done with it."

Ellen crushed out her cigarette in an ashtray that perfectly matched the decor of the room.

"My father," she said, swallowing hard, "feels that the students are undermining the efforts of our men in Vietnam. You know what's going on here and you know what's going on there!"

"Yes," Colfax said, "I do."

She waited for him to say more and when it became obvious that he wasn't going to, she said, "I don't feel that the Minelli story continues to be relevant. The protests go on without him. Keep searching if you must, but I'm still killing the interview and there will be no more stories until and unless he's found. I'm tired of the whole damned thing."

Her voice was tired, her face tense. Colfax's tendency was to somehow comfort her, but she was his boss now, the publisher, and he was a reporter. Reporters didn't comfort publishers.

"Circulation is down to two hundred twelve thousand," she said suddenly. She looked deeply into his eyes, never blinking, her expression filled with weariness and realization. "We're dying."

Colfax left her with those words filling his head. *We're dying.* Was it possible that the newspaper he had longed to join was nearing the end of its century-long reign? He tried putting the notion into perspective as he rode an elevator upstairs to Stafford's room. It was a visit he had to make, reluctant homage to the architect of the *Herald*'s troubles. The memory of Ellen's words deepened and lodged itself firmly in his brain.

Stafford sat in a wheelchair, his eyes open and locked in a stare that penetrated the hospital wall. There was a kind of helplessness in them, a desperation borne of the absolute inability to move or react. The expression on his face was a scowl etched deeply into the lines of his grimace. It was the life he had lived permanently imprinted on his last conscious response, desperation combined with rage.

Seeing him that way made Colfax uneasy. He had heard that people in comas could hear even though they couldn't respond. Alone now with the man who had once determined his destiny, he felt he ought to say something but didn't know what. The attending nurse had left to give them time to visit. He was alone with the old man.

Colfax slumped in a chair facing Stafford. "What can I say? I'm sorry you're here. I'm sorry for what's happened to you and the *Herald*."

He stopped himself. It was no time to preach. Uncomfortable, he stood up and moved to a window of the room Stafford now occupied. As he did, he thought he saw Stafford's eyes shift in his direction. Colfax stopped cold and stared at his stricken publisher.

"You're in there," he said in a voice that was almost a whisper. "You know I'm here. You understand."

He moved again. Stafford's gaze followed him, his expression unchanged.

"What remains of you?" Colfax asked without thinking, not even sure himself what he meant. "Is conscious thought in there or only instinct? Do you know what's going on? If there's a spark left . . ."

He moved again. The eyes followed. Again and again the eyes followed.

"Son of a bitch," Colfax said. It was an exclamation, not a curse. He sat again in the chair facing Stafford. "Can you blink your eyes?" He waited, staring at the publisher's face. Nothing happened. "I guess—" As he was about to continue, the eyes blinked.

Colfax realized now that he was being heard. Communication had been established. The facial expression of the man was unchanging, a scowl as deep as a death. The pain and frustration remained in his eyes, fixed there from the moment the stroke had slammed him to the ground like a child's toy, but at least he could use his eyelids. The irony was implicit. A man who had once communicated through the pages of a mighty newspaper now reduced to blinking.

"Do you know what's happening to you? Blink once for yes, twice for no."

The eyes blinked once. The silence in the room was heavy, broken only by distant voices and padded footsteps in the corridor outside the door. Colfax lowered his voice to fit the mood.

"You know that Ellen has taken over the publisher's desk."

The eyes blinked twice.

"The job may be too big for her."

Once.

"The *Herald*'s position is tenuous. You helped make it that way."

Once.

"And now your daughter inherits that mess."

Once.

"I never could get the point of it all. I mean, taking on the kids, sneaking that Jew-baiting shit into those editorials . . . what was it all about?"

No response.

"If it was a circulation gimmick . . ."

The eyes blinked frantically.

"Patriotism."

Once.

"You hooked up with the wrong patriots, Mr. Stafford."

Once. That surprised Colfax.

"You knew that?"

A moment passed, then Stafford blinked once.

Colfax nodded and then stood. The eyes followed. "This has probably gone on long enough. Rest." He pressed a bell for the nurse. "I'll tell Ellen about this . . . the eye-blinking business. Maybe you can help her. I don't know. You can't even help yourself." As he turned, he hesitated and looked back at Stafford, the shell that had once glowed with power, now cast in a light as dull as his spirit. "And you sure as hell can't help the *Herald*."

Colfax left the room as the nurse entered. Neither of them saw the eyes, filling with tears, blink once.

CHAPTER
SIXTEEN

The meeting room above the Three-Oh was jammed. Doors and windows had been opened to allow circulation, but the temperature inside remained oppressively warm. A heat wave dripping with humidity lay like a bathwater over the city and lingered long after the sun had disappeared from the sky. A single large fan on a table at the far end of the room did little to ease the stuffiness, adding only a background whir to the proceedings. Shirtsleeves abounded. Women fanned themselves with folded newspapers. It was a scene from the Scopes trial.

Cliff Hammer had called the meeting. For twenty minutes he monologued in the flat, heated rhetoric of an orator, filling the wet air with invective. The cocksuckers wanted an endless moratorium. The cocksuckers weren't negotiating in good faith. The cocksuckers were trying to screw them. He wanted a vote. He wanted them to hit the bricks. He wanted a strike until the cocksuckers came around. The reaction was a roar of approval. The feeling in the room was tumultuous. What village unity still existed at the *Herald* now excluded the newspaper's management.

Colfax waited until the roar had died down before speaking. With Sally Bell gone, he was now the sole leader of the Guild at the *Herald*. He allowed the silence to build and the energy to drain from Hammer's rabble-rousing, then said in a tone meant to convey finality, "If we shut the *Herald* down now, that could be the end of it."

"Bullshit!" Hammer shouted. "The cocksuckers have strike insurance! They'll—"

"No!" Colfax's exclamation shot through the interruption. "I've checked on this. There is no strike insurance. With a company union there was never a need for it. A strike was impossible. Would other publishers rush to the aid of the *Herald*? That's unlikely. Stafford has alienated them all. We're alone."

Hammer glared and fidgeted, angry at the younger man's effort to diffuse his own rhetoric. No one challenged the Hammer. No one undercut him. *He* led the Guild, not some goddamn kid with a Pulitzer up his ass.

"What we have left," Colfax continued, "is a newspaper on its last legs without a real publisher. Stafford is reduced to communicating by blinking. That may never change."

"The cocksucker never could communicate," Hammer said, his voice growing drier and somehow deadlier.

Colfax tried to ignore the comment and the muted laughter that followed. He wanted to shut Hammer up but realized that to make his point he had to suffer the mockery. Still, a different kind of heat was rising in him, far deeper than rage, and more profound than simple annoyance.

"Circulation is down almost to two hundred thousand," he said, struggling for control. "Advertising has dropped forty percent. Look at it." He held a copy of the *Herald* in the air. "Has anyone here ever seen it this thin?" He looked around the room directly at individual faces. "Trager? McGee? Travis?" No one answered. "This is not a healthy newspaper."

"What're you saying?" Trager asked.

"I'm saying we've got a dying product owned by a dying publisher and run by a young woman who's trying to hold it all together. If the *Herald* goes down, so do we. Maybe it's time to demonstrate a little self-serving compassion."

"What compassion did the *Herald* show when they canned my ass?"

The question came from in back of the room. Colin Stern, who had been the newspaper's book critic, stood, still regal in his bearing, anger and desperation lacing his tone. Fired by Stafford, he had been unable to find another newspaper job and was reduced to managing a small bookstore off Market Street. Shouting was uncharacteristic of the man, who had always spoken in modulated tones. But now he reflected the rage in the room that had been fueled by uncertainty and ignited by Hammer.

"Strike." The single word was said by a woman from a suburban beat that had been eliminated.

"Strike." Another suburban reporter given the word by Burns said it next.

"Strike." Barry Adams repeated it.

Colfax held up his hand for silence. "I'm not saying any kind of strike moratorium ought to last forever. It would be temporary. I mean, Jesus, the man has had a stroke and a woman who knows damned little about newspapers is running the shop!"

Hammer had been leaning against the wall, waiting, like an old lion on the hidden edge of a watering hole. Now he pushed forward and faced Colfax, standing only a few feet away.

"I say your judgment is clouded by your hard-on." Hammer's words lay heavy in a room suddenly absolutely silent. The whir of the fan seemed ominous. "If you weren't fucking the publisher's daughter, would you feel the same way?" He turned to the room and roared, *"Strike!"* with all of the energy he possessed, thrusting his large head forward, the muscles of his neck straining, the vein down the center of his forehead bulging. But before the last sound of the word had rocketed into the room, Colfax's fist was flying through the air. It caught Hammer on the side of his face and sent him crashing back against the wall. He sat on the floor, stunned and hurting.

It was a move that had nothing to do with the logic Colfax had been attempting to bring to the meeting. His response had been instinctive, the heat in him rising with volcanic speed and exploding to the surface. It was a reaction to noise in the jungle behind him, a blast of gunfire at a shadow in the darkness, something moving just beyond his vision. He stood motionless for a moment looking down at Hammer, frozen in the posture of his attack, momentarily confused by his own violence. No one in the room spoke until Trager half whispered, "Jesus."

It broke the silence and allowed Colfax to focus on the man he had just knocked down with one lightning blow. Hammer had pushed himself up to a sitting position and was using a handkerchief to stem the flow of blood from cuts around his mouth. Danny Doe had been standing in the nearby doorway and rushed forward to help the Guild leader to his feet and now others were joining him, glancing at Colfax to see what he might do next.

Colfax sighed deeply. He knew an apology would make little difference and made no effort to offer one. Both men simply observed one another. They were a still life on canvas, boxers between rounds staring across the ring, sizing each other up, both afraid and anticipatory. Colfax was more afraid of himself than he was of Hammer. He couldn't explain his action. A darkness had powered his rage.

Oddly, Hammer spoke the first words. "I shouldn't have said that." He turned to the room. "Our fight isn't with each other. I was an asshole to make that comment. Disagreeing points of view are okay." He paused, holding his jaw. "I prefer them to being knocked on my ass."

Laughter broke the immediate tension, but it was too late.

"I've said and done more than I ever intended," Colfax said, his voice unsteady. "I can't be an effective leader of this unit any-more."

He pushed his way through the crowd, hurried downstairs, and left the building. The evening embraced him with the dampness of a monsoon season, wet and hot and depressing. Miami gone west. Even breathing was uncomfortable. He carried his jacket thrown over one shoulder, but parts of his shirt stuck to the sweat on his chest and back, creating splotches of moisture. He walked slowly down the block toward his car, the senses that had tingled with combat giving way to a great emptiness. He felt isolated and alone, realizing suddenly that the feeling wasn't new. Hadn't he always felt that way? As a kid he'd wandered alone through the woods, as a Marine he'd stood apart from his platoon, as a lover he was often remote and uninvolved. Laura always sensed that. "Where's your mind, Bill?" she'd ask. "Where you hiding?"

Colfax walked through the damp twilight in a daze, only vaguely aware of those who passed him. He knew that his action upstairs had severed the camaraderie he felt toward the *Herald*'s staff and theirs toward him. No one had envied his position and most had known of his relationship with Ellen, but nothing had ever been said until now. They managed to drink together and work together and support each other, because that was the nature of this family, this tribe, clustering for comfort in a world that was turning increasingly strange. But his violence had instantly separated him from them, leaving him to wonder where he belonged.

Footsteps hurried up behind him. Colfax turned, half crouched, wary. It was Cliff Hammer. "I want to explain something," he said.

"You don't have to, okay? I was out of line."

"I'm not talking about that. I've been punched in the mouth before. It's no big deal."

"It is to me," Colfax said.

"I'm still going to explain. I'm not a guy without compassion. I know the Staffords and the *Herald* are going through shit. My old man was like a fucking carrot for three years from a stroke. I loved him like I've never loved anything in my life. I sympathize with Stafford's daughter. And I don't want the *Herald* to go down. But we're not in this alone. We're in it for every fucking Guild member across the country. Publishers are out to break the unions and we're not going to let them do that here."

"So you take the *Herald* down as a symbol." Colfax shook his head. "Except that the symbol is a real thing, you know? The newspaper is real, the jobs are real, the people are real. I can't see doing that just to make a point."

"We've got no choice."

"Then you'll do it without me," Colfax said.

He hurried ahead of Hammer, who stood watching him unlock the door of his car. "We've got no choice!" Hammer shouted again across the widening distance that separated them. He was still standing there as Colfax drove away.

Colfax wandered for a while, then stopped at a dive called Hop's where the *Daily News* people gathered. It was darker than any bar he'd been in and for a moment Colfax stood beside the doorway, adjusting his vision. He saw faces he recognized but ignored them, making his way to a corner stool at the bar. Still looking around, he spotted Gwen Ballard. Her back was to him. She had one leg arched over the leg of the *Daily News* reporter Kaminsky and was purring in his ear like a cat in heat. Colfax could see from his angle that she was also back to miniskirts that half bared her ass.

Was this the same woman he had seen before? The changed woman who had given up the game of playing at sex and settled down into being a whole, normal human being? The transformation had been startling then and it was startling now to see it reversed. Was anything ever permanent anymore? She had twisted slightly in her chair to put her hand on Kaminsky's thigh when she saw Colfax sitting alone at the bar watching. Her expression, a drunken leer, faded as recognition filled her eyes. She pulled back from Kaminsky and unhooked her leg from his. Then she rose and walked, almost slithered, toward Colfax. He sipped his scotch and watched her, more intrigued by the transformation than by the image she was selling.

"Hello, big boy," she said in an exaggerated Mae West slur.

"Gwen."

"Why are you here?"

Colfax shrugged. "Why not?"

Kaminsky, turning to find Gwen, saw Colfax. He rose unsteadily. An evening of drinking had left him shaky.

"Go away," Gwen said to him.

"I just want to say congratulations to m'old friend," Kaminsky said.

"I'm not your old friend," Colfax said. "Congratulations for what?"

"Well, first for kicking the shit out of the Cocksucker King and second for talking them out of a strike."

"How the hell do you know that?"

"Hey, shit, I'm a newspaper reporter!"

"They voted not to strike?"

"Yup."

With that, Kaminsky suddenly lurched forward and fell to the floor.

"You're a newspaper reporter, all right," Colfax said.

"Trager called him," Gwen said, looking down in disgust at the man she'd been fondling a moment before. "They're drinking buddies."

If it was true that the *Herald*'s Guild unit had voted down a strike, it had been a quick vote, probably after Hammer had left. What had swung them? Colfax suspected it had been Hammer's verbal attack on him. For all of his power to persuade, the Guild leader was still an outsider. Colfax was one of them. Hammer wasn't. That was the difference. Maybe even punching him in the face helped. Colfax finished his scotch in one swallow and pushed away from the bar, standing.

"I've got to go," he said, scooping up his jacket.

"You wouldn't like to drop me off, would you?" Gwen said. There was a drunken lisp to her voice. The leer, muted slightly, remained. It was obvious. She was obvious.

Colfax studied her. "No," he said. He left her standing, only half realizing what was going on. Then he stopped at the door and turned to face her. "Who are you?" he asked. He didn't wait for an answer.

Summer became autumn and in the suburbs surrounding the city the leaves of the liquid AMBAR trees were turning to shades of red and gold. It was 1973. There was a feel of ice to the wind that blew through the Golden Gate. Fog penetrated the heaviest jacket, chilling the bones.

Colfax studied the war news with greater intensity. It was winding down. He wondered who of those he had known in combat remained alive. Who would come home when the fighting stopped and the blood ceased to flow? Weiland? Nunn? Mamarill? Henry Kissinger called it an age of trouble and triumph. Americans planting a flag on the moon and dying in the jungles of Asia.

The *Herald* clung to a precipitous existence. Ellen remained in the publisher's office, her father confined to a wheelchair, watched over by twenty-four-hour nursing, limiting to blinking his responses to any questions anyone had. Gerald Burns ran the paper from the city desk. Circulation continued to drop despite all they could do. By November, it was down to 186,000 and advertisers continued to desert like frightened children in the face of a mad dog. The mad dog now was Maxwell Callahan, who at first had marshaled Minelli's forces into bigger and better-organized antiwar marches and had turned the boycott against the *Herald* into a a loud and effective consumer weapon. Callahan mounted his campaign even though no front-page Stafford editorials plagued the radicals. But without them, the noise of the protest lacked passion. Unlike Minelli, whose oratory burned with visions of a political utopia, Callahan was without fire. The crowd sensed that and their numbers dwindled.

Rumors abounded that the *Herald* was up for sale. Strangers in suits were seen walking through the city room and downstairs through the composing and press rooms. A business reporter swore that one of them was from a firm that brokered the sale of print media. The *Daily News* carried a story that Ellen was in secret negotiations with the Hearst chain. She denied it; no one from Hearst would comment. "The *Herald* is not for sale and never will be," she said. "We are working hard to reverse a temporary decline."

Radio and television commercials extolling the newspaper's history and reliability were weak and discordant. Nothing worked. They were not the rousing songs of a growing newspaper but the dirges of a failing one. In between chronicling the campus protests, most of which were now led by Callahan, Colfax continued a lessening search for Minelli. Ellen had relented. At one point, he even convinced her to publish an editorial, which he wrote, urging those with information regarding the missing radical to come forward. No one did. As often as possible he wrote of the search for Minelli, hoping that by keeping the story alive those involved in Minelli's disappearance would know that the search was continuing. To Colfax, that meant there was still hope for a successful conclusion. To Ellen it was a way of brushing off the lingering accusation that the *Herald* had been responsible for whatever had happened to him.

Gerald Burns invited Colfax over one night. No one had ever visited the city editor at his home, a sprawling ranch-style place down the Peninsula near Stanford. Colfax was surprised at the state of disrepair the house was in. Its wood siding needed treatment, its porch railings replacement. Where there had been a lawn, there were weeds. A fence was half down. It played against the tidy nature of Burns, the scrubbed look he presented at the *Herald.* His wife Helen left them alone. Colfax was certain she'd been drinking.

What Burns wanted was never made clear. They drank on a back porch that overlooked a heavily brushed hillside. Red-barked manzanita grew in thick clumps on the steep slope. Scrub oaks struggled for life against overwhelming odds. Fire had once raced up the hill toward the house, but a water-dropping helicopter clattering in low over the flames had stopped them.

"It was like watching hell coming at you," Burns said, staring down toward the homes below. "You ever see hell?" He seemed remote, almost distant. "In Vietnam."

Colfax thought about it. Memories of explosions ran through his mind, one segueing into the other. If he listened, he could hear their roar.

"Yeah. I suppose."

Burns nodded. "That paper is going through hell," he said, pouring them another drink, "whimpering away its life. It's a damned shame, William Colfax. Did you know that the American Publishers' Association once voted us the best medium-sized daily in America? I'd show you the plaque, but it's buried somewhere under a lot of crap. We're all buried somewhere under crap."

They watched the day fade and the darkness come, never reaching a point in their conversation. As he thought about it later, Colfax decided Burns simply wanted him to know that there had been greatness once at the *Herald*. It had not always been this way. But Colfax already knew that. It was why he was there, why the desire to get there had always been a part of his most elemental ambitions. And now he had become a part of its tailspin. Colfax brooded about it as he drove home and fell, fully clothed and half drunk, onto his bed. Burns stayed on the porch half the night, looking out toward the blackness and remembering.

Colfax found Strickland a week later living like a hermit in the mountains northeast of Sacramento. He had built a shelter on land owned for 120 years by his father's family. No one thought to look there until Colfax, nosing into the family background, came up with it through county records and hiked up to the open space in a forest where Strickland was camping out. It wasn't a terrific find, he guessed, since Strickland was still talking to God and wasn't a lot of help when it came to Minelli's disappearance. In fact, he knew damned little about him. But Colfax, who had learned how to squeeze words from a carrot, worked Strickland until he'd gotten everything he could and then turned him over to an elated Hagen. The FBI agent was still on suspension and almost gloated as he marched Strickland past a row of television cameras up the stairs of the Federal Building. He couldn't arrest Strickland, but he could sure as hell take him in.

The *Herald* had an exclusive and it was sweet. The first edition hit the streets with a seventy-two-point head that screamed, KILLER BOMB SUSPECT ARRESTED! The old guy who sold papers at the corner screamed, "*Wuxtry, Wuxtry!*" until he was hoarse. It was a sound Colfax had come to love when one of his stories was involved, like an announcement from the stage singing his praise. The banner wasn't one he'd preferred, but the choice wasn't his. Ellen, beginning to reflect her father's emotional bombast, had written it herself. Colfax shrugged it off. It was mattering less these days. The story ran ten inches on the front page and twenty inches after the jump. Hagen got credit, a spit in the face of the Bureau that had suspended him, and Colfax kept the rest for himself. By now, the city was expecting the unexpected from him. A Colfax story was not to be missed even in the fading days of the *Herald*. His prose had toughened under fire but continued to soar with a lyrical cadence that set him apart.

"Excellent," was all Burns said after editing his piece, but that was tantamount to dancing naked on his desk and screaming hallelujah. Burns rarely praised.

"I've never heard him say 'excellent' before," Trager said later. "I remember him saying 'good' in '52 when a guy named Sackett caught a wife-killer and wrote about it, and 'very good' '64 when Rosebud did some stuff out of 'Nam, but never 'excellent.' "

Up for seventy-two hours and too weary to really care, Colfax headed for the back door. He didn't get far. Jill caught up with him, pushed him aside where no one could hear, and said, "The fruitcake's willing to talk."

It sailed over Colfax's tired head. "Who?"

"The queer. Jason Blackwell. *Korchek's driver, for Christ's sake!*"

Now he understood. "He'll talk to me?"

"He'll spill his guts!"

Colfax was enthusiastic in spite of himself. "How in the hell did you manage that? If the guy's queer, you couldn't have slept with him."

"No, I did. I mean, yes, I did. He's bi. A switch-hitter. Not bad, either. Korchek dumped him for another cutie and he's pissed. Get him before he changes his mind."

"This afternoon soon enough? I've been up all night."

"Go for it."

It was night before Jill came pounding at his door. It took ten minutes to awaken Colfax and he reacted groggily. A cold shower electrified him awake, then together he and Jill drove in his car to a meeting with Jason Blackwell. Colfax talked to him, Jill took notes and, using a tape recorder hidden in her purse, secretly recorded the interview. Blackwell's apartment in the Oakland hills was the epitome of good taste. Each piece of furniture, done in shades of blacks and reds and gleaming silver, complemented the other, contributing to an art deco theme that was out of place in the woodsy environment of the hills.

Blackwell was not reluctant to talk. He and Korchek had been lovers. The apartment was paid for by the chief and was where they frequently had sex. Korchek preferred a blow job, but—Blackwell smiled—he was adaptable. What intrigued Colfax was not the chief's sex life but his relationship with Max Callahan. Blackwell had twice driven Korchek in an unmarked car to a house in Berkeley that from the description Colfax recognized as Callahan's.

"I have no idea what they talked about," Blackwell said in the high-pitched, nasally drawl of his native Houston. "I had to stand in the middle of that pigsty while they rapped in another room. God, I felt positively *soiled* by the time I left that place!"

The chief had said nothing to his driver about the conversation except that you had to sleep with a Commie to know a Commie.

"I assume he meant it figuratively," Blackwell said, "but who in God's name knows? He could have been fucking that pig right under my nose. So to speak."

"Is Callahan homosexual?"

"Of course, dear boy. He's probably my Wally's boyfriend now!" Pause. "I do remember something the chief said. He said that the other radical, what's his name, the dago . . ."

"Minelli?"

". . . yes, him, was on his way out."

Any remaining weariness Colfax had felt was gone. He gleamed with a clarity of perception he had never known before. Everything was pointing to a conclusion.

"Jason," he said, leaning closer, "would you be willing to sign a statement based on what you've told me and testify to it in court if necessary? I don't think it will be necessary, but if it is?"

"Instantly!"

"Do you have a typewriter?"

He led the way into another room. Jill brought out the hidden tape recorder with a sheepish smile and began typing its contents while Colfax and Blackwell talked in another room. In a little less than an hour, the statement was ready. Blackwell signed it, Jill and Colfax witnessed it.

"What this amounts to," Colfax said to Jill as they drove back to the city, "is a hint of collusion between the chief and Callahan. The left and the right in bed together. Maybe literally. And maybe that's what happened to Minelli."

"Can I share the byline?"

"When I write it. But first I want to use this in a face-to-face meeting with Korchek. We'll let him deny it all."

"Jeez, I can't believe this is happening," she said.

"You're the one who did it. And by the way, enough of this copygirl shit. I'm strongly recommending that Burns hire you as a first-year reporter. You won't make a hell of a lot more money, which is probably why you'll get hired, but your foot will be in the door."

Jill leaped at him, arms around him and lips pressed hard on his face, causing Colfax to swerve across two lanes of the bridge. Providentially, both lanes were empty.

"Great Christ," he hollered as she licked the side of his face, "get off me or you'll kill us!"

"I don't know what to say, I've been waiting all my life!"

"Just say thank you and stop licking my goddamn face!"

She was still trying to crawl all over him when they reached his apartment. Inside, she thanked him properly.

At first, Korchek wanted nothing to do with Colfax, instructing his secretary to have the reporter thrown out.

"He asked me to give you this," the secretary said, handing the chief an envelope.

Korchek read it. His expression never changed, but the secretary would recall later that his hands trembled. Finished with the note, he said curtly, "He's got fifteen minutes."

He was sitting at stiff attention at his desk when Colfax entered. There were no preliminaries, no chitchat, no sparring before combat.

"You print any of this," the chief said, "and I'll sue you for libel."

Not asked to sit, Colfax stood before the desk. He could remember during his first interviews for the *Herald* how uncomfortable he'd felt face-to-face with powerful people. The discomfort no longer existed. Eight years of newspapering had hardened him. What he faced today was a victim rather than an opponent. Colfax knew that the power was in his hands, not the chief's.

"We can prove it all," he said. There was no challenge in his tone. "We have affidavits and tape recordings. Truth is on our side, Chief."

"You have shit!" Korchek roared, his stare burning into the reporter. "Words from a driver I had to replace because of drunkenness? What the hell proof is that?"

Colfax felt a little sorry for the man. He was a great, wounded grizzly fighting until the last breath of life, holding tightly to his composure. Colfax had done his work well. After interviewing Jason Blackwell, he had confronted a shaken Callahan and had wrangled a jailhouse interview with Strickland. What emerged was a story of complicity that tainted them all, but never explained Minelli's disappearance.

"Our story will quote Strickland as saying you played upon his overwhelming feelings of guilt in Leonard Rose's death and brought him in as a player. He's talking now because he realizes what bastards you are and how badly he was used. He wanted Minelli to pay for Rose's murder . . . but he didn't want him killed. He is dead, isn't he?"

"You're crazy!" Korchek's words sailed without conviction. He had slumped within himself. "Why are you telling me all this?" he finally managed to ask, his voice choked.

"It's your opportunity to deny, to comment . . . whatever."

"And you'll print that crap Blackwell told you?"

Instead of answering the question, Colfax bore down. "What did you do with Vito Minelli?"

"Fuck you." The chief stood. "You'd better watch your ass, mister!"

"Is that a threat, Mr. Korchek? Because if it is . . ." Colfax opened his jacket to reveal a tape recorder. "It's your call," he said.

"Get your fucking ass out of here!"

Korchek's large hands were doubled into fists. The grizzly had drawn from his last fiery pit of energy to stand tall, to bellow defiance, to burn brightly in his final moments.

Colfax nodded. "See you on the front page, Chief," he said, and left.

Korchek's secretary would testify during an inquest that she entered her boss's office when the reporter had gone and found the chief slumped at his desk. When she asked if he was all right, he only nodded and gestured her out of the room. She had never seen him like that but felt powerless to help unless he wanted help. She did as she was told and left the room.

Korchek sat at his desk for long moments without moving. The afternoon sunlight that slanted through the window behind him turned the buttons of his epaulets into gold. He loved that uniform and kept it in immaculate condition. It flashed his pride and his power. He was a leader among men in a war that had been waged with dedication in the face of overwhelming odds. But leaders fall and deep within him Korchek knew that he had been mortally wounded. He wondered now as he looked up how he would be remembered. His gaze swept the office as though absorbing every detail, from the large photograph of Douglas MacArthur on one wall to that of Richard Nixon on another. A flag that flew over the nation's Capitol, a plaque from the American Legion, a parchment of appreciation from the City of Oakland. It occurred to him as he finished that the memory of him would not survive tomorrow's newspapers. They would damn him and hold him up to ridicule and hatred. His terrible secrets would emerge and he would become everyone's object of scorn. He couldn't take that.

Korchek was crying as he reached into his desk and placed his chrome-plated .45-caliber automatic in front of him. It was a gift from his men. He leaned close to the weapon, drawing from it the comfort it provided, an ability to shut out pain, to end with explosive suddenness the ache of loneliness he had always felt. It was right that he should perish in thunder. There was pride in thunder. There was power.

His secretary was on the phone when she heard the roar of the gun. She dropped the receiver and rushed into the chief's office. Her screams followed the thunder.

The two men who had helped Minelli bomb the FBI office were arrested and indicted along with Strickland. They all testified that the bombing had been Minelli's plan. He was indicted as a fugitive coconspirator. Based on Hagen's investigation, the FBI linked the bullets that had sprayed Minelli's apartment to weapons used by the Oakland Police Department. After Korchek's death, the city ordered an investigation into the private army he had formed within the department.

Ellen emasculated Colfax's story. Her genes were showing. Reference to Korchek's homosexuality were deleted. His involvement with Callahan was blue-penciled.

"I see no reason to defame a dead man," she insisted when Burns and Colfax complained.

They stood before her desk like pleading children. It was a position that neither man liked, stating their case to a woman still in her twenties, gifted with authority over them only by the caprice of her father's dysfunction.

"It's not a question of defaming anyone," Burns said. "It's the truth. We don't sit in judgment. We offer facts."

"By your logic," Colfax said, half leaning against a wall, "Hitler would emerge as a pretty nice guy."

"That's not the same!" she shouted, glaring at him. The fire of her words engulfed him, bearing the heat of their past emotional involvement as much as their professional disagreement.

"When do we stop protecting dead people?" he demanded. "When do we decide who should be debased and who shouldn't be? It's bullshit, Ellen!"

"This isn't newspapering," Burns said, his voice always soft. "This is editing by whimsy."

"It's my decision," she said, regaining her lost composure. "Period."

Both men knew they had lost.

"I want my name taken off the story," Colfax said. "That's *my* decision."

He left the room. Burns remained.

"It's not a dishonor to change your mind," he said.

"I don't intend doing that, Mr. Burns."

Her voice was as cold as steel. It reminded the city editor of her father in the final moments of his questionable decisions.

"Then," he said, still speaking softly, "you will do it without me."

He had not preplanned it. The words emerged from frustration that had been growing for years. The *Herald* he had known no longer existed. This was a child's toy. He would seek the island of his dreams.

Ellen gave no ground. "You will be missed," she said.

When Burns left the room, she stared at the door without blinking and without a single show of emotion. The lion's head stared with her. Both remained firm in their positions and righteous in their execution of power.

Word swept through the city room. Questions flew. Disbelief brought work to a halt. Burns too had decided. There was no changing his mind. He packed the few personal belongings from his desk, stood for a moment observing the staff, waved, and headed for the back elevator.

Trager, standing in the copy desk slot, began a rhythmic clapping. Colfax joined him. Others took up the slow, purposeful applause, acknowledging the passage of the man who had been their boss and their conscience for as long as anyone could remember. Burns paused as the elevator door opened and looked back. He smiled the small, secret smile Colfax remembered from that first day, except written into it now was relief. A burden had been lifted. He was free. He stepped into the elevator. The door closed and he was gone.

The clapping continued for a moment in its slow, steady cadence and then faded. That afternoon and far into the night they would meet at the Three-Oh and conduct their ritual for the dead. But as Burns disappeared all knew with grim perception who the dead were.

Silence filled the city room. It was their tomb.

CHAPTER SEVENTEEN

C allahan's army massed around the *Herald* like a herd of angry bulls. The indictments had stirred them again, but this time any element of the good-natured undergraduate romp that had characterized the Minelli years was missing. This was no symbolic protest. Minelli had understood the value of theatrics to promote himself. He knew the point of the war lay in his vision for the future. Callahan saw only the here and now, and the bedlam of the crowd reflected that limited view. There was only fury here and it was all directed at the *Herald*.

Colfax left the building through a back alley that led away from Mission Street. He had known from anonymous tips that the protest was coming, but it somehow didn't matter. What had mattered to him as the months passed was what happened to Minelli, but it seemed now that he would never know. Only the slimmest of evidence implicated Korchek and Callahan, but Korchek was gone and there wasn't enough to indict Callahan. Minelli had simply vanished like a leaf in the wind.

Ellen named Trager city editor, but he refused to occupy Burns's old desk, leaving it empty, moving instead to what had once been Sam Perkins's spot next to Burns. No one objected because the copy chief was one of them, a regular at the Three-Oh who had refined "Danny

Boy" to a virtuoso level and played it for them on the evening Gerald Burns had walked out of their lives. But Trager wasn't Burns and the absence of the legendary city editor left a hole that no one could fill. It was as though they had lost a father and a close friend and a lover all in one, so powerful had been his presence in their days. He was an era all his own, a hallmark by which all others would someday be measured.

Colfax knew he could have and probably should have stayed to cover this latest assault on the tower but had left it to others instead. When Burns walked out the door, it severed a connection that Colfax had come to rely on. The loneliness in him deepened and for a moment he thought about seeing his father again but gave up on the idea. There wasn't the same kind of linkage between them, even though in some ways he admired his old man. Granger had finally gotten a phone, so Colfax had telephoned instead, unwilling to once more submerge himself in the dampness of his redwood forest past. Granger, as tough as a rhino, had survived pneumonia. Remarking on his recuperation, he would only say, "God moves in mysterious ways." Colfax had never heard his father refer to God before. Old people turn to the unknown for answers. Faith billows or dies in last moments. It was that way in combat. He remembered praying quietly before patrols and under mortar barrages. He hadn't prayed since.

He had barely hung up after talking to his father when the phone rang.

"This is Vera Epstein. I am telling you not to worry."

"Mrs. Epstein? Vito's mother?"

"His name is Jules."

"Yes, I'm sorry," Colfax said, surprised at her sudden call. "Have you heard from your son?"

"I am just telling you not to worry."

Colfax thought for a moment. Not to worry? "You've heard from him."

"I'm not telling you this and I am not telling you that, Mr. Colfax, I am just saying to save your gasoline money. You're a nice boy and I don't want you running around the country looking."

"If you've heard from him, it's important that you—"

"I'm not saying more, Mr. Colfax."

"He's a fugitive, Mrs. Epstein. They'll find him."

"God's will be done, Mr. Colfax." And then she hung up.

Colfax stared into space, the dial tone of the vacant line humming into the stillness that surrounded him. Then he said aloud, "I'll be a son of a bitch."

December 1973. The staff of the *Herald* was called together after the day's final edition. Reporters were summoned to the meeting from whatever beat remained active. Ellen had shut down the police beat and ordered Trager to find ways to cover it from the office. Two police reporters had been "laid off," along with editorial cartoonist Billy the Bug, the gloomy little man who had taken to calling his boss "Tits." Cheap syndicated cartoons took his place. His last shot was a caricature of her with her head up her ass. He put it up on the city room bulletin board. No one took it down.

What her great-grandfather had begun, Ellen was ending. The *Herald* had become a kingdom isolated in its tower. Its lower windows remained boarded up from the last protest. Rocks and scrap iron had smashed them open and the boards added a bleak and vacant look to the newspaper's Mission Street front.

Ellen emerged from her office exactly at six P.M. She was never late. Editors, reporters, and photographers stood or sat in a semicircle. She set herself in front of the city desk.

"I have bad news," she began. No one doubted there was any other purpose to the meeting. "We can no longer continue the way we are. I have been informed by our business manager, Gloria Seaton, and our advertising manager, Rich McAuley, that in a short time the *Herald* will no longer be able to meet its financial obligations, and that includes payroll and operating expenses."

The city room was silent. Ellen tried to avoid individual faces, peering over the tops of their heads as though addressing something on a high wall behind them. Rain was falling over the city. Christmas ornaments strung across both Mission and Market Streets glowed in the moisture. Tinsel swung in gusts of wind that accompanied the precipitation. For Colfax, there was a funereal quality to the adornment. This was the end.

"It's too much for me to speculate why this has happened. Other afternoon newspapers are in trouble across the country. Television is making inroads. The costs of labor and newsprint are soaring. Ours has borne a special burden. You've been here. You know what's been going on. Someone will analyze it someday, but not now. The result is that the *Herald* has been officially offered up for sale. I know you all heard the old rumors and, at the same time, they were just rumors." Her voice broke. She steadied herself before going on. "Now they are no longer rumors."

Milton Travis raised his hand. "What if—"

"Wait." Ellen silenced him. "There's more and it isn't any better. We have sufficient funds to continue for another ninety days. If the *Herald* isn't sold within that period of time"—she inhaled deeply— "we will be forced to cease publication."

What Colfax was hearing, what they were all hearing, was what had been anticipated but unaccepted. The *Herald* had been a solid, moneymaking venture, as firm and permanent as the tower that housed it. Now the very earth had moved beneath them.

"I am telling you this now so that you might consider your options if worse comes to worst," Ellen continued. "We have put a fund aside for severance pay. We owe you all. What is happening isn't your fault. We will help as much as possible in obtaining new jobs for those who want to leave now. If the *Herald* should cease to publish, we will nevertheless continue our efforts to find other employment for those who remain. Thank you all and God bless you."

As quickly as she had entered the city room, Ellen was gone, leaving a vacuum, that sucked them all into the space she had occupied. During the final moments of her speech, Colfax had spotted Cliff

Hammer entering from the rear elevator. They had exchanged glances and now the Guild boss was approaching him.

"Well," he said to Colfax, "I guess it didn't even take a strike."

Colfax nodded. "I don't know what the hell most of these people are going to do."

"What about you?"

"I don't know that either."

The staff dissipated slowly, merging into the far corners of the city room and down the hall to the sports and women's departments and into the small alcove offices where the specialists sat. Clusters of them grouped together, whispering, talking, not believing. One or two of the women cried.

"God," Colfax said, "what a world."

Hammer shook his head. "The cocksuckers," he said.

The *Herald* shut its doors two days before New Year's Eve. A conglomerate of buyers was interested in continuing publication, but that was before both of its ancient Hoe presses broke down and they realized how antiquated its equipment was. The Age of Computers was edging into newspapering. The *Herald* could never be made ready for it. Many speculated that sabotage had played a final part in the drama and a police investigation was conducted, but it really didn't matter. How this once-grand newspaper died was incidental now. Like an old lady on life support, its doom was inevitable.

Those working on stories knew something was wrong. When the presses were running, the very building shook, a vibration they had become accustomed to every afternoon as each edition slapped its way down the rollers to the bailing equipment. Word spread quickly that one of the presses was down and then, shortly thereafter, the other. It came in the middle of the home edition, the day's most important press run. Reporters stopped writing. Editors stopped editing. Colfax looked up when the presses stopped, listening. They were a still life in the city room and the waiting seemed interminable.

Telephones rang, but no one answered them. Staff members gathered in clusters, speculating, wondering. Trager had vanished into Ellen's office and now they emerged together, the young woman of radiant beauty and the limping older man with the lines of his years etched like trails of a long journey on his face.

"This isn't what I wanted . . ." Ellen began, but was unable to continue.

"There will be no home edition today, ladies and gentlemen," Trager said, taking up the burden. "Nor will there be a *Herald* tomorrow. It's not the way anyone planned it. Both presses are irreparably damaged. There's just no point in fixing them. I don't like being the bearer—"

"No," Ellen said suddenly, interrupting. "It's my family's newspaper. I must be the one to say it. We are ceasing publication. There will be . . ." She hesitated, fighting for control. "There will be no further editions of the *Herald*." Pause. "Thank you for all you have done. We were great once. And now we're gone."

Colfax felt as though he were standing by the bedside of a dying king. Someone ought to play taps.

The wake for the *Herald* was held at the Three-Oh on New Year's Eve. Trager played "Danny Boy" and Travis brought his monkey. Carter Blake, three drinks toward heaven, offered a prayer. Paul Lowin, remaining in character, drank alone. Glasses were turned upside down so often, Patty the barmaid had to take some back to wash them for the next hundred rounds. Gerald Burns came by to say good-bye and Gwen Ballard, sober and wearing a dignified pants suit, took the names of those who might want to join the *Daily News*.

"How about you?" she said to Colfax.

"I'm going to L.A.," he said. "They've made an offer I can't refuse."

"You'll hate it there."

"I can't stay here. The *Herald* was unique, the *News* isn't. That was the last city room, Gwen. There'll never be another like it."

She kissed him on the lips and then moved on into the noisy crowd. He saw her talking to Jill and hoped there'd be a place for the onetime copygirl. Colfax had said his good-byes, kissed all the kisses, and hugged all the hugs. It was over. Only Burns saw him slip out the door and half smiled, the way he had when he hired Colfax. What did he know? Colfax wondered. What secrets had he discovered?

The streets were filled with New Year's Eve revelers. Noisemakers cluttered the night. Rain had fallen earlier and the streets were wet. The glow of streetlights reflected in pools of water. Colfax looked up at the tower, its clock outlined in brilliant red neon, its hands dead at eleven-fifteen. He had to see the city room one more time. As he crossed the street, he heard his name shouted and looked up the street. Bruno Hagen approached.

"Now what?" Hagen asked, reaching his side.

"I'm off to L.A."

"You're leaving the party early."

"It's been over a long time. How about you?"

"The Bureau took me back. I'm a G-man again."

Colfax nodded. "Good luck, G-man," he said.

"I hear you're taking the midget with you."

"Is there anything you don't find out? You're like an anteater sucking up everything in sight."

"Anteaters don't suck. They lick up things with their tongues. I haven't licked anything for years."

Colfax laughed and realized as he did that he hadn't laughed for a long, long time. The sound was different and, in its way, purifying.

They shook hands. "I'm still trying to figure the whole thing out, who was doing what to who," Hagen said. "Korchek, Stafford, Minelli, all the other shit."

"Let me know if you do."

Hagen nodded. "I think I'll go drink with the boys. They've been a good bunch."

"That they have," Colfax said.

Hagen turned to leave, then hesitated. "If what that old lady hinted is true and Minelli's still alive, I'll find him," he said. "There's a score to settle. The bastard won't get away." Then he waved and disappeared into the Three-Oh.

Colfax entered the *Herald* and took the elevator to the third floor. The city room was empty. A few lights remained on, casting the room in the eerie half glow of a dream. It was the kind of light Colfax recalled from combat when the smoke of artillery had diffused daylight and created an illumination all its own. Papers were scattered around, the Teletype machines were silent, the police scanners had been shut off. The old wooden desks, the ancient Remingtons, the telephone headsets, the high-backed desk chairs, stacks of copy paper . . . all elements of a dream.

Colfax wandered through the room, found a copy of the *Herald*'s last edition, and stuck it in his back pocket. He wondered if he should call Ellen or see her father to say good-bye but decided against it. Thinking of them, he wandered into the publisher's office. It too had been emptied except for one vital artifact. The lion's head was still there.

Colfax climbed on a windowsill, reached up for the head, and jerked hard. It crashed to the floor, its face staring up at him. For a moment he thought about putting his foot through it but instead picked it up and tucked it under one arm. The lion's head and the last edition were all he would take from the *Herald*. There was nothing else it could give him. The realization dropped to the pit of his stomach. He fought back tears.

Walking through the newsroom, he paused by the desk Gerald Burns had once occupied and remembered the bottle the city editor kept in a lower drawer. Colfax opened the drawer. The bottle was still there. He brought it out, rummaged around for a paper cup, and poured a drink. He held it up in silent tribute, drank it down, and then, in the style of a good *Herald*'s man, very carefully placed the paper cup upside down on Burns's desk, scooped up the lion's head, and hurried out.

He drove home, packed quickly, and headed south, going by the tower one last time. As he passed it, he could have sworn he saw Minelli in a car moving in the opposite direction. The man, clean-shaven, his hair blond, glanced at Colfax and seemed to smile and then was gone into the rain and the traffic. Colfax made no effort to follow, but the very thought that Vito Minelli was still in town was too much to even consider. He would leave it at that.

On the way out, he stopped to pick up Corona McGee. She was also L.A.-bound, just as Hagen knew. The Haight was no place for dreamers anymore. Like the fading powers of an aging illusionist, the magic had glittered off and vanished. They drove in silence, the reporter and the dwarf, each seeking new lives, each abandoning old ones. The car pulled up onto the freeway past the Cow Palace and Candlestick Park and the airport, heading south.